Murder at Highfields

A Berkshires Cozy

Andrea Kress

Murder at Highfields

A Berkshires Cozy

Andrea Kress

Copyright © 2021 by Andrea Kress

Table of Contents

Chapter 1 5
Chapter 2 10
Chapter 3 21
Chapter 4 27
Chapter 5 35
Chapter 6 42
Chapter 7 51
Chapter 8 58
Chapter 9 66
Chapter 10 78
Chapter 11 83
Chapter 12 91
Chapter 13 95
Chapter 14 106
Chapter 15 115
Chapter 16 121
Chapter 17 129
Chapter 18 136
Chapter 19 143
Chapter 20 150
Chapter 21 161
Chapter 22 165
Chapter 23 170
Chapter 24 173
Chapter 25 187

Chapter 26..192
Chapter 27..197
Chapter 28..203
Chapter 29..213

Chapter 1

1931

Friendship and love. Two deep, compelling emotions that define our lives. I was lucky in one and not the other—but I am getting ahead of myself.

Glenda and I had become friends during our three-year nurses' training in New York City where our single rooms were side by side. Most of the students' innocuous chatter and gossip took place in a shared bathroom at the end of each corridor; the more private conversations occurred in our rooms since we were carefully monitored in our deportment elsewhere in the classrooms and on the wards.

We were serious students but also had fun as we nervously awaited our exams, graduation, state certification, and final placement as registered nurses in a City hospital. One June morning, Glenda was called out before breakfast and told her mother had suffered a stroke, so she packed and left by the morning train home to the Berkshires in western Massachusetts.

I got a brief letter during exam week, telephone calls being expensive in those days, saying her mother was stable but not improving, life in the town was boring, and she missed us all terribly. A week later, just after my board certification exam, a telegram came telling of Glenda's mother's death and begging me to come to the funeral.

The Head Nurse gave me leave, and late on an overcast Friday afternoon, I boarded a train north, carrying a small suitcase for my weekend stay. As I looked out at the expanse of green farmland, browsing cows, and dense woods between the multiple stops, I realized I had spent entirely too much time in the city. Through the open window, I inhaled the mown grass scent of the countryside and heard the sounds of birdsong. Despite the sad circumstances, I was enjoying the pleasure of being by myself, with no exams or work on my mind, observing the passengers who stepped down to the platform or boarded the train, no longer recognizing the names of the towns we passed through. After several hours we rumbled into Pittsfield and I could see Glenda's small frame leaning against the wall of the train station, hands in her pockets, looking expectantly at the travelers descending.

"Oh, Aggie!" she said, running toward me and pulling me into a hug after I came down the steps. We must have looked a sight: me, a tall, slim girl with dark hair next to the pretty, petite blonde. She looked exhausted, her hair bedraggled, no makeup to speak of, and circles under her eyes. "I'm so glad you came. Here, let me take your bag," she offered. "The car is just outside."

"Don't be silly. I can manage." All my suitcase held was a black dress for the funeral, a nightgown, a change of undergarments, and some toiletries.

We drove through Pittsfield, the lights of the stores dimmed for the evening, through a residential neighborhood, and onto the Cheshire Road winding around the dark hills north toward West Adams thirty minutes away. The windows were down, the wind cooling my face and making conversation impossible. A final turn and we entered the town of West Adams.

"It's really lovely," I said, inhaling deeply the scent of the flowers hanging from the basket planters on the streetlights. We passed through the limited commercial area and drove into the gloom, seeing occasional lights on in the sitting room of one house or another, although most homes were obscured by trees until she turned into a driveway and slowed to a stop.

"Here we are," she said brightly, as we made our way across the front lawn before pushing open the unlocked front door. At my astonished look, she added, "We're not in New York City anymore. Nobody locks their doors here."

It seemed reasonable enough considering how hard it would be to find a front door in the dark neighborhood with few streetlights.

The foyer opened onto a sitting room to the right, spacious yet a bit over-furnished; I put my suitcase down and nonetheless commented on how charming it was.

"Have you had supper? Would you like something to drink?" she inquired, taking me across the hall toward the dining room.

The long table was piled with dishes and platters set out as for a buffet although no food was in evidence. To my surprised look, Glenda added, "The neighbor ladies have been busy preparing for tomorrow." The post-funeral buffet.

She led me through to the kitchen and rummaged in the icebox, taking out a plate of cold chicken covered in waxed paper.

"Just the thing," I remarked, realizing I hadn't had a proper meal since lunch.

"Oh, no," Glenda said, lifting an eyebrow. "*This* is just the thing." Using a chair as a step stool, she pulled out a half-full bottle of brandy from a high cabinet.

"Let's do the chicken first, shall we?" Ever sensible, I was not going to have strong alcohol on an empty stomach.

I washed my hands at the sink and sat at the enamel-topped table while she put the chicken on a plate, gave me utensils, a napkin, some pickles, and a slice of bread, and poured two small brandies. She sat and motioned for me to begin eating.

"How's old Nurse Watson?" she asked.

"Missing you terribly, as you can imagine. No glamour left in the nurses' digs."

We both laughed, remembering our first day in training where we sat in an auditorium, arranged alphabetically—me, Burnside, Glenda Butler to my right—and Nurse Watson read out our names. After getting through an Ethel, a Margaret, a Rose, and me, Agnes, she got to Glenda's name and stopped a moment and repeated it.

"Glenda? Rather a glamorous name for a student nurse."

We all laughed a bit at the jibe, but when Nurse Watson looked down again to the list to find her place, Glenda plumped up her blonde curly bob with one hand like a movie star and fluttered her lashes making the auditorium erupt in laughter. It quieted instantly when the Head Nurse looked up to see what or who had caused it, only to meet the wide-eyed innocence of Glenda Butler returning her gaze.

"How were finals? I bet you aced them," Glenda said.

"I did well. The practical was ridiculous with Watson and one of her cronies scrutinizing our every move, waiting for someone to spill a bedpan or not fill an icepack correctly. I don't know why they bothered since we had been through it a thousand times."

Just talking about it made me realize how I had missed her while my life and obligations had gone on. I stopped eating for a moment and looked back at her face trying to read her expression.

"Is there any chance you can come back and finish?" I asked. I couldn't imagine life in the hospital without Glenda's presence.

She shrugged her narrow shoulders. "I haven't asked yet, but I'm sure they would make it as difficult as possible. I missed the last few weeks, the finals, the practical, and I would still have to take the board exam." Her voice drifted off.

I nodded, wondering if she might not have been as invested in completing the course as I had been. During our application interviews, I am sure she, like all of us, professed our deep attachment to helping mankind by our service as nurses. How many of us harbored the belief, I don't know, but in my case, I had to work, and of the three choices available to me, nursing was preferable to teaching or office work. In the orientation lecture, Nurse Watson had reminded us we were there to learn to be professionals, not to be husband-hunting. The look on everyone's face said, "Of course not," but we all knew better. An intern or new doctor might hope to marry someone with money or social connections to set him up in practice, but the reality was his work hours didn't allow for much of a social life and there were so many pretty, available nurses right there all the time. Nurses understood the nature of medical work, the long hours, and even better, could be partners in the future practice as receptionist, assistant, and nurse at no cost.

I continued eating, watching Glenda's face as she pondered. "Let's get through tomorrow, and then we'll talk," I said.

She nodded, her eyes filling with tears, turning away to hide them.

I changed the subject and told her who had been assigned to which hospital to date.

"I'm scheduled to stay put. I've become accustomed to the place," since all duty nurses had to live on site. "But I have wangled a bit of a holiday for myself."

"You lucky dog!" she said, wiping at the corners of her eyes.

"Nothing too exciting. A graduation present from my parents. And for my brother, too."

"That sounds really nice, Aggie," she said with a twinge of envy.

"If you have some time, you could come to visit me here for a while."

"Of course." I gave her a hug and kiss and told her she needed to get some rest. I was fairly certain I would never see West Adams again. How wrong I was.

Chapter 2

We were up shortly after eight the next morning, anticipating the neighbor women's descent upon the house in preparation for the funeral. They drifted quietly in the back door an hour later with sympathetic looks, arm squeezes for Glenda, and approving nods to me upon introduction; somehow I was always perceived as the pillar of reason and probity where the two of us were concerned, although maybe it was my simple bob and sensible clothes that gave me away. I marveled how Glenda's neighbors came freely in the unlocked back door and seemed to know where everything was in the house. Our offers of assistance were brushed aside as they ferried in covered dishes of food, pitchers of lemonade, and bunches of flowers picked from their gardens. Although introduced to each one, I promptly forgot the names except for Miss Manley, who lived next door and had been a great friend of Glenda's late mother. She was tall and elderly, with a funny habit of tilting her head to the side when particularly interested in what was said, a bit like a bird. My telling her about my nursing career elicited just such a response.

"What an enterprising young woman you are," she said.

"Saturday's child must work for a living," I replied, a bit embarrassed about the cliché response I often employed to deter further questions or assumptions about my marital prospects or my family's financial standing.

While Glenda and I stood aimlessly in the kitchen, one of the women discreetly took a dust cloth out of a closet and made her way to the sitting room to make it more presentable.

"They are going to drive me crazy," Glenda said under her breath.

She stood on a chair, reached up into the high cabinet, produced the brandy bottle and poured some into a teacup, took a sip and handed the rest to me.

"I'd better get changed," she said, disappearing up the stairs.

I was already outfitted in a sedate black dress with long sleeves, perfectly suited to the cool June day, so I wandered into the dining room to offer my assistance although I could see it was hardly required. The old-fashioned wallpaper looked tired and the drapes were faded, but the women had livened up the room with flowers and colorful china filled with food that didn't need refrigeration. Last touches were made by adjusting the stem of a daisy or brushing an invisible crease in the tablecloth, but for the most part, the women seemed content with the arrangements. Miss Manley approached me, smiled, and took both my hands in hers.

"I was one of Sarah's oldest friends," she said. "Women's friendships are so important, don't you think?" She was referring to Glenda and me and I thought she was trying to hint I should keep in touch with my friend.

I nodded and wondered how often these women had been in contact with each other—not just by the years of residency in West Adams but seeing one another in the daily rounds to the shops, out in their gardens, at school events, in the church fussing with the floral arrangements, the rummage sales, and the town's July 4th parade.

"How long are you staying?" Miss Manley asked.

"Just until tomorrow, I'm afraid. My family has a holiday arranged beginning next week so I must be getting back."

Miss Manley glanced at a watch pinned to the lapel of her black dress. "I had better pop back next door to finish getting ready," she added and then surprised me by going into the sitting room.

I followed, puzzled by her action, and discovered she was exiting through the French windows, leaving one side open.

"Bit stuffy in here, don't you think?" She disappeared into the garden, presumably to her own home next door to put on a hat and gloves.

***

    I could hear the scuffle of feet as pews filled up behind us, and I reached for Glenda's hand and squeezed it. Miss Manley sat to her right, erect, an old-fashioned, black, peach-basket hat covering most of her gray hair, which was pulled back in a bun. On the other side of the aisle sat the bevy of women who had been at the house earlier, mostly widows or spinsters as few men sat beside them; they nodded their heads at me in recognition. An organ was playing softly while the clearing of throats quieted down in anticipation of the reverend's beginning the service. It was heartening to realize he knew Mrs. Butler so well as to speak of her attributes in great detail and her health travails toward the end of her life with appropriate gravity. A final hymn was sung, and six men stepped forward to take the casket down the aisle of the church and out to the graveyard beyond. We solemnly filed out onto the porch into the sunny, cool day, a beautiful one except for the purpose for which we were there. Glenda stoically took her place and shook the hands of those who exited, accepting expressions of condolence with a simple word of thanks. Many of those in the church had already proceeded to the gravesite and the reverend spoke the customary words as the casket was lowered into the ground. It was at this point Glenda finally broke down, and I put my arm around her narrow shoulders as she sobbed. She only had to get through the after-funeral buffet and then the worst of it would all be over, I thought.

    Even though Glenda continued to refer to them as 'those women' only in my presence, they were formidable allies shepherding people back to the Butler home, making sure those assembled had something to eat and drink but not encouraging second helpings, patrolling the dining room, porch, and sitting room for stray plates or glasses, and bringing them into the kitchen where a young woman washed them up. They moved efficiently among their neighbors, smiling a little tightly at the reverend's wife, a pretty, animated woman clearly years younger than her husband. A tall, well-built man, who I later learned was the doctor, spoke softly to Glenda, and judging by her reaction, he was probably uttering reassurances that her mother hadn't suffered toward the end and everything that could be done had been done. Other neighbors were there, storekeepers, a local judge with a booming voice who introduced himself and his wife to me, and a roguishly handsome artist who rented a studio from the reverend located behind the parsonage next door to Miss Manley. It was an overload of names, professions, and places of where people lived, for example, "You know, across from where the large oak used to stand near the green." I let the names, places, and words wash over me since I didn't anticipate meeting any of them again.

The talk flowed as people moved to and from the food laid out on the table, but I caught Miss Manley's eye across the room as she was following a different sort of movement. It was almost a slow-motion dance as the judge's wife was trying hard to stay on the opposite side of the buffet from the artist who had his gaze intently on her. This strange pavane was not lost on Miss Manley, me, or the judge whose face began to turn a deeper shade as he seemed to grind his teeth. At the moment where angry words might have been spoken, Miss Manley broke the tension by putting her hand on the woman's arm, turning her away and asking some detailed questions. The rhythm was broken, the artist stopped in his tracks near me, introduced himself and began an innocuous conversation about how I knew the Butlers, all the time glancing back across the table. The judge had narrowed his eyes in our direction and Richard Fairley took the hint, excusing himself quickly and leaving the house.

As the food and talk dwindled, the small army of women tacitly signaled to the guests it was time for the remaining people to express their last sympathies and go home. When everyone had left, Miss Manley intercepted Glenda, who was making a halfhearted attempt to clear up, and propelled her upstairs to lie down with a cool cloth on her forehead, the time-honored remedy for an exhausting emotional day. By the time Miss Manley returned downstairs, the dining room was entirely cleared and the last of the dishes washed and dried. One last glance through the downstairs rooms for lingering people or dishware and the women assembled in the kitchen.

"Thank you, Annie," Miss Manley said to the young woman who had done the cleanup. She nodded in response and left out the back door. Then to me: "If you or Glenda need anything, remember, I am right next door."

"And I am on the other side, but two," another said. Another geography discussion began about who lived where, next to whom, across from whom, how long, etc. I smiled through this recitation although I was sure my head would burst.

"Perhaps you'd better lie down, too," Miss Manley suggested to me.

"Yes. It's a good idea. Thank you all so much for helping Glenda," I said.

They tut-tutted at me, and as efficiently as they had arrived and directed the entire operation, they left through the back door. I stood there, inhaling the still, cool air and some sort of jasminelike scent from the garden before closing the door. By reflex, I turned the key in the lock but then felt I had violated local custom and unlocked the door before going upstairs for a nap of my own.

***

A tapping noise roused me from a dreamless sleep and the door opened to Glenda's head peeping in. She came in and sat on the bed looking down at me.

"What now?" she asked.

I was overwhelmed by my inability to get my thoughts together. What now, indeed? What would she do? Take her mother's place here with the other women in the town? Not likely.

But what choices did she have? I cleared my throat attempting to formulate an answer, and she saw my struggle to respond.

"No, silly. What do you want to do now? It seems there are plenty of little sandwiches in the icebox and I'm starving." She got up and preceded me down the stairs, looking rested with mussed hair and wrinkled dress, me following, still groggy from my long nap.

"Just look at all this!" she exclaimed, pulling out platter after dish of tiny sandwiches, miniature cakes, stuffed eggs, and celery sticks.

"Those women were terrific," I stated.

"I'm sorry I called them 'those women'," she said, scrunching up her nose to indicate she wasn't too sorry about it. "But why I call them that is because they are such gossips. The poor reverend's wife, Nina, just because she is young and vivacious was once referred to as a minx." She took a bite of a watercress sandwich.

"One of our neighbors had a Minx cat," I said with a straight face.

This got her laughing. "Manx, darling. Manx. After the Isle of Man."

"Oh, yes," I said, pretending not to have known.

"I'll have to watch my p's and q's here, something I haven't had to worry about for a while. There isn't anything done in this town without every last person's knowing about it within the hour."

"It sounds stifling."

"I'll say. I was lucky enough to go away to Miss Hall's in Pittsfield and have four years of peace from the constant commentary. 'Mrs. Butler, I am sure I saw Glenda wearing lipstick!' 'Mrs. Butler, I believe Glenda has bobbed her hair!' The horror!"

I tucked into a stuffed egg. "These are good."

15

She huffed at me and picked one up to taste it. "Yes, they—or their cooks—are superlative, I'll give them that."

"To return to your original comment or question, what now? Are you going to stay here or come back to New York to finish?"

She put her hand under her chin. "I talked to my mother's lawyer last week and got a good idea of the finances. My father had invested heavily in the stock market and lost a pile in the crash. This is why I ended up going to nursing school instead of college, as you know. He did leave my mother an insurance policy that comes to me."

"What about nursing?"

"I think I'm done with it."

"Why? I'm sure they would take you back under the circumstances. They wouldn't make you start all over, maybe just repeat the last term, finals, and board exam, and you would be done."

"No, I don't think so. I'm not cut out for it. I could be a rich doctor's wife, however." She smiled mischievously.

"Remember what Nurse Watson said. No husband-hunting!" I shook my finger at her.

"Ha! Husband-hunting may have been a moot endeavor for her."

"True," I said, thinking of the head nurse's ferocious face. "What will you do, then?"

"If I rent out one of the bedrooms—city people want to come to the Berkshires in the summer, you know—cut down the minimum expenses to just a weekly cleaner, I think I will be all right."

It not only sounded like a bleak prospect to me but totally unlike the Glenda I knew who could barely boil an egg, much less make an entire meal, and certainly needed someone to pick up after her.

"If there is a drugstore in town perhaps you could get a job as a pharmacist's assistant. You had an entire semester's experience working in the dispensary and you seemed to take to it quite well."

"True. But don't worry," she said brightly. "The lawyer advised me not to do anything precipitous for the next six months. For instance, not to decide to sell the house or become a missionary."

I laughed. "I gather he doesn't know you too well."

"Very funny. On the whole, I think it's good advice. And in the spirit of going slowly, why don't we tidy up and take a walk through the town since you haven't seen much of it?"

We put all the food away and went out the back door into the garden in full bloom, though in a state of recent neglect, and through a gate onto a lane running to the right, past the back of Miss Manley's house, ending in the back garden of the parsonage where Glenda pointed out the artist's studio. There were roses in bloom, tall pink hollyhocks, enormous sunflowers, purple foxglove, white daisies, as well as petunias, pansies, and begonias. In the other direction, almost directly behind Glenda's house, was another path leading up through the woods.

"Let's go up this way instead of into town. The path is welltrodden and easier walking than tramping through the deep, dark forest," Glenda said, trying to make it sound menacing and pointing to the right. "Or having people gawp at me in the town."

"Hardly deep and dark," I replied. "But thank you for the suggestion since I didn't bring appropriate footwear for a hike." I inhaled deeply. "This air is so wonderful here. I'd almost forgotten what clean air smells like."

"Do you think New York City air is so bad?"

"It seems there are more taxis, buses, cars, and factories every day. Perhaps it's just because I am stuck inside the hospital rather than outside in some lovely garden."

"When you marry your rich doctor, you will have your enormous garden. And a fleet of servants to tend to your slightest wish."

"And who might this person be?"

"What's-his-name you went out with a few times."

I grimaced. "A nice young man, but boring. I was hoping he'd be a bit more dashing or something. Anyway, it fizzled, and it is no more. I don't know why Nurse Watson made such an emphasis on husband-hunting. It seemed to me most of the med students were so focused on their studies they had little time for romance."

"The next time you're ill and need a doctor, you'll be glad they were focused."

"I suppose," I muttered, wondering what my marriage prospects would be.

"Don't worry, you'll find the one. Or he'll find you," Glenda said.

"Your doctor here is rather dishy."

Glenda turned to me and raised one eyebrow. "You think so? I think he has a rather plodding nature. Too much science training probably."

"I don't have a problem with that. What about the artist fellow?"

"Not my type at all. I think he considers himself some kind of matinee idol. Well, he certainly has the looks for it, but he is too self-consciously handsome."

Nodding backward toward the studio that looked more like a shed, I asked "You should cross him off your list anyway. He doesn't look as if he's done too well, if that's all he can afford."

"He doesn't live there; he rents a house down the street, so I suppose he is financially stable. The studio is where he paints. Mostly portraits from what I gather. He asked to paint me."

"How charming!"

"For money." "Oh,"

I laughed.

"Cottage industry. He is currently painting the wife of the judge who lives at Highfields. I am sure it was what the tension was about earlier with judge Nash. He was the large man with the big voice. He sits on the local bench for the district, earning a reputation as a harsh adjudicator. His wife was the lovely woman in the navy blue silk dress."

Glenda would notice what every woman wore.

"Younger than her husband?" I asked.

"Yes, he has a daughter, Christine, from his first marriage. He is as rich as Croesus and has a fantastic collection of ivory chess sets he got in his travels to the Orient. What he was doing there, I don't know. There it is, Highfields," she said stopping while we were still in the shade of the trees. It was the perfect spot for admiring the large home perched on a small rise, giving vast views of the valley beyond.

"Mount Greylock," Glenda stated, pointing at the mountain visible from the top of the path.

"Come on, since the weather is so nice, why don't we drive over there?" she asked, taking my hand and pulling me back the way we had come.

"Are we done sightseeing in the town and environs?" I asked.

"Nothing much to see. No haunted houses. Just more shops, closed, of course, by now, and then the farms as you go out into the country a bit."

Glenda led me to what I had thought was a small barn at the bottom of her garden, so covered with ivy I hadn't even noticed its existence. She jiggled the handle and pulled opened the right-hand door to where she had parked the car sometime yesterday.

In just a few minutes we were off along the main street of the town, past closed shops and the church, and within a mile we were out into the countryside, the open windows blowing our hair all around.

"I lobbied hard for a convertible when it came time to buy the family car, but my mother was aghast at the idea. Too showy, she thought, so this is what Daddy got."

"Surely you are aware you are incredibly lucky to have any kind of car at all?" I said. In my world, adults owned cars, not young, single women.

"Don't be pompous."

"I'm not. As long as you can afford the gas, you are not 'stuck in the town,' as you put it yesterday."

"True." She gave me the Glamorous Glenda smile and laughed. "Leave it to you to point out the difference in perspective."

The roadway wound up and down and in places, the vegetation encroached upon the road, in others we were exposed to fields on either side with wildflowers blooming in profusion. The rocky soil and hills didn't lend themselves to much in the way of agriculture, but the scenery was stirring. My peace of mind was interrupted by the reminder of why I was here in the first place and then I let it slip away to enjoy the immediate pleasant sensations of wind and sun. We spent the rest of the afternoon scaling the mountain by car, then getting out at the top to admire the view of the towns and forest below. How lovely it would be to live out here—if only there were job opportunities, and it was summer forever.

We slept in on Sunday and Glenda offered to drive me to Pittsfield to take the train back home in the early afternoon. She entreated me to come back for a visit if not soon, then in autumn. Fall might be the next time I could get away for a holiday, and the thought of all these maples and elms in their autumn colors was tantalizing. Although the Berkshires were not far from New York by train or car, I harbored the nagging thought I might not ever get back this way again.

Chapter 3

The day after I got home, our family began its weeklong holiday in Atlantic City, a bit of a family tradition. My parents had taken their honeymoon there and we had gone every summer for as long as I could remember, except for the two years my father was in France during the Great War. He was gassed badly and discharged when I was about eight, old enough to know that what had happened to him was serious and life-threatening and would affect the family's future. My mother, a natural worrier, developed a deep crease between her eyes as she looked after my father and continued her maternal role. There was talk about scrimping, being careful not to use too much hot water, and turning cuffs on shirts, and a lot of shaking her head at the rapid growth of my brother and me. This stage didn't last long, since my father recuperated to the extent he could return to work at his former law firm in New York, but the notion of the wolf at the door stayed with me. It was not too long after, while the Great War was still raging, I announced my intention to enter the nursing profession when I grew up. It seemed a heroic goal, based on my mother's example and the images of tending to young soldiers in need, and it relieved the fear my parents would not be able to support us if my father's health became further compromised. As I grew older, the notion of the smart nursing uniform and living an independent life took root in my mind and I read all I could about what sorts of things I should prepare myself for, such as biology and chemistry.

The public high school in Pelham Manor was excellent, which meant my parents were freed from the cost of sending us to private school. I was a diligent pupil and received top marks in most of my subjects, made friends and had the cocooned life of the suburbs of New York City. My parents approved of the nurses' training bent of my life, having informed me university funding would go to my brother, not me, and for a while, I was resentful of those girls who had the opportunity to attend college. Nurses' training turned out to have many of the same aspects, however; it was academic, moving toward a well-respected profession. We studied together, lived together, made lifelong friends, and felt we were sharing a defining moment in our lives.

This Atlantic City holiday was likely the last one we would take as a family foursome since my brother was off to Brown and had visions of being invited on exotic holidays with his classmates in the future. And because he and I felt it might be the last vacation together, by tacit agreement we decided to enjoy ourselves thoroughly. More recently, we had considered ourselves entirely too sophisticated to walk on the beach or eat ice cream; that summer, however, we indulged in the most childish of activities despite the fact that my slim figure in a bathing suit attracted the attention of young men on the beach. He and I played tag, collected shells, built sandcastles. enjoyed the boardwalk, and even sneaked off to a speakeasy to have a surreptitious alcoholic drink. We were in exuberant spirits most of the time, which greatly amused my parents and made us all cherish this final time together. Vacation over, we returned home with our sandy clothes, bags of shells, sun-lightened hair, and browner skin to a pile of mail and newspapers bringing the real world back into stark focus.

"Two for you, dear," my mother said, handing over a letter from Glenda and one from the hospital. My stomach tightened; I was supposed to start work the following week and there was a letter from Nurse Watson. I tore it open and read 'something had transpired' and could I please stop in at my convenience. It was Sunday and the restful day I looked forward to now was fraught with worry. I was convinced this was not good news. Had I done something wrong? Was there some mistake in my board exam?

After a fretful night's sleep, I appeared at the hospital early and found Nurse Watson in her office, all smiles, which could be a good thing or a bad thing. She looked appropriately sad when asking about Glenda Butler and the funeral, then brightened up when asking about my family and my vacation until I wanted to scream for her to get on with it.

"Something has occurred, Miss Burnside, and I would like to know if you could help me solve this little problem. Nurse Miller, whose position you were to take next week due to her upcoming marriage and relocation to Virginia, has had a setback in her marital plans. Unfortunately, her fiancé has contracted rubella and her wedding date has been pushed forward by approximately two months."

The knot in my stomach relaxed but I still wondered where the conversation was going.

"As a young couple, they, of course, wished to be in the best of financial situations as they start their married life. He naturally cannot work at the moment, so Nurse Miller has requested her resignation be delayed by six weeks."

I nodded. "What you are saying is rather than start next week, I will be starting at the end of six weeks?"

"Yes, that's right. I don't believe you have signed your contract yet so we will just adjust the dates."

"All right." It was disappointing but a relief compared to what I had imagined.

"Thank you, Miss Burnside, I should say Nurse Burnside, for your understanding. I hope my decision will not affect you adversely?"

The first thing that came into my head was how this decision affected me wasn't the most important part of this conversation. She hadn't thought to ask if perhaps I needed the money or a place to live. As it turned out, I didn't, and staying with my parents for another few weeks would be fine.

"I think I'll manage," I said.

Standing up abruptly, Nurse Watson came around to my side of the desk and shook my hand.

"Thank you. You were an excellent student and I know you will be a good nurse."

I shook her hand and left in a bit of a daze having moved from an initial sense of dread to one of calm, if a bit of confusion; after all, I now had weeks of unplanned activity ahead that I wished to use wisely somehow.

When I got back to Pelham Manor, I told my mother the news, which she took with her usual look of slight worry, then I went to my room to read Glenda's letter, pushed aside earlier in favor of my concerns of the night before. It was brief: she was coming down to the City on Tuesday and wanted to meet for lunch at our usual place. It made me smile. Just like old times.

The next day, I got to the speakeasy near the hospital before her, remembering how Glenda had discovered this location where we could have a cocktail in peace knowing neither Nurse Watson, the interns, doctors, nor the other student nurses would dream of walking into such a shabby place. It hadn't gained any charm during our recent absence and the regular barman was just as nonverbal as ever when I ordered my martini, which came in a teacup. I sipped it as slowly as possible, yet was halfway through it before Glenda burst in, her hair tucked under a cloche hat, a purse and papers under her arm, and plopped herself into a chair opposite me.

"I am parched!" she announced, taking off her gloves and waiting for the barman to approach to take her order. "The usual," she said.

"What are you doing in town? Visiting the mystery boyfriend you never wanted to tell anybody about?" I asked.

She made a face at me indicating she still had no intention of admitting who the person was that had the entire nurses' quarters speculating. The top guess was a married man, then a married doctor, all the way up to John Barrymore, whom she would have bragged about rather than hidden.

"Had to see a man about an old life insurance policy my mother took out when she still lived in New York, something I knew nothing about. It's funny how you think you know someone and yet there are still surprises." She paused a minute. "As a result, the good news is I am not as destitute as I thought. And by a strange surprise, I already have someone renting a room."

"Two pieces of good luck," I said. "Other than that, how are things going?" I asked.

"The house was and is in kind of a cluttered state. One closet had my father's old golf equipment and all kinds of boxes of papers. I thought my mother had sorted through it all, and now I have to attend to it, but there is her paperwork to plow through first. I'm afraid my mother wasn't the most organized of people."

"Unlike you?" I teased. "How are you holding up?"

"I am all right, and I suppose the burden of sorting the clutter and throwing out papers has kept my mind occupied as well as my hands. I might get through it all by the end of the summer."

The barman brought her drink over to our little table and she thanked him, put her pinky out when she picked up the teacup just to be silly, took a swallow, and sighed contentedly.

To take her mind off her difficulties, I filled her in on where each of the other girls in our graduating class was assigned to work and how next year's incoming class would have a more rigorous academic load than we had. But I noticed as I prattled on she seemed less interested in what her former classmates were doing, so we sat in silence for a few moments.

"My big news is my near future has just been turned upside down by a certain man's case of German measles," I said. I related my conversation with Nurse Watson and in doing so regretted that I had not been more forceful with her in expressing my wish to start right away.

Glenda's eyes widened. "I hope she's not going to cancel the entire wedding as well as their move out of state! Although even if she decides to stay on, another position will open up soon for you, I'm sure."

"That is exactly my hope. But I don't know what I'm going to do in the meantime. If I stay at home, the constant comings and

25

goings of my brother's friends will drive me to distraction. The telephone and doorbell ring constantly, and he has come to consider us his private secretaries, taking and relaying messages; I think he is trying to make himself as annoying as possible so that we won't miss him when he goes to college."

"Interesting strategy!"

"What's new in West Adams?"

"It's the same boring place and I suppose I should be thankful for stability. Say, in my conversations with Doctor Taylor—you remember meeting him—he mentioned he is filling in for another physician's practice over the summer and he is looking for a receptionist or assistant."

"Oh, Glenda. How wonderful! When will you start?" I asked.

She looked shocked. "Not me, I'd be hopeless. What about you?"

I was speechless. "I couldn't commit to the entire summer. Do you think he would want someone for a little over a month?"

"I don't know. We can ask. Any little bit would help, I'm sure. Oh, Aggie, just think." She smiled broadly, contemplating our future fun times, no doubt.

So that is how it came about I was going to West Adams again. The arrangements with the doctor were made over the telephone later that day, and he was thrilled to be getting a registered nurse to assist in his office half days. Glenda regretted having rented out her room to someone else but assured me Miss Manley would be glad to oblige and pleased to make a bit of money from the arrangement. Within a few days, I was on the train north again, this time with three suitcases and the anticipation of a small adventure. Never in my wildest dreams did I imagine it would turn into a betrayal of the worst sort. And a murder.

Chapter 4

When I arrived in West Adams in the early afternoon in June, the town was a hive of activity, with trucks in from the countryside delivering milk and vegetables from local farms, delivery boys on bicycles exiting the shops, women with baskets on their arms popping into the butcher's, the greengrocer's, the baker's, the general store, the drug store or stopping to chat with one another. The school term was over, as well, which meant children in the street chasing one another with the end-of-school enthusiasm.

"Things are about to get exciting," Glenda said, as we drove slowly past the clamor. "We have been invited to tea at Mrs. Lewis's this afternoon. The reverend's wife, you know. And the regiment of women will be there in force."

"How nice to be included in the social life so soon." I was not going to be pulled into Glenda's view of the female population whether they gossiped or not. Surely they would detect any disdain I might show and besides, many of them might be the doctor's patients: I needed to be mindful of that.

"Miss Manley has been in an absolute tizzy all morning getting your room ready. I stopped by and saw her puzzling with Annie over which sheets to put on the bed. It made me feel a little guilty about not having taken more care with the arrangements for my tenant."

"How is it going?"

"She's only been here a few days but so far, so good. She is quiet, an art student at Wellesley who is assisting the interior decorator hired to do an overhaul of Highfields. She leaves to go up there in the morning and only returns in the evening."

"Where is the decorator staying?"

"They've given him a room at the house, if you can believe it. I am surprised the judge allowed the hired help to have a room.

Landon Whittaker—what a perfect name. Wants to tear down walls and redo the entire place, from what I hear."

We had safely navigated the motorized and human traffic of the main street and were entering the more sedate pace of the residential area beyond. Glenda pulled the car into her narrow driveway and toward the ivy-covered garage. We walked across the garden toward Miss Manley's house, then entered through the French windows opening onto an empty sitting room. It looked remarkably like Glenda's house in the style of furnishings, crocheted antimacassars on the chairs, and the sofa facing the windows. We found Miss Manley in the kitchen with Annie, who was not only the maid but also the cook, as they were discussing the menu for dinner.

"Well, there you are," Miss Manley said with a warm smile. She had the usual polite questions about the weather in the City, the condition of the train, the level of my fatigue, etc. "But just listen to me, let's get you upstairs and settled in. Then we'll have a light lunch because I am sure there will be plenty to eat at the tea."

The bedroom I was offered was at the top of the stairs and had a broad view of the back garden through two windows as well as a vista of the lane behind the houses where Glenda and I had walked the last time I was here. It looked as if I had been assigned the master bedroom and I commented I felt somewhat guilty at having displaced my hostess.

"Oh, no, my dear. My bedroom is at the front of the house where I can see what is going on in the street. So much less distracting." Her eyes twinkled and she went back downstairs.

As I unpacked my suitcases, Glenda stood by the windows watching the activity in the back lane and beckoned me over to observe. A young girl with light blonde hair wandered slowly toward the parsonage next door and disappeared from view, likely going in one of the French windows each house here seemed to possess. All unlocked, no doubt.

"Christine Nash," Glenda said. "The judge's daughter."

The artist poked his head out of the door of his studio as if to see who had recently walked past and just as quickly closed the door. A few minutes later we saw the reverend toward the town end of the path coming home, intercepted by a sickly-looking young man who appeared seemingly out of nowhere and spoke with intensity although we could not hear what he said.

"That's Thomas Kirby, his assistant. Strange fellow. Always in a dither."

Their conversation continued almost directly in our line of sight from the rear windows upstairs and I stood still hoping they would not see us looking down on them. The reverend had been the epitome of calm during the funeral service, but today he seemed frustrated and irritated by the excited monologue of the other man. He threw up his hands, shook his head, continued to the parsonage, and went in through the sitting room windows as had the young girl earlier.

Glenda and I exchanged glances.

"Busy place," I said.

"You have a much better view than either Miss Manley or I do."

"Perhaps she has no idea of all the traffic?"

"I wouldn't count on it. I'd better get changed for tea," Glenda said.

I looked down at what I wore and asked if it was suitable and she assured me it would do just fine.

I resumed unpacking, pulling out the three starched nurses' uniforms I had brought with me, now slightly crumpled, and hung them in the closet next to the few other outfits I had imagined were appropriate for casual town events and one fancy dress in the hopes I might get to wear it somewhere. I gave myself one last glance in the full-length mirror attached to the closet door and wondered if I really was dressed appropriately for a tea in West Adams, knowing some excuses could be made for my being an out-of-towner. My dress was a mid-length, powder blue that accentuated my slim build and the color of my eyes. Wide set, those were my best feature; they and my strong, straight nose resulted in the usual description of my looks were as 'arresting' or 'handsome.' I had always wished to fall more into the 'pretty' category, but I came to realize 'pretty' didn't last as long or wear as well as 'handsome.'

"Time to go," Miss Manley said from the doorway a few minutes later, and I bent to view my hair in the vanity mirror, combing a few strands out of the way before following her down the stairs and out the back garden to the lane, meeting up with several of the women I had seen at the funeral. Now I wished I had paid better attention to names, but they kindly reintroduced themselves for my benefit. Many Misses and only a few Mrs. if my hearing was accurate. By the time the lot of us began the trek across the parsonage's garden, I had once again lost track of who was who. They admired the roses and had a lively discussion of the intricate interaction of sun, shade, soil amendments, and insecticide entirely beyond my comprehension, since I didn't have much interest in gardens except to walk through them in admiration. As we passed, we could see Reverend Lewis, standing in the middle of his study talking to someone seated on the sofa, and he nodded in our direction as we made our way further along the bed of hostas through French windows open to the sitting room where tea was laid out for us.

His wife, Nina, wore a daffodil yellow dress, welcoming by its color and lighting up the features of her bright, impish face. She stood to greet us and thankfully used her guests' names, making me feel I might eventually figure out who was who. As we positioned ourselves on the sofa, a loveseat, and various chairs, she didn't sit down but left the room to get her husband from the study. We could hear them coming down the hall in our direction and there was an embarrassing moment when all the women in the sitting room had momentarily stopped talking so the reverend's voice came through loud and clear to us.

"Judge Nash is going to be the death of me or I of him."

"Hush, darling. Here we are," his wife said brightly leading him into the stunned silence of the sitting room. He had the grace to look sheepish at being overheard and cleared his throat a few times, scanning the group and looking relieved that Mrs. Nash was not present.

"Good afternoon, ladies," he said and took his seat in an empty chair across from his wife.

The talk was about gardens again, and whose looked as if they might win the floral show prize in late July.

"Poor Aggie won't be here, then," Glenda said frowning, in what I knew to be her sly, teasing voice.

The room broke out in all manner of sympathetic noises aimed in my direction and questions about when I would begin working for their doctor, was this my first job, how long could I stay, couldn't I make a special effort to return for the show, and so on. I was trying my best to remember who asked me what and wondering if I should just follow one line of inquiry at a time rather than responding to each question in turn, which would come out as a string of non-sequiturs. Glenda smiled devilishly at my discomfort over the rim of the teacup balanced above the saucer in her hand.

I managed to make something of a coherent reply touching on all the topics thrown at me before one of the women began talking to her seatmate in tones spoken softly enough to seem a private conversation but was just loud enough for everyone to hear. As the gist of the narrative was an accusation about some missing church funds, the more polite members of our company began a series of side conversations to make enough noise to drown out the chatter that would surely offend the reverend.

Nina said in a clear voice, cutting through other conversations, "You're not the only newcomer in our town, you know."

Some were quiet waiting for the revelation while others nodded their heads knowingly.

"Judge Nash and his wife have hired someone to 'do' their house."

There was murmuring around the room.

"That's why Mrs. Nash isn't here today. Working on the drawings and all." She took a sip of tea with a smile indicating she was glad to have surprised her company with the news.

"What's his name, dear?" she asked her husband.

"Landon Whittaker," the reverend said.

"His assistant, Sandra Logan, is staying with me," Glenda offered. I liked the way she phrased it as if she were a guest rather than a paying customer. Glenda was trying to catch my eye to acknowledge her slight deception, but I avoided her gaze, afraid I might giggle.

There were murmurings around the room suggesting several had noticed a new face or two in town but now were able to put an explanation behind it. Then, someone took the conversation in the direction of the issue of the artist, Richard Fairley, whose studio was visible from the sitting room windows. Just as we turned to look in that direction we saw Christine, the judge's daughter, walk to the studio door and enter without knocking. Where had she been since we saw her go into the reverend's study earlier? Had she confided something to him, leading to his comment about the judge?

The women turned to the reverend to see his reaction, perhaps expecting him to stand up and intervene in what might be a cause for further gossip, but he did not. He pursed his lips and sighed loudly instead, which got one of the women to widen her eyes in disapproval.

"She seems to want to cause all manner of disruptions with her father," the reverend said with resignation.

"Perhaps at her age, it might not be so unusual," I suggested.

My remark brought an outburst of comments along the lines of, "When I was a young girl…" "Back in my day…," which then simmered down to a low murmur of disapproval.

A few minutes later, we all saw the daughter leave the studio and go up the lane toward Highfields where she lived. I assumed she could not have done anything too scandalous in her short time with the artist and also thought her quick exit exonerated her, but a few of the women shook their heads or sniffed in disapproval all the same. The look Glenda gave me was as if to say: see what I mean about the women?

The tea was winding down, further hastened by the reverend being called away to the telephone, and using it as an opening, Glenda and I made to leave with Nina's and Miss Manley's nods of approval.

"Whew," I said when we were out of earshot of the French windows as we walked across the grass of the back garden. "I had no idea things were so lively in this place you called boring." It gave us both a bit of a laugh.

"Come help me finish unpacking," I suggested.

"I always loved this room," she said, walking about my new place and looking out the side window toward her own house. "It's too bad my bedroom faces the other way, or we could just open the sash and yell to one another. Then the entire town would know all of our business immediately without having to wait for people to tell one another."

Her idea of helping me unpack was to sit on the bed and poke through the clothes in my suitcase.

"Isn't it funny we were so used to seeing one another in our training uniforms that looking at your real wardrobe is a treat. Where did you get this?" She had picked up a recently purchased beige sweater.

"My mother got it for me at Lord and Taylor's."

She opened the other suitcase and gasped. She had found two nurse's caps specific to the hospital where we trained; they differed from other institutions either in height, presence, or placement of a black band. Part of our graduation ceremony had been a procession where we lined up single file holding a candle, to invoke Florence

Nightingale I presumed, and approached the head of the hospital in our training caps, which were replaced by our formal nurse's caps. What started out seeming a bit theatrical turned out to be an emotional moment for the graduates, the staff, and the families alike. Glenda's moment of awe at seeing my graduate cap reflected this same feeling, and I thought despite what she had said earlier, some part of her regretted leaving that world behind.

She got up suddenly and walked over to the windows looking down into the garden.

"Look, there's Reverend Lewis," she said, pointing to his progress across his rear lawn to the artist's studio. I craned my neck to look.

No sooner had he knocked on the door, opened it, and put his head in than he closed it again and purposefully walked back home.

"Hmm," said Glenda, as I put a sweater into the chest of drawers. "Wait, look at this."

I walked back to where she stood and saw the judge's wife come out of the studio and make her way across the lawn toward the reverend's house.

Glenda and I exchanged glances.

"Never a dull moment," she said chuckling.

Chapter 5

The next morning, I came to learn Miss Manley's schedule was roughly as follows: breakfast prepared by Annie at a reasonable hour, then Miss Manley pottered about the house, tended to what correspondence came by the early mail, went to the shops to get provisions for dinner, pottered around in the garden for a bit more, and ate lunch at noon. It always seemed to be a modest meal accompanied by water for me and some strange liquid in a tumbler for her.

Her head to the side, she smiled at me. "As a medical professional, no doubt you are interested in what is in this glass." Before I had a chance to comment, she continued. "It is not spirituous liquor as you might imagine, but a special tonic the doctor recommended the pharmacist make up for me. He saw I had lost a bit of weight and wanted to enhance my appetite."

I nodded and suppressed a smile at her antiquated vocabulary.

"I think it was the worry about dear Sarah Butler causing the weight loss. I hope it is no more than that because this tastes awful!" She took it down in one gulp and did her best to disguise a look of intense revulsion. Oh, those elderly ladies and their sense of propriety; one must never show excess emotion.

I was informed that Miss Manley would soon have her afternoon nap, what she referred to as putting her feet up, to be followed by tea with Glenda, which had formerly been her customary tea with Sarah, then sorting through and answering the afternoon mail, further pottering in the garden, and possibly a social call or two before dinner. We chatted through lunch until it was time for me to change into my uniform and walk the short distance to Doctor Taylor's for my first afternoon half day.

The doctor shook my hand in greeting and said to place me, "Oh, yes, you were the tall young woman."

This put me off a bit because people often commented on the obvious.

"I still am. As are you," I blurted.

At least he thought that was funny and he responded, "Tall, not a woman, I presume."

The initial tension broken, we got right into the work at hand. He was polite yet professional, instructing me in his preferred protocol for scheduling appointments and dealing with patients and his contact information for the other doctor's practice where he covered in the morning. No sooner had he retreated into his office than the first two patients arrived, nodded at me, and sat in chairs across the small room from my desk. Oddly enough, the older man and a younger one, who may have been his son, did not present themselves to me or give me their names, so I felt forced to ask.

"Name?"

They turned to one another and began to laugh. Seeing my surprised reaction, they stopped.

"The doctor will know who we are," the older man said.

"Yes, sir, but I don't know who you are," I said standing.

At that moment the doctor came out of his office and shook the men's hands in turn and ushered them toward the examination room.

"Please get the file, Nurse," he said to me over his shoulder.

I stood staring at his back. When he did not see me move, he looked back impatiently in my direction.

"Name?" I asked.

He began to laugh, and the two men thought this was uproariously funny and took almost a full minute to regain their composure.

"Mr. Perkins."

"Thank you, Doctor Taylor." I felt my face flushing with embarrassment at the awkward exchange. I turned to the file cabinet behind me and it took some time to find the file because it looked as if the doctor was in the habit of putting the files back by laying them on top of the others any which way rather than alphabetically. After delivering the Perkins's file to the doctor, I spent the time they were in the exam room putting the files back in alphabetical order and then opening the second file drawer to see what was in it. The first name to jump out at me was Sarah Butler, Glenda's mother, and I closed the file drawer abruptly, unsettled at my discovery of what must be deceased patients. I looked around at something else to do and the door to the exam room opened to three smiling men.

"Name?" the old man said again as he left, laughing and slapping his cap against his leg for emphasis.

"Is there something you would like me to be doing besides ushering the patients in?" I asked the doctor.

"You could put the files in order," he suggested.

"I have just done so."

"Hmm. How about if you take an inventory of the drugs cabinet. It hasn't been done in a long time."

I nodded, took a pad of paper from the desk and went to work in the examination room while he retreated to his office, presumably making notes in the most recent patient's file. The drug cabinet was not locked, something I found shocking, since the hospital's protocols were to lock everything up—drugs, medications, towels, sheets, whatever could grow legs and walk out the door. We always knew when Nurse Watson was making the rounds by the sound of the ring of keys jangling at her waist that could unlock the precious contents of the various cabinets. Here it was in full view behind the glass and I was relieved to find at least no narcotics except for a vial of tincture of opium, often administered for problems with the lower digestive tract. Although the boxes, jars, and bottles were in some kind of order, I was not able to ascertain what kind of classification system the doctor used. Well, I thought, this is something I did not learn in our training and I might suggest to Nurse Watson it could be taught because I was sure there must have been some common system developed over time.

The list completed, I looked at my watch to see I had only been here an hour and a half and seemed to have run out of things to do. My thoughts were interrupted when the surgery door banged open and a mother rushed in with a wailing child who had hit his head and scraped his leg. And so went the rest of the afternoon: long stretches of quiet and idleness followed by the sudden appearance of someone with a pressing need, although no lifethreatening emergencies showed themselves on my first day. I left at five o'clock, surprisingly more tired than I had anticipated, and considered having a few moments with my feet up before dinner. I got home to discover Miss Manley lying on the sofa in the sitting room looking dazed, with Annie and Glenda in armchairs facing her, worried looks on their faces and an exhalation of relief when they saw me.

"Whatever is the matter?" I asked.

"You've called for a nurse?" Miss Manley asked weakly looking in my direction.

"It is I, Agnes Burnside," I said, wondering if there was a problem with her vision to not recognize me or if something more serious had happened to her faculties.

She moaned a little in response.

"Aggie, I don't know what we should do. I came over for tea and she hadn't come down from her nap. When we went to wake her, she was disoriented and muttering about something. Each time we tried to get her to lie down, she would get up and try to wander around," Glenda said.

"Why didn't you call the doctor?" I asked. What were they thinking? His house and office were next door to the parsonage, fronting the main street, a mere minutes' walk.

"I'll go get him," I said, turning around and briskly making my way back to Doctor Taylor's house. The surgery door was unlocked, and I found him putting files back into the cabinet, his back to me. I explained the situation as best I understood it and waited for him to get his bag, then we made our way back through the yards and gardens. What followed was a series of questions directed at Annie, who seemed entirely baffled by Miss Manley's behavior, and Glenda, who could provide no helpful information. I related I had last seen my landlady at lunch where she was conversational and as normal as I knew her to be in my short acquaintance.

The doctor took her pulse and her blood pressure, looked in her eyes, throat, and ears, and then put a thermometer in her mouth and waited for the outcome while we three women looked at one another.

"No fever. Miss Manley," he said a little loudly, shaking down the thermometer. "Can you describe how you feel right now?"

She cleared her throat and asked to sit up. The maid brought a glass of water from the kitchen and after a swallow, Miss Manley found she could speak.

"The oddest thing," she said. She drank more water while we waited. "I have never had such a long nap and when I awoke, I felt I had to do something, but I couldn't remember what it was."

"Do you have a headache?"

"No."

"Dizzy?"

"A little bit. I'm just feeling a bit wooly." She managed a small laugh and tried to get up but all three of us made sure she remained seated.

"It happens," the doctor said. I thought he left out the rest of the sentence where he would say, 'when you get old.'

Although he didn't say it, it was implicit and she looked at him with a bit of fear in her eyes, not yet ready to admit she, too, after the loss of her good friend Sarah Butler, could be frail and might be next.

Leaving Glenda with Miss Manley after the maid and doctor left, I went upstairs to change out of my uniform, still crisp and clean after a mostly uneventful first day. I stood near the windows overlooking the back lane buttoning up my blouse and saw the artist walking slowly toward the parsonage, his eyes to the ground as if something was on his mind.

I rejoined the two women in the sitting room and was pleased to see Miss Manley had regained some of her usual color and was talking coherently to Glenda.

"Poor Reverend Lewis," I muttered without thinking. They both gave me questioning looks.

"Sorry, it seems people are always popping in to talk to him. I can't see how he has any time for himself."

"He is good in that way," Miss Manley said.

"It's the job, isn't it?" Glenda asked.

"If more people would attend services and support the church rather than just expecting him to provide pastoral duties at the drop of a hat…." Miss Manley stopped short.

I changed the subject and asked if she would like to get a breath of air in the garden, to which she readily agreed. Glenda led her outside while I checked in the kitchen to see what Annie had left us for dinner and took the liberty of rummaging through the pantry looking for some kind of restorative. Taking the stopper out of one ornamental bottle I smelled what seemed to be homemade wine. I put it and several small glasses on a tray.

"Just the thing," Miss Manley said from her chair in the shade of the garden as I brought it out. "Elderberry Wine."

"They didn't call me glamorous for nothing," Glenda added with a smile, reaching for a cordial glass as if it were a martini.

It was lovely to sit in the shade with a gentle breeze ruffling our hair, the only sounds birds high up in the trees. And whistling. Whistling?

We turned our heads toward the lane where we saw a gangly young man with curly brown hair whistling loudly as he swung his tennis racquet against the low-hanging bushes on either side.

"Hullo, Miss Manley, Miss Butler," he said, walking jauntily in his white outfit.

"Good evening, Roger," she replied. "Let me introduce Agnes Burnside."

He came over and shook my hand and gave his name, then left, making his way into the reverend's back garden, heading for the study. I immediately thought of the artist whom we had seen enter the study but hadn't yet seen come out and was about to halt the young man, but Miss Manley stalled my impulse with a hand on my arm.

"It's the reverend's nephew, Roger, come to stay for the summer. Richard Fairley probably left by the front door already. Much easier to get to his cottage down the road."

From this, I surmised she had certainly regained her usual observational and cognitive skills. Perhaps there was something to be said for homemade wine.

Chapter 6

I was still concerned enough about Miss Manley's 'episode,' as she called it, to listen to any noises in the night, such as her getting up to use the bathroom, which could present a potential fall, but all was silent in the house. Outside, however, a bird sounding as if it were on the ground kept singing or vocalizing and regaled me with its repertoire for a good half hour. Quiet at last, a door slammed, and thinking Miss Manley had got up or bumped into her door, I got up to see all was quiet in our house, but a light had gone on in the artist's studio next door and shortly thereafter had gone out with the accompanying slam of the door. To round out the late-night activities, a long 'whooo' call seemed to indicate an owl was somewhere in the yard or adjacent woods hunting for the night.

The next day began with the muffled sounds of Annie in the kitchen making our breakfast and I was pleased to see Miss Manley had preceded me to the table, looking cheerful and erect in her posture. I had decided not to bring up the event of the day before but carry on with the usual chatter about what each of us had planned. I was going to write my parents a letter, then get some film for my Brownie camera as I intended to take photos of the town and the surrounding landscape over the weekend to enclose in future correspondence. The latter errand would take me to the shops that had just been a background to my other activities to date. Glenda could tease me all she liked about what she called the 'Ye Olde' look of the main street, but I was entranced to experience the quaint buildings with their mullioned windows and hanging signs outside and flower baskets suspended from the streetlights.

Unlike my dashed-off notes to my parents while I was in training, I decided to take time and care to give them a detailed picture of the place and people I had encountered so far. Afterward, I had to laugh at myself because I was not in a foreign country and my mother had grown up in Pennsylvania and well knew what life was like in a small town: the characters, the gossip, the shops, the metronome of daily life. As I wrote at the feminine desk facing the windows, I had an expansive view of the woods beyond the lane as well as the usual foot traffic behind the homes that ended at the parsonage but extended in the other direction to a small road perpendicular to the main street. In the space of time I sat there, the reverend's maid availed herself of the shortcut to do the daily shopping, his nephew whom we saw yesterday left in his tennis whites with a racquet in hand, Richard Fairley came from the town center to his studio, and Glenda took the path in the other direction on some errand. It seemed the only people who didn't use it were the milkman and the postman. Despite these visual distractions, it was a treat to give myself over to prose, a change after so many months of my studies, and to be able to use the sturdy, marbleized fountain pen with the gold nib, a graduation present. Reminder: get more ink while out shopping.

    I had several hours before work, so after depositing my letter at the post office I took my time wandering from store to store to see what they had to offer. All of those about foodstuffs had a busy trade as women did their marketing in the morning when all was still fresh. My mother did the same back home although there were also small trucks from the countryside that drove through the suburban areas around New York, stopping to sell vegetables, fruit, and sometimes more exotic items while parked along the main street in Pelham Manor. I remember as a little girl, before most transports became motorized, going out to the street with my mother to pet the horse that drew one greengrocer's cart. The ancient animal was exceedingly docile, and the vendor usually managed to find a damaged apple to give me for the horse's treat. The few animals pulling carts here through the town were larger and healthier, evidently actually working farm animals.

    A young butcher smiled at me from behind the counter in one shop although I had no basket on my arm and was not doing marketing. I soon realized I must be the new topic of conversation because proprietors or their assistants were standing outside on the pavement and nodded to me as I walked by; I don't think I have ever felt so conspicuous in my life. The general store was along this side of the street and I ducked in to buy ink and peruse their boxed sets of paper and envelopes made in a factory outside of Pittsfield. I glanced up to see a sign indicating the price of buying one sheet of paper and one envelope: how curious. Perhaps a farmer or tradesman did not need to send more than one letter once in a great while, so this was a thrifty solution.

As I was leaving with my new bottle of ink, I saw Reverend Lewis across the street, striding purposefully toward home. I was about to wave to him when he was interrupted in his progress by a loud voice.

"Reverend Lewis! Reverend Lewis!"

It was Judge Nash with his loud voice who took the reverend's elbow in his hand and stopped him in his tracks.

Reverend Lewis responded in what must have been normal tones for I could barely hear him from my distance across the street, but the judge must have been somewhat deaf because he cupped a hand behind his ear and said, "What is it you say?"

From then on the conversation was loud enough on both their parts for me, as well as probably half of the people on the street, to overhear. It involved a problem with church funds, and the judge was evidently on the board of the church in some capacity and did not take his position lightly. The conversation seemed to get heated, but it might have only appeared that way because Mr. Lewis had to speak loudly to be heard and the judge probably did so from force of habit. In any case, the last bit had them making an appointment for six-fifteen at the Nash residence, Highfields, and each man went his way.

On my way back toward the residential area, the reverend caught sight of me, waved, and crossed the street to join me. He mopped his forehead with a handkerchief although it was hardly a warm day, and I deduced his recent conversation had been uncomfortable. Before we had even begun to make conversation, the man who Glenda identified as Thomas Kirby yesterday talking to the Reverend on the back path now popped out in front of us from the shrubbery of a neighbor's yard, and he seemed as startled to see me as I was to see him. Without an apology or introduction, he explained to the reverend he was feeling unwell and wouldn't be able to conduct choir practice that night. Just as quickly, he turned and disappeared back into the bushes.

"What an odd fellow!" I said, instantly regretting my bold observation.

"Yes, he is. He most certainly is. Thomas Kirby, my assistant. I believe his former assignment as a missionary took a toll on his physical and mental health. I am not revealing any secrets by telling you the poor man contracted malaria and is still suffering from the effects."

"I am sorry to hear it. We had a patient at the hospital in New York, a former geologist, who had contracted malaria somewhere in South America and he suffered greatly in an awful cycle of fever, then chills, then a respite of a few days before the cycle began again."

"That's exactly what goes on with him and I do have sympathy for his situation, but it makes his already odd personality even stranger, somewhat paranoid. Is it one of the effects of the disease?"

"I don't remember such a thing, but perhaps Doctor Taylor can answer your question. I am sure just being so ill repeatedly has got to have a wearing effect on one's state of mind."

"Well said, young lady." He looked me in the eye and shook my hand as we were at the front of Miss Manley's house and his was the next one on. "Good day."

What a curious man he was and what a demanding job to juggle the spiritual needs of the community, which entailed listening to anyone and everyone's problems and complaints at any time of the day as if he had no life of his own.

Just as I turned, a short, round man with a mustache and trim beard came purposefully toward us. He had on plaid pants, a pink shirt, a red bow tie, suspenders, and a relatively sedate black jacket.

"Reverend Lewis!" he called out, quickening his stride.
Behind him was a young woman trying desperately to catch up to him.

"I'm so glad I found you at home!" the man said to the reverend's disappointed look that was quickly turned into a welcoming smile.

"I hope I'm not taking up your precious time? I'm Landon Whittaker, working at Highfields."

"Oh, yes, of course." The reverend introduced me and when the young woman caught up to the three of us standing in the street, she thrust out her arm and shook the reverend's hand heartily.

"Sandra Logan." Ah, so this was Glenda's tenant. She was as nondescript in her appearance as Landon Whittaker was outlandish in his, dressed in a brown skirt, beige blouse and mud-colored cardigan. Introductions all around and the reverend asked how he could be of assistance.

"I understand from Mrs. Nash you have something of a collection of American Indian artifacts. I'm a bit of a history buff myself."

Reverend Lewis blushed a bit. "Yes, I do. Would you like to see it sometime?"

Mr. Whittaker and Sandra nodded enthusiastically, and I added my voice to the conversation, asking if I could see it as well.
This town was full of surprises.

"No time like the present," he said.

We were led into the reverend's study, a large room with seating against one wall, bookcases on another and a desk and chair facing a wall. If this had been my room I would have had the desk facing the garden for the vista but perhaps the reverend needed to minimize distraction when he was working and chose the wall with its placid landscape painting hanging as his view. I could see a fair number of papers on the desk, likely Sunday's sermon in progress.

"Please sit down. I keep the artifacts here and sometimes when I am stumped in my writing, I take one out and contemplate its age, who its maker so long ago was, and that tends to put my mundane problems in perspective."

He went over to the bookcase and opened a drawer in the cabinet below, pulled out a tray lined with flannel, brought it over to the table in front of the sofa, and showed us about twenty arrowheads of various sizes made from different colored stone, finely chipped to create a lethal point.

"Perhaps you've seen much better, but this is my arrowhead collection."

"Very nice, very nice," Whittaker said. "Do you have a record of where you found each of these?"

"In a notebook. I'm afraid the names of the locations won't mean much to you, but we could take an excursion someday and I would be happy to show you."

"How wonderful. May I?" Whittaker picked up one knapped from some maroon-colored stone and held it up to the light. "Isn't the workmanship exquisite? It almost looks too delicate to have been used to kill a rabbit or deer, doesn't it?"

"What Indians were in this area before it was settled?" I asked.

"The Mohicans," Sandra responded crisply.

"I thought they were wiped out long ago," I said, turning to her.

"James Fennimore Cooper strikes again!" Whittaker said chuckling. "They weren't too numerous to begin with and coalesced with other tribes after Europeans settled here. But many of these tribes spoke the same language and had similar customs. Have you any basketry by chance?"

The reverend's face took on color as he proudly went to the cabinet and returned with something encased in waxed paper. He set it down on the table and carefully unwrapped a brown woven

47

scrap that didn't look like much to me. But Whittaker exhaled in delight and taking a pencil from his pocket to use as an instrument, moved it carefully.

"You can see the warp and woof, can't you?" he said, and we all nodded although I could not detect anything resembling weaving.

"It might not be so old, actually," said the reverend. "But I did find it in an area where I have found arrowheads and pottery shards." He wrapped it up again and returned it to the cabinet. Next, out came another tray lined with flannel and an assortment of pieces of clay, some with marking pressed in, others with colors applied.

"Ah, now that is something!" Whittaker exclaimed. He seemed excited by all he saw, and his enthusiasm was contagious enough to give the reverend a beaming smile. We heard footsteps and Nina appeared at the door to the hallway.

"Darling," she stopped abruptly. "Oh, sorry, I didn't realize you were busy."

"No, no, come in."

Today she was wearing a dress of printed pink flowers, so unlike the somber clothes of most of the women of the town, myself included, who dressed for practicality above all. However, now I saw what a difference her colorful outfits had on people; it immediately brightened the room, along with her smiling heartshaped face.

Introductions were made and the reverend continued explaining about the pottery bits, apologizing as he went, deferring to the expertise Whittaker seemed to display and agreeing with everything being said.

"How long have you been working with Mr. Whittaker, Miss Logan?" Nina asked.

"Just a week. I am going to be a sophomore at Wellesley, and I saw the posting on the bulletin board for an interior design assistant. It sounded interesting."

A brief pang of regret shot through me as I realized I could have been that young girl two years ago, looking at all options for my future, seeing an enticing notice on a bulletin board and having an adventure in a new place.

"I would have brought my usual assistant from New York with me, but the cost of travel was prohibitive," Whittaker explained. "And somebody has to mind the store! This way I can use the money to make sure Sandra gets paid for her time."

The reverend put his pottery tray back carefully and brought out another with slightly larger shards.

Whittaker rubbed his hands in anticipation and said, "May I?"

After a nod from the reverend, he picked up a piece. "Exquisite."

"Now you have discovered my hobby, I wonder if I could prevail upon you to share your ideas of renovation of Highfields?"

"Of course. If Judge Nash doesn't have a problem with it."

The reverend's face fell a bit at the mention of the property owner, but his wife said, "I'm sure he would be delighted with it." She sat next to him, leaning in with interest.

"Are you familiar with the layout of Highfields?" he asked the reverend.

"Yes, generally speaking," the reverend answered with a bit of hesitation as if he had been there several times but hadn't paid much attention to the overall plan.

"Mrs. Nash thinks many of the rooms are too dark, and I quite agree. Wood paneling, small windows, heavy curtains, grotesquely Victorian." There was an awkward moment when he realized he had also just described the study in which they sat.

"Part of the style can be attributed to worrying about staying warm inside the house with limited central heating. My grandmother also had a horror of sunlight on her Persian carpets, so she had thick velvet curtains and sheer curtains, as well. But she lived in Boston and I think there was a notion of not allowing people a view inside the house," Nina offered.

"My grand design will open the gloomy house to the vast views of Mount Greylock, and the natural light will pour in onto oyster-shell white walls. If you don't mind me saying so, the dreadful lumpy furniture has got to go—I envision a sleek look of white with black accents." Whittaker's face turned up to the ceiling. "And gleaming white, from floor to ceiling except for touches of grey."

"And black," Sandra added.

"It sounds like what grand houses look like in films," I said. I hadn't been inside Highfields, but his description of rooms I had seen in movies where people were in evening gowns and tails chatting urbanely seemed incongruous with the exterior of the house on the hill.

"And knocking down walls will accomplish much toward opening the lungs of the house that has such good bones. Speaking of which, we'd better get back to it," Whittaker said. "I appreciate seeing your collection, Reverend Lewis. And I'd love to take a walkabout with you so you could show me where some of your special places are."

It was almost noon after an eventful morning, and I hurried back to Miss Manley's in time for lunch and to share with her the grandiose plans for Highfields.

Chapter 7

After our meal and a quick wardrobe change into my uniform, I was off to work. The door to the doctor's office was unlocked although he wasn't there yet, which I considered an unwise practice considering there were medical instruments, medications, and an accessible file cabinet. I was wondering how best to express concern about the lack of security without making my comments appear to be criticism when he burst through the door a bit out of breath.

"Sorry to keep you waiting, Nurse Burnside. A large truck slowed down traffic into town. How are you today?"

"Well, thank you. And you?" Once again I noticed he was a big, handsome man, tall and strong-featured, but he seldom smiled. I found him serious rather than plodding as Glenda had described him.

"Tolerable. If all is quiet, I will just go into the house and get a bite to eat. Have you had lunch?"

"Yes, thank you. And take your time, Doctor. If anyone comes in, I will call you."

Finally, he smiled, quite a lovely smile.

While he was gone, I looked through the mail, which consisted of a note marked 'Personal' that I, of course, left unopened after holding it up to the light to see if I could discern the author. There was also a medical journal, a magazine, and a lumpy envelope containing five one-dollar bills and a note of thank you from one of the patients. We hadn't yet discussed if I was to handle payments, another point of clarification we could make during a slow moment in the afternoon. The phone rang and I almost jumped out of my chair because it had been so quiet. It was a man calling from a nearby farm asking the doctor to come out and take a look at his wife. I asked if I should get the doctor on the phone so they could speak directly and he said no and did not request a specific time, but abruptly hung up. I wrote down what I thought was the name of the farm—the man did not give his name—and I had been so flustered I forgot to ask. However, as the community was small, the doctor would likely know exactly who it was, and the notion of an appointment was laughable since the farmer probably wouldn't be going anywhere all day.

I was trying to adapt my thinking to how things were done here with a degree of informality, a largely walk-in practice, visits to far-flung farms, and skimpy payments. Reminding myself it was only my second day, I was still disappointed at the lack of activity and the meager remuneration in a rural doctor's practice. I wondered if he ever got paid in eggs or chickens or a sack of potatoes. In any case, whatever daydream I might have had of being a doctor's wife in a small town or village was beginning to evaporate. I turned to the file cabinet and saw he had put yesterday's files on top of the ones I had alphabetized previously. This was evidently how he did the paperwork, and it was better than his leaving the files out on the desk for anyone to riffle through.

Doctor Taylor returned from his lunch and we discussed filing, payment, incoming and outgoing mail, the telephone call from the farmer, and not much else. He took the envelope marked personal, looked at it quizzically, and put it in his pocket. Shortly after, the first of what turned out to be a dozen people during the afternoon came into the office. The medical issues ran the gamut from something stuck in the eye, fever and swollen glands for another, an almost full-body rash that could have been measles, and dramatically, a broken radius on a young boy who fell out of a tree in his first week of summer vacation. When it came to the last, I was able to assist in soothing the boy and his mother and working with the gauze and plaster, something that surprised the doctor, who perhaps didn't realize nurses were now trained in applying casts.

Before I knew it, it was past five o'clock and I was feeling tired and most definitely hungry. I walked back home and was dismayed to see the same scene as the afternoon before, with Miss Manley lying on the sofa with Annie and Glenda in attendance.

"You should have called me," I said, and bent to look more closely at the recumbent figure.

"I'm sorry, but I insisted they shouldn't," Miss Manley said. "It is just as it was yesterday, therefore I think we can expect this sensation will pass shortly. No need to call the doctor."

We looked at one another and I was of two minds about what to do.

Miss Manley pulled herself to a seated position and exhaled. "I don't feel nearly as bad as I did yesterday." She took the glass of water offered to her and drank deeply.

"Do you think it's the tonic you have been taking before lunch?"

"I've been taking it for several weeks, so I think not. I would feel better if I were out in the garden, however," she said.

We took her outside and positioned her again in one of the chairs in the shade of an elm and I could see the color returning to her face and a smile at the pleasure of being in her garden. Perhaps this event was an anomaly, even if it had happened two days in a row. Annie was preparing dinner for us but was not yet ready to leave for the day, so Glenda and I sat outside with Miss Manley for a while until Glenda, too, had to attend to her tenant's meal. I went back inside to fetch the elderberry wine from the pantry, poured two cordial glasses full, and returned to see Miss Manley looking about somewhat anxiously.

"The garden is getting to be such a mess!" she said.

To my eyes, it didn't, but for someone who took such pride in her horticultural skills and was out and about in her garden, front and back each day, I am sure she noticed each minute issue. I looked down at my uniform and picked the several pieces of plaster off it before standing to brush them into the grass.

"Do you mind if I change my clothes?" I asked, a bit anxious about leaving her alone.

"Of course not."

"On the condition you remain here until I get back," I said sternly.

"Of course."

I made my way up the stairs quickly, changed clothes, tidied my hair, took a short trip to the bathroom and was downstairs in less than five minutes, checking my watch, which said six-thirty, pleased the fast change routine perfected in nurses' training had come in handy.

As I walked out into the garden, I immediately noticed Miss Manley was no longer in the chair in the shade or anywhere to be seen. I called out and up popped her head from the rose garden near the gate to the back lane and she smiled.

"Just seeing which roses need dead-heading. Can't let them become hips, you know."

"Let me go get some garden gloves for you, at least," I said to Miss Manley. "And please, take it easy."

Of course, she wouldn't but immediately bent down, probably to yank some weed out of the ground. I hurried in the back door and looked on the low shelves holding garden shears and other implements, moved a hat and found a sturdy pair of gloves. I brought them outside and saw Glenda approach from her back garden.

"Let's go for a walk, I have been stuck inside all afternoon going through paperwork," she said, probably referring to her mother's estate.

I asked Miss Manley if she would be all right by herself for a short while and she shooed me away with a laugh. Annie was still there and would be until I returned even if I wasn't so sure I should leave her for any amount of time; but if she could garden, she was probably all right, and I was mindful of her pride as well.

Glenda and I took the path up to Highfields and as we walked I recounted the events of the day at the doctor's, evidently a rather exciting one by the reaction I received. I knew the poor young boy was over the initial shock of the accident, had likely moved to the stage of showing his cast to his friends, and was just beginning to feel the throbbing ache of the actual injury.

Glenda revealed she had been trying to figure out if the property taxes had been paid and, finding no receipt, discovered in further frustration it was too late to call anyone. Our walk was leisurely, and the smell of pine needles and the soft breeze was a balm to both of us as we came out into the sunshine of the lawn opposite Highfields and saw the most amazing scene.

The reverend was just pulling his car up to the entrance when Richard Fairley threw open the massive front door of Highfields and came down the stairs in a kind of daze. His hair was askew, and he raked his hand through it as he approached the reverend, then laughed chillingly.

"Whatever is the matter? Have you been to see the judge?" we overheard the reverend ask.

"Oh, I've seen the judge all right," he responded, jiggled around from one foot to the other and ran off down the driveway toward the town.

The reverend turned to follow his progress, spotted us staring at the strange scene, and shrugged his shoulders with a bewildered look on his face before going in the open front door.

"Hello!" he called out as he entered what seemed to be the deserted hall.

Glenda and I stood, still wondering what we had just witnessed when a few minutes later we heard a shout from inside the house and then a woman's scream. We ran across the lawn, past the driveway, up the front steps, and through the open front door. Stopping momentarily to allow our eyes to become adjusted to the dim hallway, we saw a maid at the end of the long entry hall standing in a doorway, her hands to her mouth. We raced to her and, looking in the shadowy room, we saw the reverend far over to my left, standing behind a slumped object at the desk. Reverend Lewis turned immediately and said: "The judge has been shot!"

The maid let out another scream at the doorway and I said, "We need to call the doctor. Touch nothing!"

While Glenda gaped at the scene in front of us, I pushed the maid out of the room and demanded she show me the nearest telephone, which was in the hallway near the bottom of the stairs. I picked it up and while dialing saw Mrs. Nash come slowly down those stairs with a quizzical look on her face, regarding me intensely and likely wondering who had screamed and what on earth I was doing in her house taking advantage of her telephone.

To my relief, Doctor Taylor was at home and said he'd be at Highfields immediately. Mrs. Nash continued to look at me, then followed my gaze back down the hall toward the study. I grabbed her arm.

"I wouldn't go in there just now if I were you," I said.

Mrs. Nash pulled away from me slowly yet with determination, clearly puzzled, and made her way quickly down the hallway, stopped at the open door, and fell against it in horror. I was able to catch her before she crumpled to the floor, her tight skirt buckling behind her knees as she slid down. Glenda and the reverend were aroused from their frozen position looking down at the judge's body and hurried to the doorway to assist me. We managed to get Mrs. Nash back out into the hallway and onto a chair near the telephone. A woman I assumed was the cook by her outfit and another maid came from the back of the house along a parallel hallway and stopped at the foot of the stairs. At the same moment, Christine, book in hand, and Landon Whittaker and Sandra with rolled papers in theirs, appeared and inquired what was going on.

"Glass of water, quickly!" I commanded, and while Glenda looked around wondering where to get it, the cook scurried toward the back of the house and returned almost immediately with a large glass. The reverend was lightly slapping Mrs. Nash's hands in an attempt to revive her and she was pulling them away trying to make him stop. I stepped between them to give her the glass and she drank almost half of it greedily. We stared at one another for long minutes until we heard a car roar up the driveway and skid to a halt. The doctor's strides across the gravel brought him into the darkened house. He stopped a moment to adjust to the scene, perhaps thinking something had happened to Mrs. Nash, but I led him to the study, and he took the entire scene in quickly.

"Has anyone touched the body?" he asked.

I was standing about five feet away, conscious of not wanting to get too close for fear of contaminating something.

"No," I answered. "I don't believe so."

"How is Mrs. Nash?"

"She's being looked after."

The doctor took his time examining the judge, slumped over his partially outstretched hands, a puddle of blood on one side of his head and a letter off to the left before he spoke.

"He's hasn't been dead very long. Perhaps half an hour."

Chapter 8

It was only then I began to wonder what in the world the reverend was doing up at Highfields before remembering the appointment he had made with the judge earlier. He turned toward me, his face unnaturally white and explained, unnecessarily: "He was waiting for me, I reckon. We were to meet a bit after six to discuss some church business, but I had been summoned out to a parishioner's house by a phone call earlier and it is some distance. I knew I would not be back in time." He looked at the maid, who leaned against the staircase, her eyes still wide.

"Were you the one who took the message for him when I phoned?"

"Yes," she responded. "The judge said he would wait."

"The oddest thing is when I got out to the parishioner's farm, not only was he not in need of me but the call didn't come from anyone in the family."

"Odd indeed," I said.

At this, the doctor looked up. "Aggie, Glenda, are you all right?"

"Of course," we said in unison.

"Call the police, please," Reverend Lewis instructed the maid, who returned to the telephone. While Mrs. Nash sat, the rest of us stood almost frozen in position.

Officer Reed arrived in record time from the town center and the first words out of his mouth were, "Touch nothing!" He marched into the study with the doctor, stayed there a few minutes, and came back out.

"I touched the body, naturally," the doctor was saying as they emerged, "to determine if he were alive and, if not, how long ago he had expired."

"Looks like a gunshot. Have any of you seen a gun?"

We all shook our heads "no," and he made a grunting noise and went back into the study, emerging a few minutes later saying he didn't see one anywhere.

"What are all of you doing here?" the policeman asked, and the reverend repeated his explanation. Glenda and I told of taking a walk through the woods and coming out to the scene of the reverend talking to a wild-looking Richard Fairley.

"I'd better call the inspector from Pittsfield to come out," Officer Reed said. "Where is Richard Fairley now?" "He

ran down the drive toward town," Glenda said.

"What?"

He then asked the housekeeper, who suddenly appeared from the back recesses of the house, if there was a room where we could all sit down. The look on her face indicated she had been told by someone about the recent events and without question ushered us all into a huge sitting room with floor-to-ceiling windows facing Mount Greylock. It was stunning, full of natural light and I was baffled by Landon Whittaker's earlier description of it as dark and gloomy.

"Now then," Officer Reed began. "I may as well take down some preliminary information. Did anyone hear a shot?"

The reverend answered first. "I was on my way back from a farm and didn't hear anything as I approached."

The staff were wide-eyed with fear and realized any one of them could be implicated in the murder. Officer Reed looked at the number of people who had to be questioned and decided to wait for the inspector to get there, which he said would take about twenty minutes.

"Are there any other staff in the house?"

"There is a chauffeur, but he's out in the garage," the housekeeper said.

"Please get him."

She turned to one of the maids, nodded her head, and the young girl went off at a trot. Looking at the housekeeper's bun, I thought of Miss Manley waiting for me for supper and decided I needed to let her know I would be late. I asked Officer Reed if I could make the call and although he hesitated, he allowed me to do so.

When I got back to the sitting room, the chauffeur was seated in a chair he normally would not be allowed to occupy in a room where he had probably never been. After an awkwardly silent thirty-minute wait, the doorbell rang, and the same maid hopped up to answer the door. She returned to the study with the inspector, a small man in civilian clothes who glared at each of us in turn as if he knew we were all guilty.

"What is going on here?"

Some of us stood and launched a torrent of words at him until the inspector held up his hand for silence.

"Please, sit down," he commanded. Sit we did. "Officer Reed?" he asked, indicating he wished to view the body. The doctor stood and introduced himself and was allowed to accompany the two lawmen out to the hall and the study. They were gone a good ten minutes, enough time for one of the maids to bite her lip and start crying. I noticed neither Mrs. Nash nor Christine expressed any emotion; the shock, I supposed, although the new widow twisted her wedding ring on her finger and her stepdaughter fidgeted with a gold pinky ring with a crest on it.

The three men came back, and the inspector sat with a sigh. "All right, I have to know who each of you is." He looked to his right where Landon Whittaker sat, his pudgy hands squeezing the roll of paper plans and began by saying his name and why he was present. And so on, around the room until everyone was identified. Officer Reed read from his notes, reconstructing what little he knew so far, but stressing no one had heard a shot; rather it was the discovery of the judge's body by the reverend, his shout and the maid's scream that alerted those in the house to the murder.

"There is one other thing," the reverend said, looking uneasy. "When I got out of my car, I saw Richard Fairley leaving in an agitated state. I asked him if he had seen the judge and he was nearly hysterical when he replied he had before he ran down the driveway."

Mrs. Nash gasped at this and put her hand to her mouth.

The inspector's eyebrows rose up considerably. "Who the devil is Richard Fairley? And what was he doing here? What time was this?"

"About six forty-five."

"We saw him, too," Glenda added, and I nodded.

"What were you two doing here?"

"We just went for a walk from the town below, up through the woods to admire the view."

The inspector gave an annoyed glance at us as if admiring the view was a ridiculous form of entertainment for anyone to undertake.

"The only thing I would comment on is it looks as though the judge's head hit the watch on his wrist and smashed the face of it at six o'clock," the doctor said. "It can't be right. He can't have been shot at six. All the physical evidence from the body indicates he died about 6:15."

"But this note we found under one of his hands has the time of six o'clock written at the top," the policeman said. He read out the contents of the note, which was addressed to the reverend, indicating he had something to attend to and would call…and there the missive, unfinished, ended.

I shook my head in confusion. Why would anyone write the time on a note when other people in the house could attest to when he intended to leave? Thinking about leaving, although I had told Miss Manley I would be detained for a while, I hadn't thought about whether Annie would stay with her until I got back. I was just going to have to put those thoughts aside for the moment; I certainly couldn't ask to make another phone call without the officer and inspector getting annoyed or suspicious.

The two men exited the room briefly and came back with instructions on separating us to do preliminary questioning. It seemed they wanted the staff—the housekeeper, cook, two maids, and chauffeur—to go to the dining room so Officer Reed could take down individual statements from each in the privacy of the kitchen. As they rose to follow him, he beckoned to Landon Whittaker and Sandra Logan to follow as well, to the great indignation of the decorator, who puffed out his cheeks, evidently not considering himself to be 'staff.'

The inspector then asked Mrs. Nash if there were a private room nearby and as if coming out of a fog, she gestured vaguely with her hand that there was a morning room. He turned around as if expecting to see it behind him and before fully expressing his frustration, Christine stood up and said she would show him. They returned a few minutes later and he ran his eyes over the lot of us: Mrs. Nash, Christine, Reverend Lewis, Doctor Taylor, Glenda, and me. His dark eyes settled on the reverend, whom he beckoned to follow him out of the room.

Glenda and I exchanged glances. Were we just supposed to sit here as he worked his way through all six of us? Should we be quiet in the interim? Would it be inappropriate to talk? Doctor Taylor broke the silence.

"Mrs. Nash, is there anything I can get you?"

She looked confused, then noticed she still held the glass in her hand, although it was now empty, and looked at it as if it had appeared by magic. "Water, please."

I don't know why giving someone a glass of water is the required remedy in the event of an emotional crisis, but medically speaking, it could help level blood pressure, increase hydration, and certainly give the patient something to do. I thought a good jolt of brandy might have been a better remedy, but I was not the one in extreme distress. I smoothed the nonexistent wrinkles from my skirt, tried to look at the view out the windows without being obvious about it, then settled my hands in my lap for the long wait.

Surprisingly, we did not have to wait long for the reverend and inspector to come back in and I was beckoned to the morning room for my inquisition. It was a sunny chamber, larger than our living room at home, equipped with a sofa under the bay window, a small desk facing another wall and a table with four chairs in the center. I assumed this is where I was to sit, across from the open notebook the inspector had been writing in.

"Name please," he began, and I told him. "Occupation."

It took a bit longer than he would have liked to explain why I was in West Adams and how I knew Glenda.

He squinted his dark eyes at me, possibly because he was myopic, but I suspected he was trying to intimidate me from force of habit.

"What were you doing up here?"

"As I explained before, Glenda and I decided to take a brief walk before dinner and settled on the path up to Highfields because of the view." I then explained seeing the reverend pull up in his car, Richard Fairley's strange exit from the house, the reverend's shout, the maid's scream, and our entry into the study. I described where the maid stood at the doorway, the reverend inside the study, my view of Judge Nash, and leaving to call the doctor on the phone although I was fairly certain from the amount of blood and the inaction of the judge that he was no longer alive.

"Hmm," the inspector said as if challenging my ability to tell a living person from a dead one.

"The staff began to emerge from wherever they had been, as did Mrs. Nash and Christine, the decorator and his assistant, all from different directions. Mrs. Nash approached the study and collapsed at the doorway and was taken to a chair in the hall by the reverend. It wasn't long before the doctor arrived and confirmed the judge was dead."

"How well did you know the judge?"

It was a surprising question. "Not at all. I was introduced to him not too long ago at Mrs. Butler's funeral—Glenda's mother—

and he called the doctor's office once when I was the one who answered the phone, but I haven't had any other interactions with him."

"Why did he call?"

I thought it was inappropriate for me to be too specific about his medical status, so I said truthfully, "He wished to renew a prescription."

There was a pause and then he pointed a finger at me. "How did you know it was the judge who had been shot?"

It was a perfectly logical question, but it gave me pause. "I assumed it was the judge since it was his house, it was a large man's body similar to what I had seen of him previously, and perhaps Reverend Lewis may have said so. I really can't remember."

"So, it was an assumption on your part?" He had a nasty smirk on his face.

"Yes, you could say so. Although it was the judge, wasn't it?"

I believe he thought I was being a smart aleck because he placed his pencil down on the table top emphatically, looked back at his notebook and finished with, "That will be all, Miss, um, Burnside."

He walked behind me to the sitting room and motioned for Glenda to follow him, her eyes searching mine for some clue about what was to transpire. I don't know what sort of expression I made since I didn't quite know my reaction to the experience except for distaste for Inspector Gladstone's assumption of presumed guilt and his heavy-handed predatory methodology.

"I'll wait until Glenda is done and then take you both down to town," the reverend said to my relief as I didn't envision stumbling downhill along the darkening path. As I sat, I noticed one of the staff had brought in a pot of coffee and a plate of butter cookies and I availed myself of the refreshment. A silly thought went through my head: weren't people supposed to be administered hot tea with plenty of sugar in times of distress such as these? I must have looked puzzled while thinking this and crinkled my forehead because I noticed the doctor looking at me quizzically. I looked at my watch and thought Miss Manley might be getting worried by now but let the thought pass. At least I had an idea of how long Glenda's interview might be.

I looked up to see Mrs. Nash sitting patiently with her hands in her lap while Christine had picked up a book and was leafing through it slowly. What different people they were, and now they were going to be thrown together as a family living where? Here? In this gigantic mansion that was shortly going to be renovated into some incongruous Art Deco monstrosity? If there were going to be demolition and reconstruction then they would have to move out temporarily, which could provide the excuse for them to set up separate households. I shivered a bit at the notion of how complicated and awkward things promised to be, recalling most of the town thought Christine and Richard had once been an item, although it seemed he had his eye on her stepmother. And where was the first Mrs. Nash? If she were still alive, would she be able to offer Christine a home? I pondered how one sorted through such difficult emotional relationships and was glad my family was boringly normal and middle class.

Chapter 9

The reverend was kind enough to drive us home as the trek through the woods without a flashlight could have been dangerous even if Glenda said she knew these paths like the back of her hand. She and I exchanged a quick hug to steady our nerves before saying good night, but I instantly felt safe entering the calm oasis of Miss Manley's home with the comforting smell of dinner still warming in the kitchen. She left the sitting room, Annie at her heels, both of them curious about what could have occurred to have kept me so long. I apologized, suggested we move to the dining room with an extra place set for Annie, who hadn't eaten either and was anxious to know the news. It seemed rather rude of me to dig right into the lamb stew, but I was famished, so I took a few mouthfuls and swallowed before I explained what had occurred. Both Annie and Miss Manley had picked up their forks, let their mouths hang open, shut them, and replaced their utensils on the plate.

"Annie, please fetch the Port and three glasses."

It was an old bottle of Port, by which I do not mean precious or valuable, simply old with dust on the outside as if there had been few occasions to bring it out. Annie came back with it on a tray and Miss Manley poured us each a healthy amount, then asked me to repeat all I had seen and heard.

"There seems to have been a lot of people at Highfields today including some unexpected people," she said.

"Yes, like Glenda and me, Richard Fairley—that was a surprise—and the reverend. I believe the entire staff, too, unless there are others I don't know about. And the decorator and his assistant. So many people."

"So many suspects," Miss Manley said.

Now I was speechless.

"If you had been living here as long as I have, you would know there are many tensions in a small town and frictions between people. Judge Nash was in a powerful position as a local magistrate deciding civil and criminal matters. It opens the door on quite a bit of animosity."

"I know one shouldn't speak ill of the dead, Miss, but he wasn't a pleasant man either," Annie added.

"You can say it, and you are correct. He was ready to accuse the reverend or the assistant of pilfering money from the collection basket."

"I wonder if that is why he scheduled a meeting with Reverend Lewis," I said. "Although he didn't say it explicitly in my hearing."

We resumed eating the lamb stew, which was growing cold due to my tardiness and our intense conversation.

"Surely none of the staff could have been involved?" Annie said, probably imagining the impossibility of doing something so heinous to her employer.

"The only staff I am familiar with are Alice, who lives in town and works as a maid, and Joseph, who is their chauffeur and also lives in town. Other than that...." Miss Manley shook her head.

"There are a housekeeper, a cook, another maid, and perhaps more, I don't know. It's a big household. How did Judge Nash come to own such a large house?" I was fishing for where his money came from and under normal circumstances knew it would be impolite to ask.

"He is from the Boston area originally, I know. I think the wealth is his, not Mrs. Nash's, but I can't be certain."

"I suppose it could be a motive for killing her husband," I observed.

"Except there is the matter of Richard Fairley," she said.

"Oh, I see what you mean," I said, then remembered the strange situation at the funeral luncheon where Richard seemed to be trying to approach Mrs. Nash and she appeared to be evading

67

him under the watchful eyes of her husband and later left Richard's studio alone.

There was a pause while I rearranged my thoughts.

"But I saw her come down the stairs after the fact and she appeared genuinely shocked. Richard seems to have been the one to discover the body, judging by the comments he made to Reverend Lewis as he ran from the house."

Miss Manley pushed her plate away and cocked her head to one side and asked me to explain the timing of the events as I understood them. As I spoke, she shook her head, I thought to negate what I was saying, but it turned out to be bafflement.

"No shot heard by anyone in the house? And dead approximately thirty minutes? Why then, it could have been anybody."

I saw where she was going with this. "It could have been anybody in the house and anybody from outside the house who came in and killed him and left without anyone knowing."

"Exactly. The most important thing then is the motivation of the person."

We hashed out the strange inconsistencies of the information presented: the mystery phone call to the reverend, no shot heard, the broken wristwatch, the note, and then Richard Fairley's strange behavior.

"Now why did someone lure the reverend away from his appointed meeting with the judge? And who knew of the meeting?" Miss Manley asked.

"I'm afraid many people could have known of it. I heard them discussing it out in the street in loud voices."

"Oh, dear, that voice of his!"

"Yes, any number of people were out and about. Thomas Kirby met us shortly thereafter and surely Reverend Lewis told his wife about the appointment," I said.

"Perhaps not. She went into Pittsfield by bus this morning. I saw her leave."

We were quiet for a few moments and Annie cleared her throat.

"Miss, I should be going now," she said.

"I'm sorry, Annie, yes, you should," Miss Manley agreed.

"I'll do the clearing," I offered, sure Annie would object, but she was already in the kitchen, putting on her hat and picking up her handbag; it was quite late, and all this talk of murder had spooked her. She may have jumped to the conclusion there was a maniac on the loose and she might not make it home alive.

"Now, Annie. I know you are upset but it is hardly likely another murder will take place and I'm sure the judge was a victim for a particular reason," Miss Manley explained. Luckily, Annie did not have far to walk.

As we moved the dishes into the kitchen, Miss Manley and I resumed our analysis.

"The broken wristwatch seemed highly suspicious to me. How incredible is it his head should fall exactly on the face of the watch? And, of course, the time on the watch did not match the time of death according to Doctor Taylor."

"Yes, that is suspect."

"I'm no expert in handwriting," I added, "but from what I saw, the difference in style of writing between the body of the note and the time written at the top could indicate more than one person had a hand in writing it."

Miss Manley nodded her head. "A very sound deduction. Perhaps the judge had drafted the note and someone else wrote in the time? I wonder if the police will notice what you saw?"

"I don't know if you can retrieve fingerprints from a piece of paper, but Officer Reed had manhandled the note enough, so his prints are probably all over it, possibly obliterating the ones beneath."

"Oh, dear," Miss Manley said.

"They seem to be thorough, although Inspector Gladstone from Pittsfield is particularly unpleasant, glowering at me as if I had something to do with it. You know, the more I think about it, perhaps it might have nothing to do with anyone here. Perhaps someone from his past, his ex-wife for example, or someone who resented a sentence he administered may have been harboring ill will and stalking his every move."

"Oh, my. In that case, perhaps we had better lock the doors tonight for a change." She proceeded to do so, including the French windows in the sitting room. "I would like to talk about this further, but we'd better get to bed. I wouldn't be surprised if there are more revelations in the morning."

How right she was! We sat at breakfast under the still wideeyed gaze of Annie, who had discussed the murder with her family and friends. Word had gotten around town quickly.

"Is it possible the judge did himself in?" the maid asked.

"The wound was in the back of the head, which is a decidedly difficult shot to self-administer," I said, a little sorry for sounding glib.

"Who would want to kill the judge?" she asked.

To my surprise, Miss Manley said, "As I said, I can think of many people."

The maid and I exchanged looks and then stared at Miss Manley, who continued eating as if nothing of import had been said.

The doorbell rang and Annie vanished, coming back a few minutes later with her eyes even wider than before.

"It was the reverend's maid, Elsie. You'll never guess—Richard Fairley has surrendered to the police and confessed. And he had the gun that killed the judge with him!"

"What!" we both exclaimed at the same time.

The phone rang and the maid went to answer while we sat mystified at the table.

She came back with this message: "The doctor was in a rush and didn't have time to wait to talk to you, Miss Burnside. His message was that he would like to you to come to the office as soon as possible."

I didn't have my uniform on, which probably didn't matter much, so I got up from the table and made my way quickly two houses down to the doctor's home and office.

I began to apologize for my lack of professional attire, but he brushed my comments aside.

"No matter. I've had to call off covering for Doctor Mitchell this morning and I don't know how present I can be here today either, with all this business." He waved his hand toward the examination room, which I hoped did not contain the body of the late judge. "What I would like you to do is hold down the fort this afternoon in the event my conference with the inspector this morning drags on into the afternoon. I don't know how long I'll be gone, but if anything of importance occurs, do not hesitate to come to get me."

"Did you…," I began, not wanting to say autopsy.

"Yes, late last night." He held out his hand to reveal a bullet.

Now it was my turn to look wide-eyed. He put it in his pocket.

We both left, he to the police station and I back to Miss Manley's house; she was in the sitting room knitting. I had hardly been gone from the house long, but in the short time, all kinds of details had been shared by the town's gossip network. The artist had indeed given himself up and produced a gun that he said he had used to do the deed.

Miss Manley shook her head. "I don't think he can be guilty. Mrs. Proctor saw him leaving the town when the clock struck 6:30 and he still had to walk up the road to get to Highfields, which would take at least ten minutes."

"He can't have just shot the judge before he saw the reverend because the doctor said the judge had been dead about thirty minutes," I added.

"Puzzling."

Glenda burst into the sitting room. "Have you heard?" she stated rather than asked about the Richard Fairley confession. "Why didn't you call me?" She looked at me in annoyance.

"Glenda, really," Miss Manley said. "We shouldn't treat this as a circus. A man has died. I know he was not a pleasant person. Nonetheless...." She stopped there and picked up her knitting again.

The phone rang and she sighed, knowing it was one of her friends requesting more information.

"Glenda, let's get some fresh air," I suggested. I had to mail a letter written the previous afternoon to my brother. Now, I wondered how far news of this event would travel, surely not to New York, I hoped. If my parents got wind of a murder, even in this quiet town, they would insist I come home at once. And truth be told, I don't know if I would blame them.

We went out to the back lane and Glenda glanced back.

"I don't think I've been scolded by Miss Manley since I was seven and picked one of her flowers," she said.

I put my arm through hers. "Everyone is on edge with the uncertainty as well as lack of sleep."

"Gosh, Richard wanted to paint me, remember? It's a good thing I'm too poor to squander my money or I could be dead now, too."

I had to stop her. "First of all, you are not poor. Secondly, who knows if the finished painting would have met your expectations? Thirdly, why in the world would he shoot the subject of his painting?"

"Why would he shoot the judge?"

"I think it has more to do with Mrs. Nash," I said.

"No! Really? Maybe it has to do with him painting the judge's daughter."

We looked at one another but came to the same conclusion: we did not know enough yet. We had rounded the corner, taking us into the main street; perhaps it was my imagination, but there seemed to be quite a lot of people about, talking in groups. Suddenly, my vision of the idyllic small town was thoroughly dismantled, not just by the murder but by the ghoulish relish of the inhabitants. It made me shudder.

We tried to keep up a normal attitude and casual speech, which was hard since conversations seemed to come to a complete halt as we passed by. Even the postmaster looked at us strangely over the top of his glasses as he took my letter. Back out on the main street, I saw the doctor approaching us from the direction of the police station. He smiled in a tense way and stopped to talk out of earshot of any other people.

"I believe we can open the office for normal hours this afternoon," he said.

"Yes, Doctor."

After a pause, he said, "In case you are wondering, the bullet we retrieved from the judge came from the artist's gun." Glenda and I gasped.

"But he couldn't have done it—timing's all wrong." Without another word he walked down the street toward his home and office, tipping his hat to those who nodded to him, but not saying another word.

***

I reported to work at the usual time, surprised to see several people there already, seated in the chairs of the waiting room. Only one was an appointment previously scheduled, the others seemed to have rather minor or vague ailments, which led me to wonder if their curiosity was the major component in showing up. The telephone was unusually busy as well, with calls from Officer Reed, one from Inspector Gladstone, and three more appointments made for the next afternoon. A woman with a sore throat was instructed to gargle with aspirin dissolved in water and to refrain from talking until the pain lessened; I couldn't help but wonder if this was the doctor's way of combatting gossip. The older man with lumbago was given a sheet with a list of mild exercises and a prescription to take to the drug store. The doctor later told me the people with chronic conditions would often not fill their prescriptions or do whatever physical activity he had recommended, hoping the malady would resolve itself by the mere fact of having visited the office.

"He'll be back in about two months seeking some other kind of treatment or remedy."

A late afternoon telephone call came from someone who identified herself as the housekeeper at Highfields, requesting the doctor make a house call to Mrs. Nash, who was ill and emotionally distressed.

"Come along with me," the doctor suggested to my surprise. "You've seen some of Highfields but there is plenty more to see."

It was not such a long walk as I knew from my stroll with Glenda, but I appreciated his taking his car instead, making the visit look more professional as well as saving my shoes from needing another whitening treatment.

We pulled up the gravel drive and the housekeeper opened the door before we had a chance to knock. She was the middle-aged woman I had seen the day before, soberly dressed, her hair in the requisite bun; she didn't say much but by the sound of her accent, she was not a local. She led us along the hallway to the right, past the large sitting room where we had been assembled just the night before. I tried to be discreet in my glances but met the eyes of the judge's daughter, Christine, lounging in a window seat reading a book. We went up a long stairway, down another hall to a waiting maid who led us into a feminine bedroom of light colors and white sheer curtains. Elizabeth Nash lay covered by a diaphanous coverlet, her lovely face pale, her puffy eyes closed. The maid stood near the door while we approached the bed.

"Mrs. Nash?" the doctor inquired.

"Oh, Doctor Taylor. I feel so weak. So tired." At this, she opened her eyes and began to cry. He reached for her hand in sympathy.

"It must have been an extraordinary shock," he said quietly. "I could give you additional sedatives if you like."

I was uncertain by the shake of her head whether she meant 'no' or 'I don't know' or 'what is the use?'

A distant doorbell rang, and she lifted her head in anticipation and said dramatically, "I see they've come for me already."

The doctor and I exchanged looks while he looked in his bag for the sedatives. He turned to ask the maid to fetch a glass of water, but she had disappeared into the hall, so I sought out the bathroom adjacent to windows overlooking the front drive. I could see another car was now parked behind the doctor's, likely related to whoever was at the front door. I located a glass, half-filled it with water from the tap, observing the jars of expensive face creams lined up on the glass shelf, and returned to a room suddenly filled with considerably more people.

Reverend Lewis, Officer Reed and Inspector Gladstone now stood near the bed looking down on the morose widow. The doctor held up his hand to me to indicate the sedative could wait until she spoke.

"I've called you here because I want to confess." She paused. "I killed my husband."

It was deathly quiet in the room as they let her continue her narrative.

"I found a gun. In one of his drawers. And I went into the study and shot my husband in the heart. Then I went back out and…." She either ran out of energy or plot points at this time.

The inspector employed a world-weary voice. "Shot him in the heart, did you?"

"Yes," she said emphatically.

"Where was he?"

"At his desk."

"With his back to you?"

"Yes, he turned around when I came in the room."

"And what time was this?"

"I, I don't recall exactly. Before six o'clock, I think. I wasn't paying attention to the time."

The inspector shook his head. "No, no, you have it all wrong. The time, the cause of death. And what happened to the gun?" She stammered that she didn't know.

Reverend Lewis spoke up now. "I know you want to protect someone who has confessed. Richard came to me the other day to tell me about your relationship, shortly after you did. But he also took my advice to break it off for the sake of you, your husband, and your stepdaughter. There was no reason for him to retaliate against the judge."

"And Richard Fairley was seen in the town at the time the judge was killed, so we already know his confession is false," Inspector Gladstone added.

At this, the widow burst into tears again but also began laughing. "Oh, the poor dear fool!"

"And you have no business confessing to a crime you did not commit, either," the inspector added in a stern tone making her go quiet. "The housekeeper was talking to you in the upstairs hallway about linens or some such at the time he was shot, she told us. She was gone several minutes to the linen closet to get something but said you were still there when she got back. Neither before nor after did she see you with a gun."

Officer Reed turned to me. "You were there when she came down the stairs. Was she carrying a gun?" the policeman asked me.

The inspector glared at him for preempting his questioning. "Well?" he asked me.

"I don't see how. She was wearing a slim skirted dress and it certainly didn't have any pockets."

"Was she carrying a purse or a large hat?" the inspector continued.

"Indoors? Certainly not," I said.

"How did she act?"

I didn't know how to answer the question because it was only the second time I had seen her and was unfamiliar with her usual expressions. "She looked worried as she descended the stairs, perhaps startled at the yell from the reverend and the scream from the maid."

The inspector gave me a piercing look, which he then turned on the judge's wife. "My good woman, you have every reason to be upset and perhaps act irrationally. But you have no right to falsely claim you committed a murder when you couldn't have done so. Any more than your, your…friend Mr. Fairley did. His confession has been ruled out as being frankly implausible and impossible. As has your manufactured fiction!"

I was on the verge of letting the inspector know that fiction was by definition manufactured but thought pointing out redundancy to him would likely not be appreciated. His comment sent her into a tearful collapse again and with a nod to the doctor, she took the sedative as I handed her the glass of water and the maid assisted her in drinking.

"Good day, madam!" the inspector said forcefully, exiting with the police officer, leaving the befuddled Reverend Lewis behind.

"I can give you a lift back," the doctor said, much to his relief. We stood around a bit longer until the doctor insisted the maid or someone sit with Mrs. Nash and call him if there was any change or difficulty.

"Thank you," the judge's widow said from the depth of the pillows into which she had sunk.

"Bad business," the doctor said when we were back out in the hall. "So, she was carrying on with the artist?" he asked the reverend.

"Yes, I am afraid so. I inadvertently came across them—ah— in an embrace and each of them subsequently came to me to express their feelings for each other. She was unhappy in her marriage, and who could blame her as the judge could be a bully. And Richard was madly in love. Nonetheless, I urged caution, which she seemed to agree to, and he later informed me, despite his heartbreak, he was going to leave town."

So, there may have been a motive for Richard Fairley to kill the judge, but it seemed he had been reconciled to breaking it off. Mrs. Nash may have had her unhappiness as a motive but not a weapon to do anything about it.

We walked solemnly down the long hall. As we came to the head of the stairs, we could overhear the inspector talking to the housekeeper down below and asking if anything suspicious had occurred in the past few days. We heard her say Miss Logan had been in the library with the judge and loud words were exchanged, which in the judge's case was seemingly his only form of verbal delivery. The housekeeper had been called away by one of the staff and she said she did not know the topic or outcome of the conversation.

Unfortunately, the sound of our progress down the stairs interrupted any further questions and answers we might have overhead, and we proceeded to the doctor's car a bit dazed because all three of us knew who Miss Logan was. She was the interior decorator's assistant and Glenda's tenant.

Chapter 10

As the doctor pulled his car into the driveway of his home, Reverend Lewis said, "Why don't you come on in for a drink?"

Nina heard us trooping in the front door and joined us after asking Elsie to get some ice, glasses, and a pitcher of water. From the sour look on the maid's face, she was well aware some bootleg alcohol was going to be served although she was supposed to pretend not to know about it.

"How was your day?" Nina began innocently to her husband, having no knowledge of the most recent trip to Highfields and what transpired there. He looked over to the doctor and nodded for the other man to begin.

"As you know, I performed the autopsy and retrieved a bullet from the late judge." Nina shuddered a bit at the image the bullet brought to mind. "The bullet came from a gun belonging to Richard Fairley."

She gasped and looked at her husband, horrified. "To think we allowed him to rent our studio! To think he wanted to paint my portrait!"

"He did?" Reverend Lewis asked.

"I meant to tell you, darling, but I was not interested."

"And he charges his subjects," I added, based on Glenda's information.

"He didn't mention that to me," Nina said with disappointment.

The doctor cleared his throat and continued. "Well, what a mess. Upon further questioning and information from Robert here, as well as my estimation of time of death, it became obvious he couldn't possibly have killed the judge. Once he was confronted with the reality—that he was seen in town at the time the judge died—he collapsed and recanted. He assumed Elizabeth Nash had done it and was trying to protect her."

"And she confessed this afternoon obviously in an attempt to protect him!" Reverend Lewis said.

Nina's eyes were as large as saucers hearing this information and she started in her chair when Elsie noisily brought in the tray.

"Why were they trying to protect each other?" she asked. We all looked at her in silence.

"Oh," she said, finally understanding.

"It may be the case, but she had all the details wrong, so of course she made it all up," Doctor Taylor said.

"Well, if neither of them shot him, who did?" Nina asked.

Elsie put the tray down hard onto the coffee table.

"Don't you be looking at my Sam!" she said, her eyes narrowing. "Just because the judge threw the book at him last year, he did his time, he paid his dues, and it's all behind him now."

Naturally, I had no idea what she was talking about and the others waited until Elsie left, closing the door forcefully, before they filled me in: Sam Campbell had been hunting out of season, someone complained and identified him, he was hauled in and appeared before judge Nash. Being the law-and-order type, the judge sentenced him to a short stint in jail as well as a fine and there had been bad blood between them ever since.

Nina pulled out a drawer in the coffee table and extracted a key, then unlocked a cabinet in the corner of the room and took out an unmarked bottle, holding it up to the light. "Hmm, it looks like Roger may have found the key to the cabinet."

Not a clever hiding place, I thought. One an enterprising young man would certainly find with a brief search.

"I hope he didn't refill what he's taken with water," she commented, seemingly unbothered by providing a teenager with alcohol, a situation that upset the reverend, who had to be wrestling with his conscience about condoning Prohibition in the parsonage to begin with.

"It's been a difficult day for everyone," the doctor said. "Consider it a prescription."

"Just don't write it out," Nina added, with a twinkle in her eye.

She put a bit of gin in each glass, added a splash of water and a cube of ice, and passed the drinks around. The reverend reluctantly took what was offered to him and nodded over it solemnly as it would have been somehow awkward under the circumstances to make a toast..

"The gun belonged to Richard, but he said he couldn't remember the last time he saw it," Doctor Taylor said.

"A handgun?" Reverend Lewis asked. "You would certainly think to keep track of something like the location of a firearm."

I thought about the local custom of unlocked doors and how easily someone could steal it. As long as they knew where it was.

"Elsie also cleans for Richard and said his home is quite untidy," Nina supplied.

"He seems to keep the studio shipshape," Reverend Lewis said.

Nina shrugged. "One is his livelihood and the other where he lays his head. I suppose it might mean a difference to him."

We sipped our drinks in silence until I remembered I ought to check in on Miss Manley and I got up, thanked Nina for the drink, and went out the French windows to the garden.

When I came in next door, Miss Manley was seated on the sofa knitting, with Glenda chatting to her from an armchair.

Glenda said, "What news?"

I didn't know how much to tell them but assumed the entire town would know it all soon enough, so I sat and began to relate what I knew so far.

"He had a gun?" Miss Manley asked. "Then I assume he also had bullets somewhere, too. Someone would have to know both of those things as well as knowing how to load it and use it."

"It would seem to point to someone with knowledge of firearms," I suggested.

Glenda's eyes grew wide. "Sam Campbell? He has wellknown animosity toward the judge."

"True," Miss Manley said. "I am sure the police will follow it up. But being such a strict judge, he may have made many more dangerous enemies unknown to us all."

My naïve impression of West Adams as a bucolic town where neighbors helped each other and doors were left unlocked was increasingly shattered as I now thought of violent criminals recently released from prison lurking about, seeking revenge.

"But how would such an enemy gain admittance to Highfields?" Glenda asked. Then she added, "I suppose someone could break in." It gave us pause.

"I am sorry to have brought up the idea of enemies because surely, if someone unknown to the townspeople were sneaking around to seek revenge, the stranger would have been noticed," Miss Manley added.

"Good point," Glenda said, greatly relieved. "Although if it wasn't a stranger, then it must be someone we know. Do you think Elizabeth Nash could have done it somehow?"

Miss Manley shook her head in disbelief, and then I told them about our trip up to Highfields earlier in the afternoon. By now Miss Manley had put down her knitting and was listening intently. "What an incredible turn of events!"

"Yes, I thought so, too. We have Richard confessing, retrieving his gun that was used and left on the floor of the judge's study, then Mrs. Nash comes out with a confession of her own but getting all the pertinent facts wrong."

"Are you saying neither of them did it?" Glenda asked and, before receiving an answer, added in a horrified whisper, "Perhaps it was Christine."

Miss Manley looked up at this. "What do you think her motivation could have been?"

"She complained about her father's strict upbringing, her lack of freedom, her lack of money, and there was no love lost between her and the judge's wife."

"Christine was at Highfields but upstairs, as far as we know," I said.

"She could have crept down the back stairs—if they have back stairs—shot him and run back up with nobody noticing. Maybe Christine had an unrequited crush on Richard and wanted revenge," Glenda said.

"Possibly, but from what the reverend has said, Richard and Elizabeth were in love with each other and decided not to pursue their relationship further."

"It proves my point, don't you see? Christine is in love with Richard and he is in love with another woman, her stepmother no less. She kills her father to blame Elizabeth."

Glenda's theory sounded far-fetched, especially since Christine impressed me as someone who might whine about her situation but not do anything to change it. After all, her father did support her—perhaps not to the level she aspired—and she had the choice of going to college or working somewhere; she was not forced to live at Highfields as far as I knew.

"I'm going to change out of my uniform," I declared, removing my cap as a start.

"Yes, I suppose I should be getting back to see how Sandra is getting on," Glenda replied, standing up.

"I don't want to alarm you, but when we were at the Highfields earlier, we overheard the housekeeper saying Miss Logan had come to visit the judge the night before he was killed and there was a loud argument."

Glenda was agog at this information. "Oh, no! Do you suppose she…. I could be killed in my bed!"

"Now, now," Miss Manley said. "She looks like a sensible young person, and what connection could she possibly have to the judge?"

I shook my head.

"I am going to lock my bedroom door tonight," Glenda said, wringing her hands as she left.

Chapter 11

The next morning brought another sunny day, evidently perfect for gardening as Miss Manley put on her garden gloves and hat to attack whatever weeds threatened her beauties, as she referred to her flowers. I knew the names of some of them, the full hydrangea bushes with their blue pom-pom flowers that grew in

83

my mother's garden alongside the house, but where my parents chose to use plants to accent the architecture of the house, Miss Manley chose to be as abundant as possible in her plantings for the sheer delight of it, perhaps because of the colder winters here in the Berkshires. There were daisies and daylilies, pots of red geraniums, violets in the shade of the elm and, of course, her many rose bushes that necessitated daily grooming and talking to. The one thing missing from her garden was vegetables but perhaps she left the growing of mundane plants to the farmers who could do a better job of it.

I took a book outside to sit in the shade while she pottered about, muttering and tut-tutting to the plants, the birdsong plentiful from the woods beyond. I had read approximately ten pages when loud voices came from the reverend's study, the windows to which were wide open. We could hear Elsie's voice quite clearly complaining about the police investigation.

"How can they do that? How can they continue to persecute him?"

There was the sound of Mrs. Lewis trying to mollify Elsie by asking her to sit down. Under the circumstances, we pretended we couldn't hear any of the conversation although it was close by and completely audible.

"They're taking him in for questioning!" Elsie went from outrage to sobbing.

More soothing noises from Mrs. Lewis.

The reverend, busy man as he was, now felt it was his duty to intervene and promised Elsie he would talk to Officer Reed. I suppose he couldn't vouch for Sam since the reverend was driving in the countryside at the time of the murder, but he could try to put in a good word. The promise seemed to be enough and Elsie left the study, slamming the door behind her. Miss Manley looked up at me and then back to her flowers.

A few minutes later there were more voices, this time Officer Reed and Inspector Gladstone, who wanted to go over the details of the night of the judge's death with the reverend. Once again, we were able to hear every word. I didn't think I would like the job of being a police officer or detective since they seemed to pound away at each scrap of evidence or suspicion seemingly to get someone to 'crack.' To my knowledge, the reverend had no motive whatsoever and sounded tired of having to repeat answers to questions he had already encountered. There was a lull in the conversation and Inspector Gladstone stepped out of the French windows into the garden and saw us, me with a book and Miss Manley at work among her plants.

"Have you been eavesdropping?" he asked.

"Certainly not," I said. "You have been speaking rather loudly, however."

He scoffed and pushed his hat back on his head.

"Well?" he asked, looking at me with his eyes narrowed.

His look got my dander up. I couldn't help myself from inquiring, "Why did no one hear a shot?"

This question annoyed him. "A silencer may have been used."

I looked to Miss Manley for clarification and she shrugged her shoulders.

"It's a device put onto a gun to muffle the sound of a shot," Officer Reed explained as he came out of the French windows. He stopped short and asked, "If a silencer were used, why did Fairley find the gun but not the silencer?"

The inspector was not pleased to have these questions put forward since he didn't have an answer. "Let's talk to Sam Campbell again," he barked at the policeman, and turning on his heel, went back into the reverend's study and I assumed they went through the house and out the front door.

I felt my mind churning with so many questions I could not settle to the book I had begun. Miss Manley felt the same way because she sat, rather than resuming her gardening work.

"Do you think Sam Campbell had a legitimate grudge?" I asked, never having met him.

"It may not have been legitimate, but he was displeased he was caught hunting out of season and angry about the judge's harsh penalty."

"Being a city girl, what is the problem with hunting out of season?"

Miss Manley smiled. "Many reasons. Most of the game bring forth young in the spring and it is considered unsportsmanlike to kill new mothers, leaving their offspring untended. Fall is hunting season: the animals are in rut, aggressive, and noisy, and hunters like to boast of bagging a buck with the largest rack. Also, the leaves have fallen, and visibility is better in autumn with less chance of shooting a fellow hunter, although it seems to happen at times. Regular folk such as I do not go wandering in the woods or birdwatching during hunting season for the same reason. Sam Campbell was caught in April, I believe."

"He seems to have a motive and has a knowledge of firearms, however," I observed.

"Yes, most country men do but they use mostly shotguns or rifles. Handguns are less common. He would have to go far enough away from West Adams to purchase a handgun without raising suspicion. And it seems the gun used belonged to Richard Fairley anyway. I don't imagine they travel in the same social circles."

"But Elsie cleans for him, doesn't she?"

Miss Manley looked sharply at me but said nothing. We sat quietly for a few minutes enjoying the cool breeze while our minds whirred with activity. Knowing the windows next door were open, I lowered my voice.

"Do you remember at tea at the parsonage overhearing Mr. Lewis muttering about the judge being the death of him or…?"

Miss Manley smiled. "Oh, yes, I do. It was a bit uncomfortable."

"Do you think there was real animosity on his part?"

She sighed as she thought it over. "My good friend, Eleanor, who was seated across from you at the tea, had told me she put a large bill in the collection basket last Sunday. But when the tally of the collection was done, it was obvious her bill didn't make it."

"Who does the tally?"

"The judge, in his capacity as one of the elders in the church. Of course, he is wealthy enough and why would he have taken it?"

"Who else had access?" I asked.

"The reverend and Thomas Kirby, his assistant. I find it highly unlikely Reverend Lewis took it—if my friend isn't mistaken about having put it in the collection basket in the first place. However, she did complain to the reverend and the judge as well, and it was the reason for the meeting scheduled on the fateful night. Reverend Lewis may have thought Eleanor was mistaken or, in the worst case, that Mr. Kirby may have taken it."

"I've only seen Mr. Kirby a few times and he seemed highly excitable. Perhaps it is the malarial fevers that make him appear somewhat shifty or guilty," I added to soften my suspicion. After all, he could just as well have come into the house, walked into the study and done the deed. Or perhaps the reverend was angry enough with the judge's intrusion on church matters or employee matters that he lost his temper and—realizing his error, left Highfields, drove around and came back later. No, I corrected myself, it made no sense. I was letting my imagination run wild.

Annie came out to the garden at this point to let us know lunch was ready, and I realized cogitation had certainly improved my appetite. I could see the maid was bursting with curiosity about the police presence in the yard earlier, but Miss Manley and I chatted about other things.

"I meant to tell you, my nephew Stuart is coming up this weekend—such a charming young man. He's a successful writer and has always been generous with me."

I had the sudden sensation she was going to play matchmaker, which made me uncomfortable.

"What has he published?"

"He writes adventure books, I believe they are called. I have some copies in the sitting room. The hero is a dashing young man put into impossible and dangerous situations from which he manages to escape before encountering yet another obstacle. Quite entertaining."

I nodded in agreement, thinking I should ask my brother whether he was familiar with them. As I excused myself to get changed for work, Glenda came in through the kitchen to the dining room.

"Hello, all. I hope I am not interrupting?"

"No, dear, we had just finished," Miss Manley said. "I was just telling Aggie that Stuart is coming up this weekend." "How nice," Glenda said.

"I've got to get changed. Come upstairs and keep me company for a few minutes," I suggested.

When the door was shut and I began to take off my skirt, I asked Glenda, "What's the story with her nephew? You didn't seem enthusiastic about his arrival."

"He's perfectly nice, writes some kind of books." She sat on the bed and smoothed out the chenille coverlet.

"Miss Manley said they are adventure books with a lot of action."

"Possibly. I haven't read them. Speaking of action, what was going on this morning in the garden with the police here? I swear you don't tell me anything anymore."

I stopped in my progress of changing stockings from fleshcolored to white. "Glenda! You just walked in. Give me a minute." I put the garters in place, the uniform over my head, and began to button the front. "They wanted to grill the reverend again."

"What? He is the least likely person to have done something so awful."

"Probably, but they persist in their questioning."

"How did the person get into Highfields?"

"He or she could have come in the front door, I guess and left the same way. I am assuming the door wasn't locked."

"She? I thought Mrs. Nash was exonerated?"

"I meant a theoretical 'she.' Perhaps Christine or Elsie." I fiddled with the bobby pins to attach my cap.

"Elsie! What in the world? Why?"

"She's Sam Campbell's girlfriend, isn't she? They're questioning him right about now."

Glenda stood up quickly. "Next you're going to say they suspect Nina Lewis!"

I looked her in the eye. "Come to think of it, she was a bit unaccounted for at the time, too."

Glenda stood open-mouthed as I descended the stairs.

"Got to go or I'll be late," I said airily.

***

I had no fear of being late, I just wanted to leave Glenda at a dramatic moment in our conversation, the way she had often left me sputtering, "What?" after some deliciously landed piece of information. To my knowledge the doctor was not scheduled to see anyone in the afternoon, and I doubted he had made it back from the nearby town where he was filling in for a colleague, so I was surprised to see the examination room door was closed with murmuring voices behind it. I checked the file cabinet, put the errant files in the correct place, and seated myself to begin sorting the morning's mail. Shortly thereafter the exam room door opened, and the reverend's assistant came out, looking startled to see anyone in the reception area much less a fully turned-out nurse. He just stared for a moment.

"Hello," I said cheerfully, and Doctor Taylor made the introductions.

"I don't know if you two have met before. This is my nurse, Agnes Burnside. Agnes, this is Thomas Kirby, who works with Reverend Lewis."

I held out my hand to shake his, which necessitated him shoving a prescription into his jacket pocket first.

"Nice to meet you," he said, although he seemed uncertain about it. The doctor walked him to the door and asked him to take it easy before ushering him out.

"Poor guy," the doctor said, shaking his head. "He'll get over it; it just takes time."

I assumed he was referring to malaria, but perhaps there was something else to get over. I then asked if there was anything special he wanted me to do and he retrieved a notebook from his office and instructed me to send out bills to the patients listed, some from West Adams and some from the other office in Adams. Noting no typewriter anywhere, I searched the desk for paper and envelopes and began the task of writing out the invoices in longhand, which took the better part of an hour. The only patient was Sandra Logan, who came in quietly and softly announced herself. I let the doctor know she was there and had a few minutes to observe her calm yet alert demeanor.

"I'm sorry to stare, but we are neighbors, and I haven't seen much of you," I said.

"True. I do keep to myself. Except for work, of course."

"Glenda is a friend of mine from nurses' training," I said stupidly for something to say.

"How nice for you," she said and turned her head away.

I bent to my task of trying to decipher some of the doctor's handwriting and he emerged from his office and took Miss Logan in there rather than the examination room. Curious, I thought. They spoke in low tones for about fifteen minutes and emerged with serious faces, although she managed a brief smile for me.

She was no sooner out the door when Glenda dashed in.

"It's Miss Manley again," she said, catching the doctor's eye. "Please come at once," and as precipitously as she had arrived, ran out.

The doctor took up his bag and followed, instructing me to hold down the fort in his absence. I could certainly do that, but I was of no use in getting the billing done as I was consumed with worry about Miss Manley. What if she had a stroke? Who would take care of her then? Would her nephew be of any help? Other more personal questions dogged me: would she be hospitalized and if so, should I stay on in her house? Would I be expected to care for her if she stayed home?

Time dragged on with no distractions in the way of telephone calls until the doctor returned within the hour and I peppered him with questions.

He held up his hand. "She seems to be experiencing the same symptoms as a few days ago—groggy, a bit unstable on her feet, confused, and then after a bit, she seems to come out of it. No, it does not seem to be a stroke, but there are instances when older people have brief lapses that come and go."

This was not reassuring to me since there were stairs in the house and it meant she could fall at any moment. It was worrisome that such a sharp mind could become muddled almost at the snap of the fingers and, of course, I thought of my parents, younger than Miss Manley but possibly open to the same dangers in time.

"Doctor, excuse me, but could it be the effects of the tonic she takes before lunch?"

He glowered at me and I was aware I had crossed a professional line.

"I mean, the pharmacist may have misread your prescription. Or perhaps she is just particularly sensitive to whatever is in the formula," I clarified.

He asked for Miss Manley's file, then walked into his office, and closed the door.

Aggie, I thought to myself, you've done it now.

A few minutes later he came out and shot me an intense look. "You may be right, Nurse Burnside. I'll retrieve the bottle and bring it to the drugstore and make sure it's what I ordered. If so, perhaps she just has a sensitivity to the medication. Thank you for your suggestion."

He left for the drugstore without another word and, despite his words, he did not seem appreciative at all.

Chapter 12

Since I no longer had to hold down the fort, I became positively rebellious and left the doctor's office fifteen minutes early, anxious to see what condition Miss Manley was in and if anyone was with her. To my surprise, the entire tea group from earlier in the week had assembled in her overstuffed sitting room, fussing over her, chiding her for not having told them of this problem earlier, and asking why she hadn't canceled her hosting. She looked properly abashed by the mild scolding and had no logical rebuttal to not having included her friends in this recent health crisis except she probably couldn't have mustered the energy to call each one to let them know before they showed up. She still looked a bit pale and not as sharp as usual, but she listened intently as the women continued their conversation after acknowledging my presence.

"Tea, dear?" one of the women asked me.

I gratefully received the proffered cup and availed myself of one of the tiny sandwiches these women were so adept at assembling. I couldn't help noticing how they admired my starched uniform, perky cap, and spotless white shoes.

"As I was saying," Mrs. Proctor resumed, "I know how much I put in the basket and I saw how much was recorded for the week's collection. I only told the judge about it because he serves as one of the elders. How could I know he might have been killed because of it?" she asked dramatically.

Her statement caused a buzz of speculation, although I was shocked to think any of them could imagine someone killing the judge over the matter of a five-dollar bill, for surely she hadn't put in a larger denomination. She was either suggesting the assistant, Thomas Kirby, who passed the collection basket, or the reverend, who supervised him, should have known about the theft or provided better oversight, but I hoped she was not accusing Reverend Lewis directly of theft.

It seemed to me Miss Manley was paying attention to the conversations but also was a bit far away in her thoughts so I asked if I could get her anything else. Of course, she said no, and the conversation veered toward some familiar topics: who was this interior decorator at Highfields and what was he doing here in West Adams of all places? Heads swiveled in my direction, but I kept my face pleasant and noncommittal and complimented someone on the sandwiches rather than responding as if I were more informed than they. Onward to the next topic, the reverend's wife, who was not present. Not only was she closer in age to Reverend Lewis's nephew, Roger, than her own husband, but she positively spoiled the young man, allowing him to gad about playing tennis with Christine and her posh set from Pittsfield rather than performing more useful functions at home. It led me to wonder what useful things a teenager could do besides mowing the lawn or carrying the groceries into the house; surely they didn't imagine he could assist in pastoral duties. Then the talk was about Roger and Christine as a possible couple, then Christine and Richard Fairley, then, with voices lowered, what about Mrs. Nash and the artist? How shocking!

I excused myself to change out of my uniform and saw Glenda coming in the back door. I beckoned her to come along with me and she looked puzzled at first, probably imagining Miss Manley was resting quietly, until I put my hands up to my chest as if they were cat paws and mouthed, 'Meow.'

We tiptoed up the stairs trying not to giggle but let loose once the bedroom door was closed.

"They have managed to rake almost everybody over the coals in the past ten minutes," I said.

"It's a good thing you left when you did so now they can talk about you. Miss Hunter stopped me in the general store yesterday, looked at my hair, and commented how unusual it was for someone to remain blond well into adulthood. I wasn't sure whether to laugh or be affronted so I managed to do both, turned on my heel, and finished my shopping."

"I can only imagine what they think of me," I said. "Career girl or something."

Glenda picked up the cap I had tossed on the bed and ran her finger over the black braid strip decorating it. "Oh, no. They are impressed by you and probably intimidated, too."

"Really?" I thought it over for a moment. "I think I like such a reaction. But I don't consider myself intimidating at all."

"You aren't. You just appear that way sometimes. Upright, trustworthy, no-nonsense."

"How exciting—no-nonsense," I repeated glumly.

"I have to tell you," Glenda said, lowering her voice, "one of the things most intriguing to them is imagining, because of our training, you and I know all about anatomy, if you catch my drift."

"Well, not all, of course." Then I stopped. "Oh, I see. *That* kind of anatomy knowledge." I had to laugh. "I don't imagine we've seen anything they haven't seen."

"I wouldn't be too sure. Remember dreadful Doctor Portland who finally agreed to let our class witness a surgical procedure from the balcony of the operating theater before telling Nurse Watson it was to perform a circumcision on an adult?"

We laughed again. "I thought her eyes were going to pop out of her head."

"The poor patient had no idea all of our virginal eyes were forever despoiled by Doctor Portland's perverse sense of humor."

A soft knock on the door revealed Annie, who wished to go home for the day but did not want to leave Miss Manley by herself since the guests were leaving. I had changed by then and we three went to the sitting room to see Miss Manley looking much like her old self, even managing a bit of a smile. Glenda said hello and picked up one of the remaining sandwiches while Annie went to answer the doorbell.

Doctor Taylor came in, bag in hand, and insisted on checking on Miss Manley again.

"Just so you know," he said, sitting next to her on the sofa, "Nurse Burnside suggested I check with the pharmacist to make sure no mistake had been made in filling your prescription. I know my handwriting can be like hieroglyphics, but it turns out the tonic he made up for you is exactly what I prescribed. Therefore, since this tonic is the only change we can point to in the last few weeks, your 'episodes' could suggest a build-up of the medication in your system. I'd like you to cut your dosage in half for the time being and we'll see how it goes."

"Thank you," she said heartily, as I remembered the sour face she made whenever she swallowed it down. She looked at me and smiled. "And thank you."

The doctor got up, looked at me, and smiled, too. "I'll see you tomorrow. Now off to the police station again."

"Have they arrested someone?" Glenda asked.

"The inspector probably wants to go over the details of the time of death of the judge. Again. I don't know what more I can say to help him figure this out. They did bring in Sam Campbell for questioning and he claims he was out drinking with some friends."

"It sounds like Sam, all right," Glenda said.

"What seems more like Sam would be giving the judge a black eye, not sneaking into his house and firing Richard Fairley's gun into the back of his head," the doctor said before leaving.

"Miss Manley, why are some of the women here anxious to talk about Nina Lewis?" I asked.

"I suppose because she is young and pretty and not what some people expected to see in a reverend's wife in a small town."

"Also, she may have pushed aside some others who thought Reverend Lewis might have considered them for a spouse," Glenda added.

"It's true. Gossip is a dangerous thing," Miss Manley said. "I don't know how the information came out, but it seems Nina knew Richard Fairley when they both lived in Boston. It was she who recommended he rent the studio and I'm afraid some people want to put two and two together now."

Chapter 13

We knew that Miss Manley's nephew, Stuart, had entered West Adams Friday afternoon by a flurry of phone calls to the house from her friends telling her. While I thought this was odd, since he was expected and we would see him in a few minutes anyway, the calls had more to do with his method of entry: an enormous yellow and black Packard roadster that drew the entire town's attention as he motored slowly down the main street to his aunt's house. Miss Manley looked out the front door at the approaching vehicle and tutted.

"Purchased with the inheritance from his father, I'll bet. How extravagant."

Exiting the car, he trotted across the front lawn, his wavy, reddish hair bouncing as he jogged in his flashy clothes meant to look like casual country wear.

"How is my favorite aunt?" he asked, kissing her on the cheek.

We were introduced and he guided her back inside to the sitting room.

I had been concerned he might find my presence an intrusion and worried the room I was staying in was his usual assigned guest space.

"Don't worry," Glenda had told me. "He'll take the middle room. You're teacher's pet now, anyway."

"What do you mean?"

"You've achieved great marks in Miss Manley's eyes by making grumpy Doctor Taylor alter her medication."

"I did not *make* him alter the medication. And he's not grumpy. I think Miss Manley's recent health problems have him puzzled because in most other ways she is a robust and healthy woman."

Despite Glenda's dismissal of how Stuart might react, I sensed he was a little put out at the preferential position I now seemed to have in the household. I could see why he might need the larger bedroom because shortly after his arrival, he hauled in two suitcases, a tennis racquet and a set of golf clubs which he maneuvered awkwardly up the narrow staircase to the second floor. Annie, usually quiet, noticed the quantity of luggage and asked, "How long will he be staying, Miss Manley?"

"Only the weekend, as far as I know."

Based on his expensive car and wardrobe it appeared he must be a successful writer and I was a bit embarrassed I hadn't taken the time to peruse his books filling half of one shelf in the sitting room. I didn't think action books would become my new interest, but I did want to read the flyleaf to get some sense of who he was. While he unpacked his bags, I took a copy of **Sabotage over the Seine** and had to stifle a laugh at the stereotypical author photo on the back flyleaf: the serious look with a hint of curiosity posed with a pipe in hand at a desk in front of a bookcase. Just then, Stuart came into the room and like a child caught with a hand in the cookie jar, I slammed the book shut and laughed nervously.

"Sorry to startle you," he said. "I see you are looking at my aunt's collection of fiction."

"I wasn't familiar with your work and I wanted to see what it was you write." He was dressed a bit formally for a weekend in the town of West Adams, Massachusetts, with white flannel pants, a sport coat, and paisley ascot.

"That one—not one of my best. Here, let me take down one of my favorites, if I do say so myself." He rummaged through the volumes and pulled out **The Peril of Dunbar**, which had a cover with what seemed to be a Scottish castle looming in the background and a car in motion driving away.

"Thank you," I said, knowing I was now obliged to read it and comment later. "How was your trip up?"

"Usual weekend traffic. Ghastly. But it is so much cooler here than in New York, thank God. Summer in the City can be stifling." Stuart's dramatic delivery could have been entirely in italics or bold, had he been writing, and it was accompanied with equally flamboyant gestures.

"I would think a writer could write anywhere, but you choose to stay in the City?"

"Of course! New York is the hub of the publishing world. It would be far cheaper for me to live somewhere like this but then, so dull," the last few words said in a whisper so as not to offend his aunt.

The doorbell rang and Annie brought Doctor Taylor into the sitting room. The two men nodded at one another, shook hands, and Stuart excused himself. Doctor Taylor raised his eyebrows and made a wry face at the other man's departure. I was surprised at the reaction and it must have shown in my face because the doctor seemed anxious to explain himself.

"I can't stand him. So full of himself and those silly books," he gestured at the one I held in my hands. "And that car!"

"It may not be my taste or yours, but he is successful."

"Not so much. He does get published but he still relies on his aunt for an allowance."

"I'm sure it's not the case," I countered. "Miss Manley suggested *he* supported *her*."

It was an awkward moment made more uncomfortable by Miss Manley's entering the room and knowing she had interrupted a conversation.

"Miss Manley, just dropping by to see how you are doing," he said.

I made to excuse myself but they both insisted I remain, since Annie would be bringing in the refreshments in a moment, evidently a treat for the end of the workweek.

"Just a social visit," the doctor added.

"You have been a busy man this week," Miss Manley said, sitting on the sofa and patting the space next to her for me to sit.

"The inquest is next week," he said for my benefit.

"Are they any closer to finding out who could have killed the judge?" I asked.

"The inspector seems to want to leave no stone unturned. He grilled Sam Campbell for a long time and got the same story: out carousing with friends. Now those friends will be brought in for questioning, one by one."

"It sounds like the whole town has come under suspicion," I said.

Annie came in with the elderberry wine on a tray with small glasses. I could see from the expression on Doctor Taylor's face he had been anticipating something stronger and I had to suppress a smile as it would have been my preference as well.

"I know he went up to Highfields to talk to Christine, who was her usual vague self. What a strange young girl."

"Perhaps it is our age, Doctor, to consider her strange. She has an active social life with friends in Pittsfield, tennis matches several times a week, and so forth," Miss Manley said.

I think the doctor bristled at being put into Miss Manley's age group since he was only in his mid-thirties.

"I have to disagree, Miss Manley," I said in his defense. "I am closer to her age than either of you, and I can assure you she is odd.

With all the advantages she has, there seems to be little direction in her life besides entertaining herself. I don't know what Roger Lewis sees in her."

"Entertainment, I expect. And she does have a car," Miss Manley said.

"Just as I was dropping off the paperwork for the inquest this afternoon, the inspector was pestering me about Reverend Lewis. Can you imagine? He was asking me what sort of a man he was, did he have any animosity toward the judge, and so on," the doctor said.

"Oh, dear, Aggie, you may be right," Miss Manley said. "It seems everyone is under suspicion." She glanced at me and I wondered if she, too, was remembering the bit of conversation we overheard at the Lewises' tea where he spoke negatively about the judge.

"Poor Thomas Kirby. He is next in the inspector's sights, I'm afraid. We all know he is ill and it's those fevers of his that make him perspire, which I am sure is going to make him look guilty in the inspector's eyes." The doctor tilted the glass back to drink the remainder of the wine.

"What about the staff at Highfields?" I asked.

"The butler did it?" the doctor suggested.

I gave him an exasperated look. "There is no butler as far as I know. But there are a housekeeper, a cook, two maids, a chauffeur, and who knows who else. Perhaps among all of those people, someone had a grudge to settle. Doesn't it make more sense that someone inside the house could slip into the study without notice and commit the crime rather than anyone else trying to get into the house?"

"Good point," the doctor said.

"And it would seem that a person who had to deal with him regularly and intimately might have the strongest motive?"

"It would narrow the field down considerably," Miss Manley said. Then addressing the doctor, she asked, "Would you like another?"

"Thank you, no. Must be going." He stood. "Nurse Burnside, you've had an eventful week. Plans for the weekend?"

I wasn't quite sure if he meant to ask if I were free. "No real plans as yet," I answered expecting him to say something further, but he hesitated.

"Well, then, good evening, ladies."

As he strode out to the hall, Miss Manley looked at me pointedly.

"What?" I asked, blushing for no good reason. "I imagine Glenda and I will take an excursion in her car and try not to get into trouble."

"Not so fast, young lady," Stuart said, entering the room. "I believe I have a more enviable chariot than Glenda and we three can wander around the countryside looking at beautiful homes and admiring the scenery. What do you say?" Of

course, I said yes.

"Before you do anything else, would you please tug open the bottom drawer on the desk for me?" Miss Manley asked him. "With the humidity of the summer, it seems to get stuck."

"Anything of interest in there?" he asked with a wink toward me.

"No, I wanted to put something in there that I don't have to look at until November," she said.

My interest was piqued, and Stuart approached the desk and gave it a mighty yank, which was needed to get it open. "Okay, Auntie, you can give me your Christmas list to hide away now."

"Silly boy," she said. "It has to do with paying the insurance on the house. I do not want to have to look at it in the 'to do' pile for another five months."

***

Saturday morning, after a hearty breakfast, we set out on our excursion, with the caveat to return early enough in the afternoon for the sake of making sure Miss Manley wasn't left alone for long.

"My aunt will be perfectly fine, what are you worried about?" Stuart asked as we made our way to his car.

Glenda and I exchanged glances, realizing he had not been informed about the 'episodes.' She nudged me with her elbow, indicating I was to be the one to tell him, which I did. For someone who impressed me as self-involved, I was pleasantly surprised at his concern for his aunt.

"Perhaps we shouldn't go at all," he suggested.

"I think she'll be fine since Annie is there until the afternoon and the doctor is nearby. I wouldn't characterize these 'episodes' as 'attacks' or 'fits,' which sounds more sudden and violent, and they seem to come on in the late afternoon. She has a difficult time waking from her nap and is disoriented as well as a little anxious, but after a while, she's back to her normal self."

"I hope she has seen a doctor about this," he said, keeping his voice low in the event Miss Manley could hear us from inside the house.

"Yes, Doctor Taylor has been by a few times and I think he is puzzled by it all."

Although we now sat in the car, Stuart hadn't started the engine, knowing the noise would make hearing each other difficult and he certainly did not want to speak loudly considering we were still in the driveway.

"Doctor Taylor had prescribed a tonic for her to take each day and Aggie thought it might be causing the problem," said Glenda.

I was startled by her statement. "I didn't say that at all. I simply suggested the pharmacist may have compounded the medication incorrectly or, if your aunt was not used to taking medications, it might be too strong for her system to tolerate."

Glenda smiled at me. "Your explanation is tactful. I see the doctor has another fan."

I put my head down so she couldn't see my face turn red, but why I was blushing was beyond me. I thought Doctor Taylor was a competent, pleasant, good-looking man but it was the extent of my thoughts on the subject. Once the coloration had subsided, I looked up and glared at Glenda, and she just laughed at me.

"I thought we could motor over to Arrowhead, Herman Melville's house. He found quite a few arrowheads on the property, which is not surprising. This whole area is practically littered with them," Stuart said.

"I remember we had a progressive English teacher who had us read **Moby Dick**," I said as we gained speed on the open road.

"About the whale? I've never read it," Glenda said.

"I wish I were as enthusiastic about it as my teacher had been. It seems each time I sat to read it I would get sleepy."

Stuart laughed. "Oh, I remember some books like that, too. Melville was famous around here but didn't stay too long, from what people say. None of his family live there anymore, but it's a lovely property."

We had to go through Pittsfield, the big city for the area with its central shopping district, bustling on this Saturday morning, all the parking spaces in front of the sidewalks full.

"See, we aren't entirely out in the sticks here," Glenda said.

Stuart stifled a laugh and continued driving south. After a few more streets we found ourselves heading into an area with few houses and so many trees that, if there were structures behind them, they were made invisible.

"There it is, I think," he said, pulling over to the side of the road.

The home stood on a hill, the oaks, maples, and elms on the roadside framing the view rather than obscuring it.

"He must have had substantial success to have owned this beauty," I said, noticing the size of the home and the large porch running alongside.

"I heard he changed some aspect of it to get the best views of Mount Greylock, but, of course, those would belong to judge Nash at Highfields."

"Yes, it was spectacular," I said, remembering the glimpse from the day before.

"There are a lot of wonderful spots here if you like the outdoors," he said, turning the car around to head back to West Adams. "We'll get out and about the next time you visit."

We got back to Miss Manley's in time for tea; she was up and about in an energetic and cheerful mood. I could see by the look Stuart gave me that he wondered how frequent and severe her bouts could have been in light of her current behavior.

"I haven't seen Arrowhead in years," Miss Manley said.

"Aunt, I can take you tomorrow, if you like," Stuart said.

"No, tomorrow is Sunday. Church. And you've just spent most of the day out; it would be boring for you to repeat it so soon."

Stuart didn't object and was probably looking forward to using his golf clubs or tennis racquet instead. As we sat chatting, Roger Lewis came to the French windows of the sitting room and knocked on the door jamb. He embodied the special time of late adolescence where the young man he would become was almost visible in the currently gangly, awkward male with tousled hair.

"Hello, Miss Manley. May I come in?" and launched himself into the room before she had a chance to answer. "Are you Stuart Manley? The author?"

Stuart had the grace to lower his eyes in an attempt at humility. "Yes, the same. And to whom do I have the pleasure of speaking?"

Roger sat uninvited and soon began an intense conversation, part inquiry, part commentary, on the series of books Stuart had written. Roger knew all about the protagonist, his many travels and trials, the villains who changed from one book to the other but were all affiliated with the same nefarious group of spies, killers, or other evildoers. It was a fascinating example of someone with what could only be described as a mania, emotion-laden enthusiasm with attention to detail. After a good ten minutes of this frantic conversation, he realized he hadn't addressed anyone else in the room and apologized.

"Would you like some tea?" Miss Manley inquired.

"No thanks," he said, taking a sandwich.

I suggested lemonade and went to fetch it from the kitchen. When I returned he was talking just as excitedly about the judge's death and his speculations about 'who done it,' as he referred to the deed, which made me wonder if he didn't read crime novels in addition to Stuart's action-in-exotic-places series of books.

"It's possible Elsie and Sam Campbell were working together. She goes up to Highfields on the pretext of borrowing a cup of sugar from the cook while Sam tiptoes down the hall, into the study, and Bam!"

"Roger!" Miss Manley said.

"How can you bear to be in the house with Elsie if that's what you think she is capable of?" Glenda asked.

"In that scenario, she is his accomplice, protecting the honor of her man. It's just one theory. I've got a whole bunch of them."

I was afraid he might be induced to share his theories to impress Stuart and I wasn't wrong.

"There's Mrs. Nash, of course, who stands to inherit a lot of dough, but it seems the inspector has dismissed the possibility of her doing it."

"As I told the inspector, she seemed to have been upstairs and certainly didn't have a gun with her when we saw her that afternoon," I said.

"And he's ruled out Richard Fairley because the timing was all wrong. If Doctor Taylor didn't goof up on his assessment of the time of death."

I was beginning to be irritated at him sharing high-handed opinions and went to the defense of Doctor Taylor. "I can assure you the doctor knows what he is doing. As a trained nurse, I also observed the body at close range and the judge had been dead a while." Perhaps I overstated things, but it made an impression on Roger, who was still not apologetic for his rash comments and rattled on.

"Then there is the mystery of the missing money." He let it hang there waiting for someone to ask to what he was referring. Nobody took the bait, so he was forced to explain. "The money in the collection basket that went missing."

"What has it got to do with anything?" Glenda asked.

"The judge thought *somebody* in the church took it. Which means he thought it was either Thomas Kirby or my uncle, the reverend."

"Oh, Roger. You are going too far," Miss Manley said in a harsh tone.

"I'm just being logical in my observations. The judge made an appointment with my uncle for the evening to discuss some financial issues about the church. Someone panicked and Bam!"

"First of all, Roger, your uncle was just coming back from visiting a sick parishioner—he was lured away by a phone call to what he thought was a sick parishioner. Many people saw him driving back just before seven o'clock, so it lets him out of the picture."

"More like six forty-five," I added.

"What about Thomas Kirby? Where was he? Unaccounted for, from what I hear." Roger allowed himself a smug smile.

"I can't see him killing somebody over the matter of a few dollars," Glenda said.

"And he has been so ill, as you all can see. He probably doesn't have the energy to do such a thing," I added.

"Fascinating," Stuart commented, whether on specific remarks or the entire disjointed conversation. "I wish I knew who all these people are. What a great plot for a story."

"Yes," Roger said. "I could help you write it."

"But you are forgetting some people, aren't you?" Miss Manley asked. "Sandra Logan for example."

Glenda clutched her necklace in alarm.

"What motive could she have?"

"She argued with the judge the night before he was killed," I offered. They all looked at me. "What about Christine?" I offered. "She had the most to gain if her father were out of the way and her stepmother was blamed."

Roger scoffed. "How is it even possible? She was off playing tennis with someone."

"With you? Oh, if not with you, then who?" Glenda asked.

Roger was quiet for a moment.

"How about you, Roger, as the culprit?" asked Stuart dramatically. "It's always the person who tries to look inconspicuous who is overlooked. As a young man, people are not paying attention to what you are doing most of the time. You come and go, and no one thinks a thing about it. You could have sneaked into what's-his-name's house and taken the weapon. And Bam!"

If Roger had been a few years younger, he might have burst into tears, but he set his mouth in a hard line until Stuart began to laugh and slapped him on the back. At last, all of us could relax and hope this fruitless speculation was over.

"And how about you, Glenda?" I said mimicking Stuart's dramatic question.

"And you, Miss Manley?" Glenda said.

"And you, Stuart?" both of us said at the same time, laughing now.

"This is no laughing matter," Miss Manley said sternly.

We agreed but at least the tension with Roger had been broken and his good humor returned when Stuart proposed they play a set of tennis the next day.

Chapter 14

I wasn't quite sure what to do with myself on Sunday, once sleeping in was no longer an option due to Stuart's noisy preparations for a day of sport with Roger. He began by crashing around in the adjacent room as he seemed to be rummaging in the closet for his gear, then humming as he banged open drawers and slammed them shut only to repair to the bathroom, presumably to shave with an accompanying song. I dragged myself out of bed, feeling groggy and out of sorts, but was hit with the sunshine through the windows and the birdsong from the forest and garden. Suddenly in a better mood, I thought it might be a nice gesture to accompany Miss Manley to church after breakfast.

She was already up and had put out a plate of muffins Annie had prepared the day before along with boiled eggs and coffee. It was delightful in the dining room with the windows open, the breeze and the sound of the birds coming through. I sensed she was a bit peeved Stuart had driven up here for the weekend, yet chose to spend little time with her, instead chauffeuring Glenda and me around on Saturday and playing tennis with the reverend's nephew on Sunday. My offer of going to church was welcomed, and we set out shortly after Stuart stomped down the stairs in his tennis whites, racquet in hand.

"Say, where are you two going?" "Church,"
Miss Manley said sharply.

"Oh, yes. Well, I had promised Roger a tennis match."

Miss Manley looked at him coldly. "I don't imagine his uncle will be pleased with him engaging in sport rather than spiritual development."

There was no appropriate answer to that statement, and we left before he could come up with another excuse.

"My word!" Miss Manley said as we walked down the street.

The small church was nearly filled with many faces I had never seen before but evidently all familiar to one another. A few women pointedly asked where Stuart was, and Miss Manley deftly handled her reply by saying he was doing some instruction with a young man. I was surprised to see Richard Fairley in attendance, although he sat nowhere near Mrs. Nash, who had come by herself. The reverend led a tame service with a sermon about loving one's neighbor and extrapolating it to mean all those with whom you disagree. The hymns were standard and short, and the entire experience was inoffensive and not the least bit spiritual, just comfortable; I now understood why Stuart had chosen to do something else and was glad I only had a few more occasions to attend before my scheduled return to New York.

After the service and the requisite chat with the reverend on the steps, Miss Manley took me around the side of the church to the graveyard. I recognized the ancient, weathered stones from my previous visit, tilting in all directions as if slowly sinking into the earth.

"Here are my mother and father," she said, stopping in front of a newer double headstone. "They passed away within months of each other," which was obvious from the dates inscribed.

"Have you any other relatives?"

"I may have mentioned I had a brother, Stuart's father. He too passed away but is buried in New York."

"I'm sorry."

"It is strange to be the last of your family. But…." She did not continue.

"Look, there's Sarah's grave." She strode over to the newer part of the cemetery.

The headstone was new, of course, and I could see Miss Manley was pleased that flowers had been placed on it.

"What was Mrs. Butler like?" I asked.

"Sarah was a lovely woman. A petite woman much like Glenda. She was patient and giving. Her husband was rather a rabble-rouser in his day, I don't mind telling you. Made and lost quite a bit of money and was a trial for Sarah's nerves, as you can imagine. Glenda takes after him quite a bit, but I suspect you know that."

I had to laugh and agree at her observation as I remembered the hijinks we sometimes got up to in nurses' training. "Yes, but it's all in good fun."

"It's why she went to Miss Hall's, you know. She was getting a bit wild and Sarah didn't know how to control her. By the time she graduated, the money was gone, and college was out of the question. It is how nursing came into the conversation."

I knew this much but was not aware how many others knew the story.

"This may sound terrible, but Sarah was hoping Glenda would take to nursing and marry a doctor, a professional man with a solid financial basis. She had done her share of worrying over money, so you can understand how she wanted something different for her daughter."

We had reached the far wall of the graveyard and I leaned my back against the stacked stone wall in the shade.

"I think many of us entered nursing with financial issues in mind but more recently with the crash and all, there may be more joining. I am lucky to enjoy it and will continue until I can't anymore. I was hoping to persuade Glenda to finish her coursework and certification since she is so close to finishing. There must be jobs in Pittsfield besides assisting local physicians in their practices."

Miss Manley shook her head. "I fear she is not going to do it. But I do encourage you to continue talking to her about it before she gets so settled in here, she can't envision going back."

***

Miss Manley prepared and cooked the entire Sunday dinner despite my repeated offers of assistance. It was quite a meal: roast beef, oven-roasted potatoes, green beans, and tomato aspic salad, more than enough for three people, only two of whom were participating, since Stuart was still not home by one o'clock when we began or two o'clock when we had finished. At least Miss Manley allowed me to clear the table and do the dishes while she put her feet up afterward. Once finished in the kitchen I wandered out into the garden and sat in the chair in the shade of the elm tree. Not long after, Glenda came out and sat beside me and closed her eyes.

"We can pretend we are two old spinster ladies taking it easy on a Sunday afternoon."

"And why weren't you in church this morning, missy?" I teased.

"Oops. I wish I could say I overslept, but it would be a lie." She ran her fingers through her wavy blonde hair and sighed. "I just couldn't take sitting with so many people, I suppose."

We were quiet for a few moments until I said, "Are you having trouble getting back in the swing of things?" I hesitated, hoping to rephrase my clumsy question, but she replied.

"Yes, I suppose that's it. Losing Mother was so much harder than I thought it would be. And now I'm responsible for the bills and taking care of the house. It's overwhelming to think if I don't stay on top of everything, it could all be lost."

I sat up and reached out my hand to her. "Don't worry, it won't be. To be practical for a moment, you could make a calendar list of when certain bills need to be paid and make sure to follow it. You've got me for a friend and I'm sure your lawyer can offer some support. He did say you were all right financially, didn't he?" She nodded.

"Even before you took the boarder in, correct?" She nodded again.

"Then stop worrying." I patted her arm. "You know, you could always come back and finish your training. I'll bet Doctor Taylor would take you on as an assistant or maybe you could work at the hospital in Pittsfield if you were to finish."

She pulled her hand away. "Why do you keep on about it? That part of my life is over, and I can't turn back time to be what I was just months ago, a carefree girl dreaming of someone to take care of me. It's just me now. I am the only one to take care of me."

The discussion was over, and I was not going to press what I thought was a sensible point on my part. Or at least, not at this time. She was still reeling from the changes in her life and once the summer was over, she might reconsider when she began receiving letters from me working in the hospital, crowing about the salary and the handsome doctors.

We sat in silence, enjoying the pine-scented breeze from the woods beyond when Stuart's car came noisily over the gravel in the driveway. Seeing the backs of our heads, he called out, with Roger echoing his greeting, slamming the car doors, and talking loudly as they approached.

I turned around to see their flushed and sunburned faces beaming after a long morning and early afternoon on a tennis court somewhere but was glad they were back for Miss Manley's sake so she might visit with her nephew.

"When's dinner?" Stuart asked, taking off his tennis sweater and throwing it on the small table in the yard.

"So sorry, you've missed it," I said cheerfully, recounting the menu.

"Surely there's some left? I'm famished." Turning to Roger, he said, "Come on, let's raid the icebox. No one will be the wiser." They made off for the kitchen through the back door.

"Do you think he's a bit irresponsible?" I asked Glenda.

"Because he didn't go to church this morning and chose to play tennis? Perhaps a little. But he is visiting; he should be allowed to enjoy himself, don't you think?"

It was a reasonable enough answer and was certainly in accordance with Glenda's general attitude toward life. I decided to get up and oversee what the two men were doing in the kitchen, since I didn't know what had been planned for the considerable amount of leftover roast. Stuart was making thin slices of the cold meat while Roger tackled a loaf of bread to assemble hearty beef sandwiches with tomato slices between the layers.

Not bothering to sit down, Roger mumbled through the first bite of food in his mouth, "So good."

I went back outside to assure Glenda the men were adequately provisioned and stretched my legs out in the sunshine. We didn't talk and before I knew it, I had dozed off. What woke me was the slam of the screen door to the kitchen and, glancing over at the other chair, I saw Glenda must have decided to join the feasting in the kitchen. Still drowsy, I nodded off again to be wakened by another slam of the door. For a moment I thought I was back home in Pelham and my brother was coming to get me for dinner, but it was Roger, shaking my shoulder.

"Aggie, wake up. They can't seem to get Miss Manley up from her nap."

I shook the sleep out of my head and quickly followed him upstairs to Miss Manley's darkened bedroom, trying to adjust my eyes to the gloom. Glenda stood away from the bed, her hands crossed over her chest. Stuart was seated on the bed with Miss Manley's hand in his as he slapped it lightly.

"Auntie, wake up."

There was no response, but I could see she was breathing normally at least. I pushed my way to the other side of the bed, took her left hand in mine and checked her pulse. Normal.

"Glenda, why don't you get a cold, wet washcloth and put it on her forehead. I'll see if I can get Doctor Taylor."

"Yes," Stuart said. "Call him."

"No, I'll just walk over. It might be faster if he is not in the office or near a telephone."

I hurried down the stairs, out the front door, and trotted to Doctor Taylor's back door, thankful it was unlocked, opened it, and called out for him. Luckily he was in the kitchen, drinking a glass of milk, and he had seen me through the window over the sink crossing the back garden.

"What is it?"

"Miss Manley again. Please come."

I didn't wait for an answer but walked swiftly back to her house and up the stairs. When I got there, I heard her trying to say something and tossing her head from side to side on the pillow, which released her hair from the pins securing it in a bun at the back.

"What's going on?" I asked.

"I don't know," Stuart said. "She seems disturbed about something, but I can't make out what it is she is trying to say. Auntie, wake up!"

Doctor Taylor came thundering up the stairs, still in his shirtsleeves, medical bag in hand. At his approach, we all stepped away from the bed, while Roger remained in the corner looking curiously at the proceedings. Although he was certainly old enough to observe what was going on, I thought Miss Manley would be embarrassed to know he had been present, so I pulled him into the hallway.

"Roger, I think you should go home now. You'll want to tell the reverend and Nina about this but, please, no one else."

For once, Roger was tongue-tied, nodded seriously, and left quietly.

Whatever Doctor Taylor had said or done in my brief absence had resulted in Miss Manley's eyes being open and she attempted to pull herself up but was gently pushed back to a supine position by the doctor.

"Not just yet, please," he instructed her. He took out his stethoscope, took her pulse, and reached for his sphygmomanometer and placed the cuff on her arm, pumped it up, and released it.

"Hmm," he said, removing the cuff.

Miss Manley blinked her eyes and saw Stuart, Glenda, and me. "Oh, dear. I seem to have had another episode." She struggled to sit upright and this time the doctor did not stop her.

Doctor Taylor smiled thoughtfully at her. "So it seems. Did you do anything out of the ordinary today?" he asked.

"No."

He looked to me for confirmation.

"I'm sorry, I don't know her Sunday routine well enough to know what is ordinary. We had breakfast, went to church, walked around the cemetery, walked home, and she made a roast, which we ate, then she went up to have a rest. That's all we did." Miss Manley nodded.

"Did you have anything unusual to eat or drink today?" he asked.

We three looked at each other with puzzled faces.

"No," she answered.

"Do you mind if I check your kitchen?" he asked. "Aggie, would you stay here while I look around?" Stuart and Glenda looked at each other.

"Certainly," I said.

He was gone a good ten minutes and returned to his patient, who seemed to gain clarity in his absence.

"Could I be eating something that causes me to sleep so heavily?" Miss Manley asked.

"You have been taking your tonic each day for several weeks, yet you only started having these episodes this past week," Doctor Taylor said. "And you haven't had one every day, so I think we can rule it out as a source. I had wondered if there was some food or vitamin supplement that could be interacting with the tonic, but I didn't see anything."

"Why didn't you tell me about this?" Stuart asked, looking from his aunt to Doctor Taylor.

The doctor wisely let his patient respond.

"I didn't want to worry you, of course."

Stuart scoffed. "Well, I won't be leaving tonight, that's for sure." He glared at the doctor and went downstairs, followed by Glenda.

I was glad he would be staying, although so far his idea of visiting his aunt had consisted of two half-day excursions that didn't include her; what he intended to do by staying another day I wasn't sure. I was more puzzled by his evident animosity toward the doctor who, in my opinion, had done more than was required under the circumstances of a puzzling set of symptoms of no known origin.

"Would you like to get up or stay in bed a bit longer?" I asked.

The doctor answered for her. "Let's wait a bit, all right? But if you wouldn't mind getting a glass of water," he asked me. This seemed to be high on my list of professional nursing skills so far: fetching water for the infirm.

I walked quietly down the staircase, turning over in my mind what the source of Miss Manley's episodes could be when I overheard Stuart and Glenda in the hallway to the kitchen.

"No, I can't believe it," Glenda said.

"Don't you think it's a little suspicious my aunt only started having these seizures, or whatever you call them, after your friend Aggie came here?"

Chapter 15

My heart was pounding, and my stomach dropped. I couldn't believe my ears. How could Stuart possibly think I was connected to Miss Manley's illness? At first, I was mortified, and it quickly turned to anger at the self-centered man who seemed to have no time for his aunt yet was all too ready to blame others when she was in a bit of difficulty. And now I didn't care if they knew I had overheard them. I boldly resumed my descent and glared at them as I passed in the hallway. At least Glenda had the decency to look embarrassed.

Without making further eye contact, I put my shoulders back and went back upstairs with the glass of water to Miss Manley's bedroom. With each passing minute, she seemed to regain herself and was now muttering about how disheveled her hair had become, pulling out the combs and pins and repositioning them. doctor Taylor smiled at her.

"I can always tell when a woman is feeling better. It's when she has to touch up her coiffure and makeup."

"I don't wear makeup," Miss Manley replied tartly.

He chuckled. "I'd like to talk to Nurse Burnside for a moment," he said, taking me out into the hall and closing the door behind him.

"I wish I had something more definitive to tell her but whatever is going on is rather baffling. I think I'd like to do a series of tests sometime this week, which may take quite a bit of persuasion." He gave me a look.

"Are you suggesting that, if you cannot get her to agree, I should try?"

He smiled. "Yes, exactly."

"If we don't succeed, we'll ask Stuart to step up."

Doctor Taylor grimaced at the mention of his name but didn't elaborate on a reason, so I left it and re-entered the bedroom. Miss Manley was seated at her vanity fixing her hair.

"I'm fine now, dear," she said to me. "I hope the doctor didn't suggest you hover around me all day."

"Of course not," I said truthfully, although my instinct was to keep an eye on her as much as possible and tell Annie to do the same when she came in the next day. I couldn't say what Stuart's response to all this would be except to take another sightseeing drive, but I hoped he would show some genuine attention to his aunt.

He did take the initiative to put together a light supper for Miss Manley, who seemed utterly shocked he had any culinary skills, even if it was only slicing meat and bread to make a repeat of his late lunch. She was gracious in her appreciation, as was I, and wondered if my meal was a small attempt at an apology for his earlier comment.

Sleep didn't come easily that night due to my brief afternoon nap as well as the noisy activity of Stuart next door, who seemed to stow something in the closet. He finally left his bedroom and quietly went downstairs, leaving me with the sound of birdsong and leaves rustling in the evening breeze. It was starting to be a bit chilly, so I got up to fully close the window and saw somebody near the chairs under the elm tree. Squinting to get a better view, I saw it was Glenda's shoes peeking out in the gloom, although I could not see the rest of her. Shortly thereafter, Stuart came out from the house, walked over to her and they conferred for a few minutes before each returning to their respective houses. Had they been talking about me again? I could feel my face burning as if I had overheard their conversation again and quietly went back to bed.

Why were they talking? And about what? I had the impression Glenda either didn't know Stuart well or didn't think highly of him. Had I been wrong? My mind whirled with thoughts. Did I even know Glenda? Was my friend trying to defend me or was she even my friend? I turned the pillow over to get to the cool side and resolved not to think about them or myself but replayed the romantic plot from a movie I had seen in Atlantic City until my thoughts ceased, and I fell asleep.

The next day Miss Manley was her old self when we breakfasted together. Stuart was still sleeping, so she took Annie aside in the kitchen and told her of the events of Sunday afternoon. We were no sooner done with the meal than the doorbell rang, and Inspector Gladstone entered to go over the same ground with me he had before. I was under the impression these interviews usually occurred at a police station and were done on an individual basis, but he seemed to have no qualms about Miss Manley's being in the sitting room with me while he discussed the day of the judge's death once more. We went through the same sequence of who saw what and said what and he took notes again. What this interview told me more than anything was he was no closer to figuring out who had killed the judge and what the motive might have been.

"Have Sam Campbell's friends vouched for him?" Miss Manley asked, taking the words out of my mouth.

"Yes," he answered with annoyance. It would have been all too easy to lay the blame on him or discredit his cronies.

Stuart chose this moment to enter the sitting room, looked at the visitor, and asked, "Who are you?"

To which he replied, "Inspector Gladstone. And who are *you*?" Miss Manley got up quickly and made the introductions and explained the inspector was leading the investigation into judge Nash's death at Highfields.

"Do you think perhaps the death of your neighbor may have had some effect on your physical and mental well-being?" he asked his aunt.

How could he attribute the judge's death to her 'episodes' when they had begun beforehand?

For once, Miss Manley did not have a response.

"I'm sorry, Auntie," Stuart said, genuinely contrite. "It must have been difficult to lose a close friend." He sat next to her and took her hand. She looked a bit puzzled because as far as I knew, the judge was not a close friend.

The inspector cleared his throat. "If you please, I need to continue my conversation with Miss Burnside."

"Aren't we done here?" I asked. It seemed to me my knowledge of the event had been described, re-described, and picked over so many times, revealing nothing new.

He made a show of leafing through the notes in his little book while muttering.

"Yes, I think we are done. For now." "When is the inquest?" I asked.

"Wednesday at nine o'clock. And you will be called to testify."

I hadn't thought of it and it gave me a serious jolt. I looked at Miss Manley.

"I shall stay here until then," Stuart declared.

I didn't know what Stuart hoped to achieve by remaining in West Adams for the inquest. She wasn't going to be called, he hadn't assisted his aunt in any way during his visit that I could see and seemed to unsettle her if anything. What neither of us needed was for him to request the details of that awful day to relive it again.

The inspector looked at Stuart with disdain. "Thank you, ladies. I'll be going then."

Miss Manley got up to see him to the door and likely to get out of the clutches of her nephew, who was wearing on my nerves, too. Her errand done, she made her way to the kitchen to confer with Annie.

"You and Glenda gave me just the bare outline of what occurred if you are both being called to testify." He came over to the sofa where I was seated and gave me his undivided attention. I got up.

"I need to get ready for work," I said although I had several hours to do so. "Perhaps Glenda can fill you in." I left it at that and retreated to my room.

I sat at the desk to write another letter to my parents but could not think of what to say, since Miss Manley's health problems should not be a topic of conversation and I hadn't told them of the judge's death. Instead, I picked up Stuart's book and read the first few lines of tortured prose, then flung it down on the bed. The book I had brought with me from home was much less melodramatic and positively soothing: exactly what was needed. I managed to avoid everyone in the house while I read although I heard Stuart opening drawers in his room next door and humming to himself before he went downstairs. I wondered if Miss Manley had successfully avoided him as well and, getting up to look out the window, saw she was actively working in the garden, a place Stuart would likely not follow, at least not to do work. Richard Fairley walked across the garden to his studio, stopping to chat with Miss Manley for a few moments, and after he left, she stared after him most curiously before bending to her task.

We were able to enjoy our lunch without the presence of Stuart, who had driven to Pittsfield on some errand. So much for keeping his aunt company, I thought. At the end of the meal, Glenda popped in to see Miss Manley and hung around until I excused myself to change for work; she didn't leave but followed me upstairs.

No sooner had the door closed than she apologized. "Aggie, please don't think I was suggesting anything to Stuart about you. He has enough imagination for two people! He merely asked me when you got here and then when Miss Manley's episodes began, and he jumped to a hasty conclusion."

"I'll say."

"I'm sure he doesn't think there is anything amiss here."

I pulled a hanger with my uniform on it from the depths of the closet and faced her fully.

"I don't appreciate being maligned. And I certainly think you should have stuck up for me in a more forceful way." I turned away to remove my blouse.

"Aggie! I did! I told him it was nonsense." She pulled at my arm, so I was tugged onto the bed next to her.

"Aggie, you are my best friend. Please, let's not argue." She had begun to cry.

I put my arms around her. "We won't, don't worry. I'm just infuriated with Stuart's remarks and his treatment of his aunt. That's all. It has nothing to do with you."

But it did. I stood to step out of my skirt and put on my uniform.

We had made up, we were still friends, but I couldn't get out of my head the image of Glenda and Stuart chatting in the garden last night in the dark.

Chapter 16

I arrived at Doctor Taylor's office to find the waiting room blessedly empty since I did not feel like talking to anyone. There was the mail to open and sort, files to tidy, and several more invoices to deal with. The doctor came in shortly after I finished these tasks and immediately asked about Miss Manley.

"She seems fine today. So far."

"Hmm. How odd these episodes only come on in the afternoon," he said. "And how are you?" "I'm fine, thank you," I lied.

"You seem a little down in the mouth. I hope Stuart isn't getting on your nerves."

I had to smile at that. "He puts quite a strain on things from my point of view."

Doctor Taylor let out a belly laugh. "How diplomatic you are!" Then after a pause, he added, "I thought I would stop in and see her a little later."

"She won't be there. She's got some meeting at the church."

"Well, please make sure to train your professional eyes on her when she returns and let me know if you think anything is amiss."

"Certainly." I went back to my busy work and he to his office for the remainder of the day.

I had developed a headache by the time I got home, which didn't improve when I saw Stuart's car was in the driveway, indicating his return from Pittsfield. I wondered how I could best avoid him, but it turned out to be impossible as both he and Glenda ambushed me as I walked into the yard.

"Good afternoon," he said, full of good cheer. "We're just about to have a cocktail. Won't you join us?" He pointed to the table in front of the two lawn chairs and I saw a sizable bottle of clear liquid in an unmarked bottle, likely gin. Of course, people drank despite Prohibition, but I thought from a gossip standpoint it was ill-advised since his aunt's yard was exposed to any number of people who might use the back path to the town center.

Nonetheless, I agreed, as soon as I'd changed out of my uniform. Clothed in a more casual outfit, my face washed, hair combed, and two aspirin taken with a glass of water, I felt the tension of the day leave and looked forward to whatever concoction and conversation Stuart had in mind.

By the time I returned to the garden, another chair had materialized, along with a pitcher of lemonade, a bowl of ice, three glasses, and a plate of oyster crackers. The bottle of gin had been discretely placed beside Glenda's chair, invisible to anyone strolling by on the path.

"Tom Collins, sort of," Stuart said merrily. He was ahead of us already, and I preferred this good-humored version of him.

"How was your day?" I asked them both.

"Dull up until now," Glenda said, raising her glass.

"Super," Stuart said, giving a big grin. "And yours?"

"It was fine, thank you." I took the glass offered to me and had a taste of a lot of gin and not much lemonade. I added several pieces of ice from the bowl to water it down.

"Aggie, I feel I must apologize," Stuart began.

I looked to Glenda knowing she must have said something to him, and if she had I wasn't sorry about it. I didn't say anything and let him continue.

"Here you are in a new place, a small town after all your experiences with big city life, a tragedy occurs practically on your doorstep, and I barge in with unkind words."

I made a small smile indicating I appreciated what he said but not yet letting him off the hook.

"You know I have enormous affection for my aunt—she's practically all the family I have now. It might not seem like it, but I do worry about her and that I am not doing enough. So, the mention of the murder at Highfields was shocking and I imagine it must have been so to her as well."

"Stuart, you might be surprised to know Miss Manley was probably not as affected by the event as you might imagine. She is quite a remarkable woman: logical, analytical, not at all given over to emotions."

He smiled. "You are quite perceptive, Aggie. And I agree, although I think the combination of losing dear Sarah," here he patted Glenda's hand, "and the horrific event with the judge may have been the cause of these episodes of hers."

"Possibly," I said, although not agreeing with his logic at all. "The doctor seems quite puzzled by them. They might just pass, and we'll never know the cause."

We sat in silence for a bit sipping our drinks and I was reminded of Glenda and my having a martini from time to time in the seedy speakeasy near the hospital.

"I forgot to tell you," Glenda began suddenly. "The inspector came over and interviewed the decorator's assistant." "Why is that so surprising?" Stuart asked.

I had forgotten I had told Glenda about Sandra Logan's having been a visitor at Highfields the night before judge Nash was killed and according to the housekeeper having had an argument with him. My tongue somewhat loosened by the gin, I repeated this to Stuart, whose eyebrows shot up his forehead.

"You don't say!"

"Keep your voices down," Glenda said, looking around.

"What do you think it was about?"

"Their conversation was not long, and I got the impression Sandra had no intention of telling the inspector what was said between her and judge Nash. The inspector left in a hurry with a terrific scowl on his face."

"And no one overheard the exact conversation between Sandra and the judge?" he asked.

"No one is admitting having heard what was said. And I just found out today the housekeeper gave in her notice."

Stuart whistled. "This *is* starting to sound like a plot I could use in my next book!"

"Don't you dare!" Glenda said. "You can go back to New York and scribble away, but I have to live here. My neighbors will vilify me if they know I've been gossiping." Stuart chuckled.

"This is small-town life at its best or worst." I didn't think her neighbors would avoid her; rather, she might gain some popularity with the local women.

"I was only joking," he said, pushing his hair back with one hand. I didn't believe him for an instant.

"The inquest is going to be Wednesday," I stated. "We're going to be called to testify."

Glenda's hand shot up to her mouth. "Aggie, I am not looking forward to it."

"It's all right. They'll just ask all those annoying questions the inspector has already asked us."

"I hope that's all."

We were quiet for a few minutes and I pondered getting my thoughts together before then to appear a reliable witness. I had to be sure not to talk to Glenda about it in the event we somehow colored each other's memory of the event or used the same words and phrases.

We heard some crashing noises along the back path that turned out to be Roger swinging his tennis racquet against the bushes along the way. He was delighted to see us, especially Stuart, who waved him over.

"Come join us in a drink," he said.

"I'll get another glass," Glenda said, going across the lawn to Miss Manley's back door. "Stuart, there is another chair in the garage."

Roger was well pleased to be seated with the sophisticated adults and be invited to cocktails, no less. I had mixed feelings about the gesture, which was kind by its nature and doubly illegal because Roger was underage, but I said nothing.

"Tennis again?" I asked.

"Yes, what else is there to do here?"

"Where do you go to school?"

"Not here. In Boston. Public school. The family doesn't have enough dough to put me in private school. I've only got another year anyway."

"How did you come to know Christine?" I asked.

"I just know her from around. And tennis," he said vaguely.

"She's been out of high school for a year already."

It surprised me as Christine appeared to be quite a bit younger than eighteen but perhaps it was her distracted, moody personality that affected my judgment.

"Here we go," Stuart announced cheerfully, plopping a lawn chair down to make a foursome just as Glenda emerged with a small glass from the house. I hoped Stuart was not going to pour the young man a stiff drink, but he showed restraint by putting much more lemonade than gin in the glass for him.

Roger seemed thrilled to be part of the cocktail party and took a sizeable slug of the drink before coughing for a few moments. We three tried not to laugh at the predictable reaction.

"We were just talking about the inquest on Wednesday," Stuart said when the noisy spasm seemed over.

"Christine mentioned it to me. You know, at first, I thought she was a mature and cool customer by not being visibly upset about her father's death. After all, they used to argue all the time, from what she says. But as the days go by I can tell she just masks her emotions well," Roger said.

"Of course, she must be upset," Glenda said. "He was her only relative. I never heard what happened to her mother. Just imagine being in her shoes."

"Oh, I can. My parents are in China, missionaries this summer, you know," he said for my benefit. "I know what it's like being without them. Except my aunt and uncle are pretty lenient with me and I get along with them great, unlike the relationship between Christine and Mrs. Nash."

"I assumed they didn't get on well, but I didn't know for sure. Certainly, neither would have confided in me."

Stuart leaned and lowered his voice. "What's the situation with Mrs. Nash and the artist fellow?"

We all turned our heads toward the studio as if Richard Fairley were in there, although we knew for a fact he had gone into town before our party began.

"They were lovers," Roger said in a whisper.

"You don't know that for sure," I said, annoyed at his presumption. "How could someone carry on an affair in a small town like West Adams?"

"You'd be surprised," Glenda commented. "Perhaps not lovers. Yet. But thinking about it from their reactions."

"My uncle saw them kissing. By accident."

Stuart laughed. "Did he see them kissing, by accident? Or were they kissing by accident?" We all laughed at his joke.

"One point for punctuation," Stuart said, raising his glass.

"So, who do you think done it?" Roger said, clearly feeling the gin.

"One demerit for grammar," I said. "From what Glenda has told me, it can't have been your uncle since he was out and about."

"Yes, but Aunt Nina wasn't," he replied.

"She was in Pittsfield for the day," I said.

"Ah—she was. But she got back earlier than she said. I saw her walking at the other end of town as I was coming back from tennis."

"What earthly reason would she have for killing the judge?" I asked.

"She couldn't stand him. Always nagging my uncle about church business."

I was thankful for the reverend's sake Roger would not be called for the inquest. He was so flippant about serious matters, I didn't think he understood his words could be used against people.

"What about Thomas Kirby?" Roger suggested. "He's strange and thinks people suspect him of something." "Like what?" Stuart asked.

"The missing money from the collection plate."

"I certainly hope it was thousands of dollars that went missing or what is the point? And if he did take a lot of money, what in the world is he still doing here in West Adams? He'd be gone by now."

"It was only a few dollars," Roger said, gulping down the rest of his drink. "Say, can I get a refill?"

All three of us said, "No," at the same time. The last thing we wanted was for him to return home tipsy and blab how we were complicit. He looked crestfallen but was still happy enough from what he had consumed.

"I'll put my money on Sam Campbell. He's a terrific shot and he's had a grudge against the judge—hey, it rhymes—for a long time."

"I've known Sam since we were kids. He may be rough, but I don't see him as devious. You'd have to have a plan in place to do what was done to the judge in his own house, I would think," Glenda said.

"Maybe Elsie helped him," Roger suggested.

"Are you going on about that again? How do you feel comfortable being in the same house with Elsie?" I asked.

"Oh, no problem. She's a good egg. Neither of them is mad at *me* about anything."

His logic or lack thereof was astonishing. I thought: if Sam Campbell were such an excellent shot, why wouldn't he get a rifle or shotgun and kill the judge with some physical distance between them? Walking through the front door of the house and shooting someone point blank would have been taking a tremendous risk.

"I wish I knew all these people better," Stuart said. "I could make a more educated guess at what happened."

After another brief silence, Roger had some inspiration. "I know. How about Doctor Taylor?"

Glenda groaned and I protested.

"What possible motive does Doctor Taylor have?" she asked.

"Who knows what evil lurks in the hearts of men?" he intoned in the voice of The Shadow.

Glenda threw a cracker at him. "You're impossible. We don't know what the inspector has found out or what he knows, but it seems to me one thing he is missing is the number of criminals whom the judge may have put away who could seek revenge. If he had been on the bench for a long time, there may be quite a long list. He only moved here about five years ago, but I know he was a judge somewhere else in Massachusetts. Maybe someone from his past tracked him down in West Adams and just waited for the right moment."

"But if it were someone from his past, the person would appear to be a conspicuous stranger here," Stuart said. "And would have been recognized by the judge."

"And how would he know the judge would be at home alone in the study at that specific time?" I asked. "That wasn't a smart decision."

"Criminals sometimes are not the brightest people," Roger said.

"I think this criminal seems to be an exceedingly smart person."

"Maybe the killer meant to shoot Mrs. Nash!" Glenda said.

That silenced everyone. Surely no one could mistake the judge for Mrs. Nash? My head reeled with the thought: perhaps it was a case of mistaken identity all along. There was only one person who wanted to be rid of Mrs. Nash but how likely was it she could be found in her husband's study and at his desk? Or was the intended target Mrs. Nash but once discovering it was the judge seated at his desk the perpetrator went ahead with the crime anyway? There was only one person to whom the death of either the judge or his wife would bring relief and it was Christine.

Chapter 17

We heard another set of footsteps along the back path and turned our heads en masse to see Miss Manley returning from her church meeting. The gin bottle was quietly pushed behind Glenda's skirts and looks of welcome and innocence were pasted on our faces, all except Roger, who was smiling as if he had had too much to drink. Which he had.

"Having a lemonade party," he said a bit too loudly.

Miss Manley missed nothing and smiled benignly. "It looks delicious. Do you mind if I share a glass with you?"

Stuart jumped up to offer her his seat and Glenda made to get up, remembered the bottle she was shielding and asked me to fetch a glass. It was hard to suppress a smile at the extensive machinations we were employing to deflect Miss Manley's suspicions, which she had the grace not to vocalize.

"Better be getting home, Roger," Stuart said. "Wouldn't want the family to worry, what?"

Roger cheerfully got up, remembered his racquet next to the chair, picked it up, and swung it in the air while whistling his way back to the parsonage.

"Nice boy," Stuart said, as we watched him return home.

"How was your meeting?" Glenda asked Miss Manley.

"Thank you," she responded to the glass of lemonade and ice I offered her.

"It was interesting. In the void of Judge Nash's leadership, it seems Mr. Barker is the only male remotely interested in serving on the church committee. The rest are women." "Why is that a problem?" I asked.

"It shouldn't be," she answered, removing her hat and placing it on the table before us. "I had an epiphany and where best to have one than in the church; I realized how we had been following the customs of our forebears without a thought. There is nothing in the charter of the church or orthodoxy requiring the committee to be comprised only of men. And Mr. Barker was not interested in serving; I am fairly sure his wife pushed him toward it as a salve to Reverend Lewis."

"I'll bet Mrs. Proctor wanted to put herself forward as a candidate," Glenda said with a sly smile.

"How perceptive of you, my dear. Yes, she cannot let go of the matter of the 'missing money' as she puts it. The next thing you know, she will be passing the collection basket herself! And counting it in the vestry after the service."

I had never given it much thought but, yes, it was always men who passed the collection plate—because it was too heavy? I supposed the real reason was they deemed it unseemly for a woman to be handling money, even if it were for church purposes.

"The end of the story is the reverend suggested my name and there will be a vote of the committee next week."

"Brava!" Stuart said. "I don't think we've had anyone of the ecclesiastical bent in our family." His cheeks were red, either from the sun, the gin, or both.

"That's not correct, of course. My father looked into the genealogy of the Manleys, and there were several Vicars in the last century, mostly collateral relations, in England."

The church bells rang six o'clock and Glenda got up with a start.

"I'd better see to the dinner for Miss Logan and myself." She thanked Stuart for the lemonade, gave a pointed look to where she had stashed the bottle and said good evening to us.

"We had better get started on dinner as well," Miss Manley said, getting up and taking two glasses with her.

"Stuart, in the spirit of your praise for women sharing power, why don't you take charge of setting the table for us while we finish preparing the meal?"

If he hadn't had so much to drink, he might have objected, but he was merry and laughed, agreeing immediately. It occurred to me he somehow considered himself the favored guest in the household although he had contributed nothing to date except some bootleg gin, whereas I had assumed some responsibility for assisting in the meal preparation, serving and clearing, not to mention oversight of Miss Manley's medical situation.

We had a jolly dinner with Stuart in high spirits regaling us with tales of cocktail parties at various publishing houses. Based on the details of the hors d'oeuvres served, I got the impression he might have been in attendance as much for a free meal as for the contacts in publishing. He reeled off a long list of names of his friends and acquaintances in New York asking if I knew any of them, and, of course, I did not. It seemed ridiculous I should have to explain I had lived at the hospital for the past two years with little to no activity in the City itself. If we student nurses had time off, we went window-shopping or to the cinema in Manhattan. In my case, with a free weekend, I went back home to the quiet of Pelham Manor. But Stuart, who was mostly focused on himself and his world, still seemed incredulous I didn't know a single person in his circle of friends—as if New York were a small town. As in other possibly inadvertent slights, I allowed this to pass and let him rattle on about people, places, and events of which I did not know. From the patient look on Miss Manley's face, I could tell she was similarly ignorant of his world and frankly, not particularly interested in knowing more.

During one brief pause for breath, his aunt intruded on the recitation by suggesting he need not stay another day for her sake.

"Are you sure?" he asked looking to her and then to me.

"Perfectly sure. As you know, the doctor is practically next door and Aggie is right here."

His head swiveled back and forth between our two faces and he had a tiny wrinkle of concern between his eyes. "I suppose so. But what about when Aggie goes back to New York?"

It seemed to me he was more worried about being called back to stay with his aunt than the notion of his aunt being on her own.

"Glenda is just next door. Even though we all seem to communicate mostly in person, we do have telephones in the event of some need. Remember, Annie comes in daily except Sunday, so I think enough people are looking out for me."

"Don't forget your aunt's large group of friends as well as the reverend and his wife next door on the other side," I added.

Stuart was suitably relieved of the burden and the forehead crease diminished. He then proceeded to tell us of some upcoming party friends of his were hosting, who would be attending, et cetera, another lengthy recitation of the unknown for me, to which I politely nodded my head. After dinner, Stuart excused himself to do some errand for which he left by the back door, leaving Miss Manley and me to bring the dishes into the kitchen. I could see him making his way across the yard toward Glenda's house, then he turned to look back at our house and seeing me at the kitchen window, waved and smiled. He veered off toward the back path and went on toward the town center.

"How nice of him to offer to stay on another day," I said.

"What with his busy social schedule and all," Miss Manley added.

I was a bit surprised at her comment, but she had left the room to retrieve the rest of the plates so I couldn't tell if it were sarcastic or not. A few minutes later, the back door opened, and Glenda came in and apologized for having interrupted our meal, but I explained we had finished. She peered around the corner to look into the dining room and say hello to Miss Manley.

"Has Stuart gone already?" Glenda asked.

"He'll be leaving tomorrow," I said. "He went into town on some errand."

"Oh," she muttered, sitting down at the kitchen table.

"Here, Miss Manley, I'll finish up," I said, taking the remaining cutlery from her and suggested she go to the sitting room and rest.

I washed and rinsed the glasses and Glenda stood, found a dishtowel, and began to dry them.

"It's a pity for poor Stuart his aunt doesn't like him better," she said.

I stopped in my activity and turned to her. "What makes you say that?"

"You can just tell from their interactions, can't you?"

"It seems cordial on both sides," I said vaguely.

"She hinted to my mother, who, of course, told me, her intentions to leave Stuart just a small amount of money and the rest of her estate—this house and a pile of cash, from what we all know —to the church."

"Really?" If Stuart were a published author with many titles to his name, I thought a small monetary gift from his aunt was probably more than sufficient. I turned the water back on and began to rinse the dishes.

"Miss Manley either likes you or she doesn't. And I can tell she likes you very much."

"How nice," I said, flattered.

"Have you been talking to her about me going back to nurses' training?"

"No, why?"

"She took me aside the other day and went on about it. She is impressed at what you have accomplished in your young life, as she put it. Of anyone in West Adams, I think she finds you a kindred spirit."

I didn't know how to respond as I thought Glenda was overstating the situation and then I thought perhaps I had stepped into a role Glenda herself should be in as a neighbor and the daughter of Miss Manley's late best friend. I gave her a quizzical look to see if she were upset or offended but she gave a shrug and a smile.

"Don't think about it," she said. folding the towel over the rack near the sink to dry. "It's getting dark. I'd better be getting back home." She walked out, leaving me to wonder why she had stopped by in the first place, before I joined Miss Manley in the sitting room. She was in her usual place on the sofa with a light over her right shoulder to better see the knitting in progress.

"A sweater for Mrs. Proctor's new grandchild in Hartford," she said, holding it up to review her progress.

I wondered how many such baby items she had knitted over the years for other people's children or grandchildren, having none of her own. She was active in her church and social circle, but it must be a lonely existence at times, especially in the evenings. I was glad I was able to afford her some company and, as I thought this, I smiled to myself.

Seeing us in the sitting room from the garden, Stuart came in through the French windows after wiping his feet noisily on the mat outside.

"Beautiful night!" he exclaimed.

"You're back already," Miss Manley said.

"Quick errand. Mission accomplished," he said still standing. "I'd better get my things together," he added, going upstairs.

There was the loud sound of his footsteps back and forth across the floor, presumably putting his things in the closet back into the suitcases. A dragging noise must have been the golf clubs, unused this trip, making their way toward the bedroom door for a quick exit in the morning. All was quiet for a bit and then he returned downstairs.

"Well, ladies, care for a game of cards?" he asked cheerfully.

"Thank you, no, Stuart. I'm rather tired. I think I'll go up to bed," Miss Manley said, gathering her knitting and putting it back into the basket at her feet. "Goodnight," she said, offering her cheek up for a peck from her nephew.

"Aggie?" he asked, hoping for some entertainment.

"Actually, I'm reading **The Peril of Dunbar** and I'd like to make some headway on it tonight." I stood.

"Are you at the part where—," he stopped himself. "I almost gave away some of the plot! Well, I hope you're enjoying it."

"Yes, thank you," I said, lying only slightly. I supposed some people enjoyed this type of fiction, but it wasn't to my taste. I still felt obligated to read at least one of his books in my time here since he was likely to visit again. "Until tomorrow."

I could see Miss Manley's light was still on when I ascended; however, after I had washed and finished in the bathroom, it had been turned out. Back in my room, I noticed the night birds and crickets were quieter than usual but there was some activity downstairs in the sitting room, directly below my bedroom. I stood quietly for a few minutes to see if it was just Stuart turning off the lights for the night, but it sounded as if he were perhaps opening and closing the drawers of the desk. The sounds of activity that intrigued me could not possibly be heard by Miss Manley from her bedroom at the front of the house, and I wondered if Stuart were snooping in her desk. If Glenda was correct in her assumption of Miss Manley's intentions for her estate, perhaps he was looking for some evidence of her financial situation. I remembered Doctor Taylor had remarked that she helped to support him rather than the other way around, as she had suggested to me. Whatever he was doing, I had no intention of telling Miss Manley. I lay on the bed with Stuart's book open on my lap and continued to listen to the intermittent noises. Checking the clock, it seemed he had been rustling around about twenty minutes, long enough to get the lay of the land. It reminded me of a story my father told of an older woman whose will he had helped prepare. She had a minimal estate but insisted all her books be donated to the local library. It turned out she had ten-dollar bills in all the volumes, which amounted to a substantial bequest; perhaps Stuart was checking all the books in the sitting room. In any case, he gave up on his rummaging a short while later and crept up the stairs and was quiet in his last moments before I fell asleep.

Chapter 18

I awoke to the first rainy day since my arrival, a drizzly day, I should say, where the mist lay close to the ground and the heads of the flowers in the garden were bowed by the damp. Miss Manley was thrilled as it saved her the trouble of hand watering her plants, Annie was annoyed because the wet day would interfere with laundry, and Stuart was worried about driving conditions on the slick roads. He left early, nonetheless, after much pleading to his aunt to visit him in the city and a vague invitation for me to 'keep in touch.' I couldn't help but notice the air of tension dissipated as we waved to him from the front door and each one of us returned to the business at hand. When the rain let up a bit, Annie went with Miss Manley to do some shopping in town, so I found myself alone in the house for a while, examining the bookcase for something more suited to my taste. There were some Victorian-era travel books from the perspective of an American traveling in Egypt that might be fun to browse through, some volumes for bird identification, many books on horticulture, and old magazines. I heard the back door open and close and went to investigate.

"Rain's almost gone," Miss Manley said, removing her hat and gloves. "Annie is still at the butcher shop."

"I hope it was enough for your garden?"

"Yes, indeed. It had been raining since before dawn, so we got a good soaking. Now all the slugs will be out, and we will do away with them!" She was looking forward to the massacre and left the room to don her garden gloves and boots by the back door.

The house was surprisingly quiet that morning, perhaps due to the weather but also because the excitement after the judge's death had quieted down. No constant telephone calls asking for or supplying gossip and rumors. However, anticipation was mounting for the inquest on Wednesday, although there didn't seem to be any additional information pointing to any one person. Glenda had concocted a fantastic story about the decorator's being one of the criminals whom the judge had sentenced in the past and who had gone unrecognized due to his effective disguise of mustache and beard. But if it were the case, why had Landon Whittaker waited until Thursday to do the deed? Was it because it was only then the judge recognized him? How absurd to imagine a former criminal was now an interior decorator. Unless he wasn't a decorator at all. Had the judge checked his references or just assumed the man was legitimate? All this speculation was starting to hurt my head.

The French windows opened a crack and I saw Roger peer around the opening.

"Is Miss Manley here?" he asked, so she was not yet in the garden.

"Yes, she's about somewhere. Come in," I said. "Don't forget to wipe your feet." I knew she was particular about her rugs.

He scuffed them noisily against the wet exterior mat and noticed while no longer muddy, his shoes were still wet, so he turned around, sat on the dry rug inside, and took his shoes off to enter in his stocking feet.

The Roger I had come to know was usually in motion, whistling, or talking loudly but now he was quiet and worried.

"Whatever is the matter?" I asked.

"I've got to get this off my chest. I was going to tell the reverend at breakfast this morning, but I lost my nerve. Then I thought I could talk to Miss Manley and she could intercede on my behalf, but she is strict sometimes."

I waited but he just chewed the inside of his cheek and looked down at the rug.

"Can I help in some way?"

Unexpectedly, he threw himself onto the sofa next to me and said in a relieved voice, "Oh, yes. Would you?"

"All right. What seems to be the trouble?" I was expecting he was about to confess to having depleted the gin in his uncle's house, the illegal alcohol the reverend was uncomfortable enough about harboring.

"It's pretty bad," he squirmed. "You know the phone call my uncle got?" he asked.

I couldn't imagine what he was talking about.

"The phone call that took him out to a farm on Thursday?"

"Yes?" I was puzzled.

"It was me."

"What? Why?"

"It's a bit of a long story."

"Let's get your aunt and uncle over here."

Miss Manley chose that moment to come into the sitting room. "I thought I heard voices. Hello, Roger."

He groaned in response and hung his head with his hands thrust into his curly hair.

Miss Manley was taken aback by the lack of greeting and his wretched appearance.

"I'll call," I offered, retreating to the kitchen telephone for more privacy. Poor Roger, he'd done it this time. Annie had just come in the back door and stared as I made the call.

The reverend and Nina came over almost immediately with looks of worry on their faces. We all sat, perched on the edges of our seats while Roger told of his little prank phone call that had taken the reverend out on a hapless errand the night the judge was killed.

"Oh, my," Miss Manley said.

"What an inconsiderate thing to have done!" the reverend said.

"But why did you do it?" Nina asked.

Roger closed his eyes. "Because I wanted to have Christine over to the house while you were gone."

"You were alone with a young lady in our house!"

Roger didn't answer.

"While Nina was in Pittsfield for the day?"

Roger nodded.

"And where was Elsie?"

"In the kitchen with the door closed."

"Well, one part of the mystery is solved. It was not the judge's murderer who tried to get me out of the way—it was my nephew!" the reverend said. "We have to call the police and tell them this important piece of information."

"No!" Roger protested, his eyes wide with fear.

I got up and escorted the reverend to the kitchen phone. Annie turned away from the sink, her eyes wider this time if it were possible.

Then we sat silently in the sitting room waiting for Officer Reed, who had indicated Inspector Gladstone was in town and would be coming as well. That got Roger cracking his knuckles in anxiety. Annie quietly appeared in the doorway and asked if she should bring refreshments. Miss Manley suggested coffee be brewed and I went to assist with cups, saucers, and a tray, hurrying as I did so in order not to miss a moment of the impending explosion.

It came with the genteel ring of the doorbell, not the thumping of fists on the door, although the look on the inspector's face was thunderous. He was escorted into the sitting room, where he removed his hat to reveal wiry tufts sticking up on either side and was offered some coffee. The suspense was terrifying to Roger, who gripped the edges of the sofa and waited for the inevitable storm.

"So, Master Lewis," the inspector began in a sarcastically cheerful mood. "What do you have to tell us?"

Roger cleared his throat. "The reverend is my uncle," he started.

"I know that."

"We sometimes play little tricks on each other."

The look on the reverend's face told me it was Roger who played the tricks, and they were not necessarily appreciated and seldom reciprocated.

"I thought it would be funny to send him out on a wild goose chase to a parishioner on Thursday."

"I fail to see the humor," the inspector said.

"It seemed funny at the time."

His face had lost some of its color and I felt uncomfortable for his distress.

"And...?" the reverend prompted.

"Because I was with Christine Nash at the time. Here. Not *here*, but in the parsonage."

The inspector put his cup and saucer on the table next to him and used both hands to scratch his eyebrows and then smooth down his errant hair.

Silence all around the room.

When Gladstone didn't say anything, I offered, "I suppose it takes Christine out of the picture."

He glared at me. "I believe that is my call, young lady." Then to the Reverend and Mrs. Lewis, "This is all highly irregular!" the inspector shouted. "Have you no control over your nephew?"

The inspector got up abruptly, his face an alarming shade of red. "That's all for now!" he said loudly, picked up his hat, jammed it on his head and made for the door, Officer Reed scrambling to catch up.

"Thank you, Miss Manley," he had the grace to say before they left.

Deathly silence reigned in the sitting room for a few minutes.

"Uncle, I am so, so sorry," said Roger.

"It was a wicked thing you did," he replied.

"I guess I am out of the hot seat," Roger said with an ingratiating smile.

The reverend and his wife looked at him sharply. "Not hardly," Nina said. "Thank you for the coffee, Miss Manley. Miss Burnside, thank you for contacting us about this matter." She rose to go, as did the reverend, but Roger continued to sit on the sofa as if not accompanying them would mitigate the verbal reprimand or punishment he would get.

"Roger!"

It produced immediate results and he bolted to his feet, walked to the French windows and put on his now-dry shoes, taking an inordinate amount of time tying his shoelaces, probably trying to buy time between the present and the inevitable. After they left, Miss Manley looked at her watch and sighed.

"What an eventful morning!"

We heard the back door close and footsteps in the hall. It was Glenda, who must have seen part of the parade of people coming and going and wondered what was going on.

"Well?" she asked.

"Good morning to you, too," I said cheerfully.

"Oh, no, you don't. I know something was going on here this morning and you are going to sit down and tell me all about it."

"Why don't you go upstairs to chat," Miss Manley suggested. "I have the mail to sort through." She moved to the desk and sat to begin her task.

The door was barely shut behind me when Glenda peppered me with questions. "I saw the inspector's car out front. What's going on?"

We sat on the bed and I related the sequence of events to her.

"Roger! What an idiotic thing to do. And on top of everything, not to tell anyone until today."

"Exactly. I wouldn't want to be in his shoes now. He is probably getting the lecture of his life."

"What does it all mean? We saw Christine at the house, but it wasn't until after the doctor got there, I think. Why didn't she come downstairs after hearing all the commotion?"

"She did appear before Doctor Taylor, but I wasn't paying attention to where she came from. I looked up and saw her, the decorator, and Sandra all at the same time," I said.

"I still think this points to a criminal mastermind." To my dubious look, she elaborated. "It takes a criminal mind to think of all the details to commit such an act. To get a gun—."

"Let's be exact: Richard Fairley's gun."

"Yes, but he, like everyone else, leaves the studio and his house unlocked, so anyone could have taken it. Especially a devious person with evil intent who has been watching the activity in town. And then to falsify the note to suggest he was killed at a different time. Whoever it was probably wasn't expecting the reverend to be there when he arrived or for us to be there, either. More importantly, he didn't expect the doctor to get there so quickly and determine the time of death."

"I agree. It was well planned. But why leave the gun behind?" I asked.

"Why not? The murderer probably used gloves, which is why only Richard's prints were on it when he picked it back up."

"Or maybe he panicked and dropped it. But why didn't anyone hear the shot?" I asked.

I remembered the inspector's explanation of a silencer, whatever that could be, but it was still puzzling. I got up and shook my shoulders as if to rid myself of the thoughts and realized it was almost time for lunch, a quick change, and then work.

Chapter 19

Back home after work, I saw Glenda and Miss Manley sitting in the chairs in the garden now the sun had come out again. I suggested a walk; Miss Manley was not interested, but Glenda took me up on the offer after I had changed into street clothes and sturdy shoes to tackle what might be muddy ground. We started up the path leading to the town center and veered off onto the trail up to Highfields. Although I was intrigued by the thought of looking at the house, I was more interested in walking and we changed course onto another trail, Glenda assuring me she knew these woods well and where we were going. Unusual for us, we did not talk but took in the cool air provided by the tree canopy and watched where we put our feet, skirting shallow puddles, watching for rocks in our way, and being careful not to come into contact with the poison ivy growing on the ground and up tree trunks. A bit of sun came through the trees to expose a glade of ferns, their damp, newly emerging fronds curled up like otherworldly beings ready to hatch. Glenda stopped beside one large plant and pointed to the curlicue about to unfurl.

"My mother knew an old woman who used to gather these fiddleheads in the spring and cook them. She knew all about mushrooms, too. We never learned although I wish we had."

"You'll have plenty of time now since you have become the old crone of the forest," I said.

It got the expected rise out of her, and she chased me back down the trail a bit before I leaped over a log and escaped.

"Fins!" I cried, crossing my fingers, the universal claim for a truce. Behind me was a log with large fungus projections. "Come look at this," I said.

"Oyster mushrooms," she said.

"Are they safe to eat?"

"I think so, but I don't want to try and see. Let's look for more types."

What began as a walk or a hike turned into a hunt for mushrooms at the base of trees, fallen branches, and logs that we poked with long branches picked up from the ground. Yellow, orange, white, smooth, lumpy, and some oozing as we jabbed at them.

"Hey," Glenda said, putting her finger to her lips and pointing ahead. It was Richard Fairley far down the path, visible by his red ascot, his most noticeable affectation, bending over and digging through the leaves. We crept down the path, keeping out of sight and hiding behind trees to peer out.

Glenda gave me a questioning look, as in, "What is he doing?"

I shrugged my shoulders. Collecting mushrooms? Or burying something? Or retrieving something? I peeked out and saw he was now standing and scratching his head as if to remember something. Then he started in our direction, looked up and around, sank to his knees again, and drew a stick through the undergrowth.

Glenda covered her mouth so her giggles couldn't be heard, and I was hard-pressed not to succumb myself. It was quiet and we dared to stick our heads out and see him standing up again, looking at the ground.

I motioned to Glenda to get back on the trail with me and we began a nonsensical but plausible conversation about nothing as we approached him to announce our presence. As expected, he turned quickly, smiled, and came close.

"Hello, ladies! Enjoying the cool, wet day?" He kept coming toward us, intent on keeping us away from whatever he had sought.

"We're just going down the path a bit more before dinner."

"I'd be careful if I were you. There is poison ivy all along the sides of the path. And you two do not have long pants on—that spells disaster."

Taking an elbow, he gently redirected both of us back the way we had just come while chatting affably. "Aggie, I don't think you've seen my studio. Why not come in for a look?"

Glenda gave me a look suggesting he was asking me to see his etchings, a silly line we used to repeat when referring to someone trying a seduction, knowing it would make me smile.

"That would be lovely," I said and wondered if he would next propose to paint my portrait.

The shed that seemed small from the outside was quite spacious inside, mostly because it was one room and had so little furniture. A loveseat sat below a north-facing window, prompting another smirk from Glenda, and a tall stool constituted the only pieces in the large room. The rest of the space was taken up by canvases stacked against each wall and a table with an open can of turpentine, brushes, and mangled tubes of oil paint. It struck me that Richard must be a fastidious person because I had never seen remnants of paint on his clothing, shoes, or hands. I hadn't had time to observe him close at hand much and was not familiar with many artists, but it still seemed strange.

While Glenda bent to flip through some canvases, I asked him what he was currently working on, looking toward the sheetcovered square resting on a tall easel. He hesitated a moment before saying, "It's a portrait of Elizabeth."

He drew the cloth off the large canvas to reveal Mrs. Nash, seated and leaning toward the viewer with a slight smile on her lips. The skin of her neck and arms was highlighted in pink, mauve and purple giving her a voluptuous glow and a knowing look. Just his use of her first name spoke of intimacy; I felt myself begin to blush before such a sexual portrayal more blatant than had she been naked.

He cleared his throat. "I haven't been able to finish it, what with all this business."

Glenda came around to look. "It's gorgeous! Now I regret not having you paint me."

"The offer is still open. And it looks like I'll be staying here a bit longer until Elizabeth gets things sorted out."

"And then what?"

"She might sell the place and we'll go to New York. Better for my art career than Boston, I should think."

I thought about Christine; what about her? She hadn't gotten along well with her father or with her stepmother for whatever reason. She couldn't just float along as she had, driving around in her car and playing tennis with whoever was available and sneaking about with Roger. With her father's death, she might be a wealthy young woman, which generally didn't guarantee a happy life considering all the impoverished young men left over from the Crash who would consider her a 'catch.'

"Oh, Highfields…," Glenda sighed. "Such a lovely place."

"But the upkeep is tremendous. A housekeeper, two maids, a cook, a chauffeur, cleaners who come in daily, and gardeners—it's a fortune just to staff the place. Oh, could I offer you a drink?" he asked.

Before answering, he went to a small cabinet on the other side of the room and took out what must be West Adam's favorite choice of bootleg alcohol, a small bottle of gin. He held it up with a flourish and Glenda clapped her hands in approval and sat on the loveseat. I followed suit while Richard searched for paper cups next to a sink in the corner. He sat on his high stool and poured us each about two shots' worth, more than I was used to drinking at a time and then waved his hand over each cup.

"We'll pretend I have blessed it with the spirit of vermouth."

Glenda got the giggles before her first mouthful.

"Speaking of Highfields, the most incredible thing happened yesterday. I bumped into Officer Reed on Main Street and he was embarrassed and blustery, but what was amazing is he asked for my help."

My eyebrows went up. "How?"

"He said he had interviewed the staff at Highfields but since they knew him to be a policeman they clammed up and he didn't think he'd get much information from them. He thought because I was a young man, I might have better luck talking to the maid, the cook, and the chauffeur, seeing as how they are closer to my age and perhaps would not be so intimidated."

I thought it was a curious thing for Officer Reed to have asked and wondered if the inspector had any idea about it but said nothing. It might have been a clever thing to request since the staff now knew who the new husband of the owner would be and therefore more likely to comply.

"What a good idea," Glenda said. "What did you find out?" She looked conspiratorially at me, neither of us expecting he would answer. However, he was more than happy to share the details of each conversation.

"The cook is a tight-lipped, middle-aged woman, and rather unpleasant, but once I complimented her on her wonderful scones, she loosened up a bit. Although she has been working for the Nashes for as long as they have been married, she didn't have any particular impressions—or maybe she didn't care to share them—of their personalities or their marriage. She only interacted with Elizabeth over the menu and special purchases for the kitchen. The housekeeper was their intermediary."

"Do you think...?" Glenda asked, her eyes wide.

"What?" I asked.

"The housekeeper?"

"Do you think the housekeeper had some resentment against the judge?" Richard asked.

"Maybe her husband or her son was someone the judge had sentenced to prison and she bided her time under an assumed name until she could seek revenge."

I gulped gin. It was an entirely plausible theory.

Richard was quiet for a few moments, then continued. "Just wait. I talked to the maid, Alice, a pretty, young girl who lives in town but comes up to the house daily. She was talkative about the Nashes, what they did each day, where they went, the young people who called on Christine and went to Pittsfield with her. I asked her about the visitor the judge had the night before he died."

"Sandra Logan?" I asked.

"How did you know?" he asked.

I shrugged rather smugly.

"You're right. It was Sandra Logan. Alice knew who she was."

"Anyway," he continued, "she led Sandra into the study and the judge came in and before Alice had a chance to get very far down the hall, they had a heated argument behind the closed door. You know how the judge had such a loud voice, it was impossible for Alice not to overhear his part of the conversation, although by her abashed look in relating this to me, I suspect she might have crept up to a closed door and listened intently."

"The housekeeper also heard a loud conversation but had no details to share," I said. "Or at least, she didn't share them when I was at the house."

"Alice said the judge told Sandra 'there wasn't a chance' and she ought to 'leave well enough alone' and 'he wasn't going to be threatened.' What do you make of that?"

"Oh, my gosh! I could be killed in my bed!" Glenda said.

"Don't be so dramatic," I said. "What possible problem could she have with you? Overcooked eggs or burnt toast in the morning?"

The sharp look Glenda gave me suggested I may have inadvertently hit one nail on the head.

"No, listen," Richard said. "Sandra was up at Highfields with Landon Whittaker."

"Yes, we both saw her," I said, looking at Glenda for affirmation.

"But she could have sneaked off at some point, because she was familiar with the house, shot the judge, and returned to her work with no one the wiser," he said.

"How in the world did she get your gun?" I asked.

He looked puzzled. "Hmm, don't know." He looked down at our empty cups.

"Refill?"

"Why not?" we both said at once and broke into laughter.

He obliged, giving us slightly more than we had before.

"Then I talked to the chauffeur."

I immediately thought of the stereotype of the lady of the house and the chauffeur but knew it couldn't be the case because this story was about the lady of the house and the artist.

"He didn't seem to be a very communicative person to begin with, and unfortunately I didn't learn anything of importance. His days consist of coming up from town by bicycle, putting on a uniform, getting instructions from the housekeeper about who needed to go where and when, washing the car, polishing the car, and driving one or the other of the Nashes here and there. Christine has her own automobile, so he didn't have to deal with her much."

I was trying to imagine what wealth the Nash family had to have purchased Highfields, to maintain so many staff and two cars, to have decorated it so lavishly and then be in the process of redecorating it. Elizabeth must be a wealthy widow now; with all decency in mind, Richard had better work fast to seal the deal, I thought to myself, or someone else might step in and get the lovely woman.

"The other maid, Marie, was the one who followed the reverend into the study. She was still upset about it all these days later and very jittery. I think Officer Reed didn't get much out of her because there wasn't much to share. She didn't say much although under the circumstances Elizabeth may cut down on the number of staff and somebody will be out of a job. It's all I found out, which wasn't much. I hope it helps the authorities in their investigation."

We were quiet for a while, sipping our gin and mulling over the information he had just provided. The church bells rang sixthirty.

"Oh, my gosh, I have to get home and put the dinner on the table," Glenda said, gulping down the last of her drink. She giggled. "If I can."

"I have to go as well. Thank you, Richard." We got up to go.

"I'm glad I rescued you both from poison ivy and other perils of the woods: twisted ankles, rabid skunks, and wolves." He made a fearful face.

"Don't worry," Glenda said. "We are used to plenty of skunks and wolves!"

Chapter 20

Wednesday morning arrived with the impending inquest at nine o'clock. I can't say why I was so nervous in anticipation of the event, but it had interfered with my sleep all night and then with my appetite at breakfast. Miss Manley took notice, I was sure, but did not comment. I thought when I got to be her age and had experienced so many things, perhaps I wouldn't be nervous about anything anymore. My fingertips were cold although it was not chilly in the house and my stomach was in a knot. I was most apprehensive that as a nurse I might be expected to give an expert opinion and then the opposite occurred to me—suppose I made a statement or conclusion of some sort and was accused of pretending to have the expertise I did not possess? How was I going to navigate the sly questioning of the person in charge? And who was it going to be? I forgot to ask anyone. That brought on another pang of anxiety. I hoped it wouldn't be Inspector Gladstone.

"Who is presiding over the inquest today?" I asked, aware my voice sounded thin.

"It's the County Coroner who is coming from Pittsfield."

"I'd better finish getting ready," I said, having an urgent need to use the bathroom and hoping I didn't vomit. I had terrible nerves when it came to important exams or public speaking and the event that lay before me presented both of these situations for which I had no prior experience.

"Take your time, dear. You are not on trial."

I managed to calm myself and we were ready to go when the doorbell rang. I opened the door. Doctor Taylor stood before us, all smiles.

"Good morning, ladies. I thought I would walk over with you."

Instead of being reassuring, his presence made me nervous all over again, obvious in my face I supposed, since he patted my arm and reassured me everything would be fine. What I was not expecting when we arrived at the inquest location were two men with cameras and popping flashbulbs, accompanied by two others who were asking for people's names, asking for the central figures in the case to be pointed out, and then trying to run them down before the inquest began. We managed to get through the gauntlet because the doctor propelled me quickly after instructing me to keep my head down. I could hear the pop of the camera's bulb and was horrified to think it might have been aimed at me, but if it were, all they got was a hand on the top of a hat and the broad expanse of Doctor Taylor's chest.

The inquest took place in the town hall's meeting room, large enough for a town council gathering, with tables and chairs at the front and limited seating in what was the audience. It seemed no one had taken into account the intense curiosity of the locals or the notoriety of the case, which was a regional phenomenon and had packed the room to overflowing. Those of us who were to testify were seated in the front row on chairs marked 'reserved,' which put us in proximity to all the principals in Judge Nash's life. Mrs. Nash sat toward one end of the row next to Richard Fairley, next to him the reverend, Glenda, me, the doctor, Officer Reed, and Inspector Gladstone. Across the aisle were the housekeeper, the cook, the two maids, the chauffeur, Landon Whittaker, Sandra Logan, and Christine, who wanted no proximity to her stepmother.

The coroner had such deep lines from nose to chin it was possible he had not smiled in years and the glare from his eyes over his reading glasses proclaimed he did not suffer fools. He barked for order several times, not having a gavel to bang on the table, until the crowd settled down and then asked someone at the back to close the doors. He began the proceeding by outlining his duties, the process, and stating those attending were not to comment or make any noise during the inquest or they would be removed by force. I turned around to see who might do that, but the looks on the faces of those in attendance told me they would behave themselves because they didn't want to miss a thing. Yes, it was a murder inquest, but I thought—or maybe hoped—there would be no salacious evidence given.

Richard Fairley was called first as he had been the first to find the body. The Coroner asked his name and address and how long he had resided in West Adams, a question each one of us was subsequently asked. Richard was remarkably calm in his recitation of the events and had done an effective job of downplaying his film star good looks by wearing a dark suit and sober tie rather than his usual corduroy jacket, open shirt and ascot; the bohemian artist had succeeded in transforming himself into looking like a junior clerk in a law firm. He told of coming up to the house to have a private conversation with the judge, although the Coroner did not ask the intended topic of the conversation. Finding the door ajar and not seeing anyone, he went to the study at the end of the hall. He said he knocked on the door jamb of the open door and noticed the judge slumped over the desk. Thinking he might be ill, he called out to him and getting no answer, approached the desk where he saw the blood and assumed the worst. He was made to tell more exactly the position of the body, the partially written note, and the gun—his gun—on the floor. In a level voice he related he was overcome with panic, knowing he would be accused of having shot the judge although he had not, having been in the town center at the time. When the Coroner asked him why anyone would have suspected him of shooting the judge he colored slightly and looked down.

"Because it was my gun," he said, deftly avoiding the more obvious reason of which the crowd was either aware or suspected. He added it was why he picked it up off the floor, put it in his pocket, and went out the front door as fast as he could.

After several more questions about where he usually kept the gun and who knew of its existence, about which he was vague, there were more personal inquiries, and it came out he had 'great respect and affection' for Mrs. Nash, who had confided her unhappiness and intention to leave her marriage. Despite the Coroner's previous warning and most of the town's knowing this already there was an audible gasp. Mrs. Nash looked down into her lap. Richard related he had falsely admitted to the police killing the judge for the sake of protecting her although he knew it was wrong. The Coroner's next question ought to have probed into why he thought she needed protecting, but he didn't pursue this further.

Mrs. Nash was called next, looking appropriately sad yet exquisitely turned out in a black silk dress and hat with a short, netted veil. She clutched her purse in her lap and seemed to have a hard time deciding where to look—certainly not at her fellow townspeople, not at Richard Fairley, and settled on the Coroner during most of her testimony.

She said she was unaware if her husband had any enemies but as his previous judicial work had been on the criminal bench in Boston it was entirely possible someone from his years of prior service might have ill will and acted upon it. This last statement was met with the murmuring of the crowd that put Judge Nash's past in a different, more dangerous light as well as summoning visions of unknown felons creeping about the town. She told of the day of the murder, working with one of the maids organizing the linen closet before coming downstairs after hearing the commotion, and said she had not heard a shot but could tell from my telephone call in progress to the doctor and the eyes of everyone in the hall directed at her or the study that something serious had happened. She said nothing unusual had occurred that afternoon at Highfields and she certainly did not hear a shot. The Coroner did ask her why she admitted to killing her husband the next day—again a collective gasp from the audience—and she said in her grief she wasn't thinking properly at the time. She added she knew Mr. Fairley had confessed and, knowing him to be an upstanding and protective person, assumed he had said it to protect her. She admitted she hadn't shot her husband and fabricated the details, then looking down in her lap said she regretted having done so.

The reverend was up next and answered the questions about the appointment having been made to discuss a church matter and his tardiness due to what was later revealed to be a bogus phone call. When asked who else knew of the impending appointment, he thought a moment and had to answer that, due to the judge's loud voice, anyone who had been on the street in the morning certainly overheard the conversation as well as anyone else the judge may have told. In addition, Elsie the maid was informed but not his wife, Nina, who had already left for Pittsfield. He told of seeing Richard Fairley outside Highfields' open front door, what he perceived was Fairley's agitated state of mind, and his own inability to grasp what had occurred until he entered the study and saw the judge's body slumped over the desk. He then went through a recitation of who came in next, who came down the stairs, which staff appeared from where to the best of his knowledge and the sequence of events that brought the doctor and eventually the police.

I was impressed and relieved the Coroner did not ask, 'What did you think happened?' to the reverend or anyone else during the inquest. He kept focused on what each witness saw, heard, or did, rather than speculating on what may have occurred, which the entire town had been doing for the past week.

Marie, the maid who was present when Glenda and I came into Highfields on the day of the murder, was called next. She had a small voice and just as Richard had indicated, was non-committal in her comments. Her job was 'fine,' and everyone was 'nice.' She said she heard someone call out, "Hello," and she went to see who it was. The front door had been left wide open, and she saw the reverend moving toward the study and then enter it. She did pause a moment and said viewing the judge's body, even from the distance of the doorway, was the worst thing she had ever seen in her life.

Next up was the local girl, Alice, who revealed she had been in the kitchen with the cook and only knew something was amiss when she heard the reverend call out and Marie scream. She testified she enjoyed her job and had no complaints about her employers and didn't know of anyone who did. I thought it was interesting either the Coroner didn't know or didn't think to ask about the conversation overheard between the judge and Sandra. And judging by Alice's state of discomfort, she was not going to reveal in public she had been eavesdropping. She confirmed to the Coroner the house had front stairs and back stairs for the staff. She had nothing to add to the atmosphere of the house or the relationships except to say things were proper, which made me wonder why anyone would assume otherwise.

It was my turn then, having been the next person to see the judge. After I related that I was new to West Adams, having a job with Doctor Taylor for the month during a busy period in his practice, the Coroner led me through the events leading up to entering Highfields after hearing a shout and a scream from inside. I then had to relate what I did and when I did it, with the Coroner's stopping me at times to ask when various people appeared on the scene. My ordeal was over fairly quickly once I had answered questions about the sequence of events after the body was found.

I exhaled in relief as I was dismissed and noticed Glenda, the next to be called, was exhibiting some of the anxiety I had felt before going up to the witness chair. She was precise in her answers, relating events to particular times according to her watch or the chimes of the church bells, which I hadn't thought to do. The Coroner asked her the same questions he had asked me, eliciting similar answers, although she looked over at me from time to time as if to verify we had seen the same things.

The judge's daughter, Christine, was called next, mostly out of deference, since she had only come on the scene after all of us were already gathered at the bottom of the stairs. She was dressed in a black dress, draining what color she had from her face, and a fashionable black hat pulled low over her forehead. She said she had been reading in her room on the second floor and had heard nothing unusual until there was a scream and people seemed to be racing downstairs. She said she did not know of anyone who wished her father harm although there had been some occasions of threats when they lived in Boston.

"Threats?" the Coroner asked. The entire crowd was silent with anticipation.

"I was away at school, not at home in person to witness anything. And this was before my father remarried, so I don't believe
my stepmother knew of it unless he told her." At
this Mrs. Nash shook her head.

"He was the judge in a high-profile case involving a gang of criminals of some kind. He contacted the headmistress and asked her to be vigilant on my behalf, which meant I was not allowed to go off-campus on the weekends with the other girls. It only lasted a month or so, if I remember correctly."

"Do you recall the names of those who were on trial?"

"I'm sorry, I don't. I don't know if I was ever told their names or what became of the case. My father didn't like to talk about his work at home."

Christine, who had already seemed to be a rather vague person, cemented the impression by not knowing of anyone who could have had the motive to harm her father. Well, she had just alluded to a possible gang of them! Names unknown, of course.

The housekeeper, who had given her notice, was still in town and was next up. She had a tight manner to match the bun at the back of her head and she answered with precise diction that came across as condescension. She also scanned the audience as she spoke as if giving a performance, which it turned out to be. I didn't know the woman at all, but she struck me as disingenuous when she spoke of what a wonderful, fine, upstanding man the judge was, admired and respected by all. Well, it was not true, or he might still be walking the earth. She said she couldn't imagine who would have wished to harm him, emphasizing her words for additional drama. Then, down to the meat of it, she described where she had been at the time the judge was killed, and her explanation of being somewhere upstairs rang true but certainly did not put her in an innocent position. She was also asked if she had any information about other staff in the house and if there was any friction with the judge. She answered no, the staff were exceedingly polite to the judge and deferential, which told me she probably ordered them never to speak a word to the man unless necessary. Then she slyly brought up the incident of hearing Sandra Logan in an argument with the judge just the night before. Of course, she had not been eavesdropping, but the judge had a habit of speaking in a loud voice and she could tell he was angry although she could not make out the words of the softer tones of Miss Logan. While the housekeeper did not imply anything specifically negative about Sandra, her smug expression spoke volumes and she held her head high when walking back to her seat. Glenda and I exchanged a glance.

The chauffeur was Randy Morgan, whose father owned the garage in West Adams, so a logical choice for someone to take care of their automobiles. He had a normal workweek except was sometimes called to come in on the weekends as he still lived in town with his parents. However, he had been allowed to stay in the small apartment over the garage if he needed to be available for an especially early morning. He said he could not hear much of anything from the main house and certainly did not hear a gunshot of any kind. He happened to be outside and noticed a car driving at a fast speed toward the house, which attracted his attention, and seeing Doctor Taylor emerge was concerned someone in the house was ill. After a few minutes, he went through the back entrance into the kitchen and finding it empty, heard voices in the hall and went into the main house to see what the matter was. He testified he enjoyed his job, had no problems with his employers, and could not imagine who would wish to do the judge harm.

By the time Landon Whittaker was called, the audience was murmuring at the large number of people at Highfields that day, especially this gentleman whom few had seen before. He practically strutted up to the chair next to the Coroner's table and glared at the assembly, annoyed to have been put in this position. Once settled, he turned his attention to the Coroner, who seemed to have taken an instant dislike to him that didn't abate when Whittaker corrected him to say he was an interior designer, not a decorator.

"Designer?" the Coroner asked, the scowling face settling into ever more deepening lines.

"Yes. I design the rooms that include architectural and structural changes as needed, as well as recommending the furnishings and so on."

I was sure few people had ever been inside of Highfields, known as the largest, most impressive house in West Adams, and even if they had only seen the exterior, they probably assumed it hardly needed an internal makeover. The murmur from the crowd indicated many were contemplating how incredibly rich the judge must have been to want a renovation of a house of that size, although Whittaker took the crowd's tones to mean they were impressed with him and he sat a bit straighter in the chair. He said he was staying at the house and on the day in question he and Sandra had been in their workroom on the third floor, looking at designs for the sitting room, when they heard someone call out and scream. It was then they ran down the long hallway and the front stairs to see what the matter was. He said he had made contact for his job through Mrs. Nash and did not have much interaction with the judge except at dinner if they all ate together.

Sandra Logan's testimony was brief, explaining how she came to have the job as Whittaker's assistant, she lived in town and came up to Highfields daily to work. She had little contact with the family and reiterated her employer's version of events on that day. The Coroner picked up a piece of paper, glanced at it, and asked her about the loud conversation with the judge the night before he died.

She shrugged. "Oh, that! He was angry that the renovations were going to cost too much and for some reason, he thought that I could influence those decisions."

Based on her age and position, it seemed that the judge had been his overbearing self and off the mark to challenge her about the design scheme when he could have talked to Whittaker instead.

Doctor Taylor took the chair next and was concise in his description of being called to Highfields, who was there, in what state he found the body, and his estimate of the time of death, which he maintained was six-fifteen. He described further examining the body and seeing that the lividity indicated the judge had most likely died in that position over the desk. He began to explain what lividity was, but the Coroner cut him off.

"I am well aware what lividity is; you don't have to lecture me, and you are not here to educate the people assembled here."

Brought up short for a moment by the brusque comment, Doctor Taylor continued his testimony about the autopsy he had performed and the bullet he removed from the back of the skull. At this point, Mrs. Nash seemed to tip to the side and Richard Fairley caught her before she fainted right on top of him.

The crowd let out a gasp and Doctor Taylor rushed over to where Mrs. Nash still sat in a slightly crumpled manner and asked for some water. The Coroner declared a short recess and not surprisingly, hardly anyone left their seats as the scene continued.

A glass of water was brought, she took a sip, the doctor dipped his handkerchief into it and dabbed her forehead and wrists, while I got up to lead them through a door off to the right, which I assumed held an office of some kind. We propelled her into a seat and Richard Fairley, following us, fanned her face with a pamphlet he picked up off a desk.

"I'm sorry," Mrs. Nash said, her face and lips pale.

"Put your head down," Doctor Taylor urged, and she followed his instructions, breathing deeply as he told her to.

Our interlude in the back office only lasted about half an hour, at which time the Coroner came in to check on Mrs. Nash's condition. Although he let her know her presence was not necessary now she had completed her testimony, she insisted on going back until the completion of the proceedings. He shot a look of contempt at Richard Fairley, who was still holding her hand, but he dropped it immediately, stood up, and cleared his throat. We trooped back into the meeting room, which was abuzz with conversation and the doctor resumed his testimony, seeming to now use descriptive medical terms in an attempt to objectify what surely seemed a personal horror to Mrs. Nash.

Officer Reed testified next. After giving his first impressions of the crime scene, he wished to defer to Inspector Gladstone, who nodded his head in agreement to him and then to the Coroner with whom he must have had many dealings in the past. The inspector recounted the pertinent movements of the judge, the times he was seen, and the time of death according to Doctor Taylor, the note, and that no one had been arrested for the crime. This was strictly true, but he omitted the fact that two people had in succession admitted guilt, only to have their actions proven impossible according to the time of death and their presence elsewhere.

The murmuring increased in volume as the crowd realized they were coming to the end of testimony and no definitive culprit had been named. The Coroner looked over his glasses and demanded order, which was promptly restored. He pursed his lips, annoyed at the lack of a clear conclusion to the murder investigation and said in his opinion, reluctantly given, death was due to misadventure by a person or persons unknown.

Another eruption of sound came from the assembled townsfolk as they noisily pushed back chairs, the scraping sound and the murmuring continuing until they had all left. The Coroner thanked us all for our helpful information, shook the hand of the inspector, took up his papers, and left the room. The rest of us milled about for a bit, waiting for the noise outside the room to dissipate, and then forged ahead through the gauntlet of photographers from Pittsfield and Springfield. I had ducked my head reflexively from the popping bulbs and hoped my photo wouldn't appear anywhere my parents might see it, but I was being ridiculous—they were waiting for Mrs. Nash and Richard Fairley and may have assumed incorrectly that the doctor and I were those two. We escaped the press and the clumps of people outside the meeting hall and walked swiftly down the street, Miss Manley having been escorted separately by the reverend.

"Well done," Doctor Taylor said to me. "You were succinct in your statement and came across as credible."

"Thank you, Doctor."

"Come now, isn't it about time you called me John outside of professional interactions?"

"Very well. John."

He gave me a warm smile, took my arm, linked it in his, and confidently walked me back home.

Chapter 21

Miss Manley and I had a cold lunch of ham and salad, which suited me fine after the emotion-packed morning. I was overcome with intense relief it was behind me, but I was curious to know her take on the testimonies we had heard, and she gave herself a few moments to ponder.

"Something is decidedly not right," she said. "Nothing fits, not the time nor the whereabouts of all the persons concerned. It is puzzling."

"If the inspector couldn't make head nor tails out of it with all his efforts, I don't know who can." Then I remembered I hadn't related to her the peculiar conversation Glenda and I had with Richard Fairley just the day before, where he told us he was recruited to assist in the questioning and, omitting the part about the gin cocktails, proceeded to do so.

"How extraordinary!" she said.

"I thought so, too, but tell me what you think," I said.

"Richard was a suspect in the murder of the judge not so many days ago and confessed to the murder before the timing proved it impossible. It seems extraordinary the police would ask him to aid in the investigation. His confession, well-meaning or noble in intention, tells me he is adept at lying even if the motivation was to protect someone else."

"By the same logic we can say Mrs. Nash is a liar, as well," I said.

"Exactly. It does not speak well for either of them. I'm sure some romantically inclined individual like dear Glenda would think their actions exemplary in the spirit of 'love,' but it does give one pause."

I looked at her and nodded my head in appreciation of her summation, a little abashed to note I had initially leaned toward the explanation of the force of love. However, something about Richard's manner in his studio continued to gnaw at me: his ability to ascertain what a person was expecting from him and then delivering on it. I don't imagine he did this deliberately; I think it was part of his nature and demonstrated a lack of ballast, for lack of another term. He could bend to whatever a situation required of him and it had me wondering if he had played to Mrs. Nash's unhappiness with his charm and attention. He may have begun with Christine and the never-completed portrait, but his attention could not have been more devoted to Mrs. Nash, the lovely, unhappy, wealthy woman married to a big, loud, important man who likely could never appreciate her as Richard would. It made me shake my head a bit in frustration.

"And you?" Miss Manley said, her head cocked to one side in curiosity.

"I should stop my imaginings of what people thought, felt, and acted, but somehow I don't think Richard Fairley is a sincere person. And I also don't know if Mrs. Nash cares one way or the other."

Miss Manley let out a hoot of laughter, making me embarrassed to have been so frank.

"Oh, my dear. I think you have it exactly!"

***

After lunch, I sat to read a letter from my brother, an utterly silly note dashed off quickly for the sake of having said he had written, informing me he had received the name of his roommate, was looking forward to getting out of Pelham, and sorry, had to go swimming with Gerald, whichever of his myriad friends that was. A letter from my mother was more informative, of course, stating all the preparations toward getting my brother ready for college and, while missing me and anticipating missing him as well, she was fed up with his erratic hours and scores of young men and women calling or dropping in at all times of the day. She asked if I needed anything as if West Adams were the wilds of Alaska rather than a four-hour train ride from home.

I put the letters down and looked out the window and considered whether staying here would be a good choice. My room at the hospital in New York would essentially be the same as when I was in training, but the excitement of living in a dormitory would wear thin when I was putting in long days and possibly even a graveyard shift. There would still be late-night card games, pranks, and loud voices—but I would be the one squawking for a little peace and quiet rather than a participant. I certainly wouldn't have the comforts of this lovely room, a view of the woods, homecooked food served by a maid, my best friend next door, and a kind man for my boss. Perhaps it would act in my favor to put in one year here, get my feet wet, so to speak, make my initial missteps here rather than in the glare of a big institution.

Another issue giving me pause was going back to where I had trained and being still treated as someone just learning the ropes, although, of course, I would be. Could Nurse Watson see me as fully qualified and treat me with respect or would I always be Aggie, student nurse, to her? Probably the best course of action was what I used in difficult decision situations: get out pen and paper and make two columns, Pro and Con. I took out a paper from the desk, took a deep breath and looked out the window. I was instantly distracted by seeing Christine make her way along the path and I abandoned my task and stood for a better look. She was intent on getting to the parsonage, not looking in any direction but at her feet quickly moving across the garden. Richard poked his head out of the studio door as she walked past, then ducked back in. I could only imagine how awkward the family's dynamics were going to be now it seemed obvious his relationship with Mrs. Nash would continue. I checked my watch and began to change for work.

As I walked to work later, I was wondering how awkward things were going to be from now on: when did I address my employer as doctor and when as John? Doctor when other people were around and John when we were alone? Doctor in the office at all times and John outside of the office? What about when other people were around in a social setting—wouldn't it sound familiar to call him by his first name? Should I even try to puzzle this out myself or ask him how to handle it? Was he just trying to be nice or was this going somewhere else entirely?

I know I have a habit of thinking things through a bit too much, but this was not so troubling, just a situation I had never encountered before. By the time I opened the door, I had it—I would wait to see how he addressed me. If it was 'Nurse' then it was 'Doctor' or if was

'Nurse Burnside,' then it would be 'Doctor Taylor.' "Good afternoon," he called out as I entered.

And then, the obvious solution: not to address him by any name.

"Good afternoon," I said, seating myself at the desk in the reception area and sorting through the mail. Another medical journal, two letters marked 'Personal,' and three payments, judging by the heft of one and the hand-addressed envelopes. I busied myself with logging the payments, writing out receipts to go into the patients' files, and assembling the checks and cash into an envelope for the doctor to deposit the next time he went to the bank in Adams, the nearest commercial center just a few miles away.

I looked in the appointment book and didn't see anyone scheduled, closed it, and checked the files for the usual clump stuck on top of the others. An 'In' basket would have made a lot of sense but then patients going into the examining room might see the names on the files, a terrible breach of privacy. His seemingly erratic system made sense to me then.

Chapter 22

Later that afternoon, Richard appeared at the doctor's office, and we chatted for a few minutes, now on friendly terms since our recent cocktail hour in the studio, and he said he might be going to Europe in the coming months and would likely need some vaccinations. He followed the doctor into the examination room and Doctor Taylor came out a few minutes later, closing the door behind him.

"I haven't had anyone request vaccinations for overseas travel in a long time. I'm just going to look it up while he gets dressed." He went into his office and pulled down a book and then a medical journal whose pages he flipped through before finding what he sought. He read as he slowly made his way back to the exam room, knocking on the door and waiting to get permission to enter. The door closed and they continued to talk for a little while before the door opened and both left.

"I think it will take at least a few days for me to get it from Boston," Doctor Taylor said. "It makes no sense for me to stock those medicines since so few people request them here."

Sometime after he left, Thomas Kirby showed up for a brief visit in a more normal state of mind since my earlier encounters with him, when he was distracted and overly emotional. The rest of the afternoon was slow, and I went home a bit early to change my clothes and visit the dressmaker in town to see if she could make over the one fancy dress I had brought with me. I loved the deep blue color, but the top never hung properly on my thin frame and I wondered if an alteration could be made.

To my surprise, the dressmaker, Miss Smith, was one of the women who had helped at the funeral luncheon and was at Miss Manley's tea although I hadn't put the name and face together. She had a space off to the side in the only dress shop in town, owned by her sister, and between the two of them they could provide ready-to-wear clothing as well as tailoring, original designs, and hats. They made an odd pair, the shop owner, the older sister I thought, was stiff and dour while her sister was congenial and talkative. They both nodded to me when I came in with the dress on a hanger and indicated the tailoring alcove. Miss Smith the seamstress was all smiles, said she was delighted to see me, and seemed surprised I would utilize her services since she thought there must be so many more experienced people in New York City.

I assured her it might be the case, but I was not from the City but a suburb, which seemed to relax her and thaw out her sister as well who, as business was slow, hung around to see the dress I brought in and what changes needed to be made. I went into the dressing room and came back out in a few minutes, needing help to have the zipper pulled up the back.

"Of course, I wouldn't be wearing these shoes," I said, looking down at my walking brogues as if they would care. "Lovely dress," Miss Smith said. "Turn around, please." "Hmm," said her sister, nodding her head at the bodice.

"Exactly. I don't like the way it just. Hangs. Not flattering at all."

Miss Smith took some pins from the cushion around her wrist and carefully made adjustments to the neckline and straps.

"What do you think? Is it too low now?" she asked.

"I think it's perfect."

She unzipped me and told me to step out of it carefully. Back in my street clothes, we talked about when it could be ready and who had recommended her. I thought it was an odd question since we had met already, but I confessed it was Mrs. Lewis.

The older sister huffed a bit and busied herself with straightening out a hat on a stand. I was getting annoyed with the snide comments about Mrs. Lewis from everyone as I thought she was a lovely woman with no ill intent, and I decided to say something.

"I know she has used you in the past and when you think of it, Nina goes into Pittsfield quite regularly and could buy all her clothes there. But instead, she chooses to patronize the local businesses." I was startled at my brash defense.

"I'm sorry," Miss Smith said, looking contrite. Her sister was not going to let up, however.

"She goes into Pittsfield all the time to do whatever she does. But I can also tell you last week when she said she came back on the late bus she did not. She came back by the earlier bus and what she did between then and the time the judge was shot, I cannot say."

Miss Smith and I stared open-mouthed.

"Why didn't you say something at the inquest?" I asked.

"Nobody asked me to, did they?" she replied, going to the door and turning the 'Open' sign over to 'Closed.' "We're closing up for the day now," she said, narrowing her eyes at me while she held the door open.

I felt as if someone had kicked me in the stomach and knocked the air out of me. What kind of a place was this to harbor such venomous sentiments toward a neighbor? And if she thought Mrs. Lewis was up to no good, as the words and looks seemed to imply, why hadn't she said something to Officer Reed or the Inspector Gladstone? Did she think she was doing the reverend and his wife a favor by withholding the information? If so, why did she tell me, someone she hardly knew? I looked up the street to where the bus stopped in West Adams in front of the store selling newspapers, magazines, candy, cigarettes, and bus tickets. If Mrs. Lewis got off the bus there, she would logically walk along this side of the street, past the dress shop on her way home. Was she on her way home earlier than she said? Or did she stop somewhere else for a long time before she got home?

I turned in the direction of going home, a perfectly natural thing to do if the Smiths were watching my movements although I walked slowly as if thinking. Instead, I was looking at the shops and buildings I passed trying to find an excuse for Nina's tardy arrival. The general store—a good candidate for a long browse—or the drugstore with its fountain service. Perhaps she stopped for ice cream or was having a prescription filled by the druggist. I walked in and browsed the shelves and found limited inventory for women: cold cream, face powder, cologne, deodorant, and manicure implements. Anything more sophisticated would have to be purchased in Adams or Pittsfield. But she had just come from Pittsfield, so what would bring her in here? The pharmacist's wife came forward to help me and I let her know I was just looking.

Next to the drugstore was a recessed doorway with several names on plates over mailboxes. One was a dentist on the second floor and the other three were surnames, one of which was Kirby. Did Thomas Kirby live upstairs? I stepped out on the sidewalk and looked upwards as if I could see him and realized it seemed a bit conspicuous. Had Nina gone to visit Thomas to see if he were all right? Or to question him about the missing money? Surely there was no possible romantic involvement. I shuddered at the thought. Perhaps she had not stopped here at all.

I walked past the remaining shops, peering into the windows to ascertain the likelihood of a stop: a hardware store, not likely; another general store, possibly; café, maybe; furniture store, and then I stopped wondering. I was letting town gossip get to me and I had enough thoughts buzzing in my head for one day. It was a relief to come to the end of the commercial section and onto the sidewalk of the residential space with tall peonies and arborvitae bushes planted at the front edges of the properties. Some folks favored the white picket fence, and I wondered if they were visible in the winter due to the snowfall. Again, I pushed those thoughts out of my head and vowed not to think about the future, which presented too many options.

As I got closer to Miss Manley's front door, I could see Nina Lewis coming toward hers from the other direction. We waved and I caught up with her.

"I've just been to see the Misses Smith," I said. "Thank you for the recommendation."

"The one Miss Smith is a delight, and the other is a bear." She giggled. "I think she doesn't like me because I sometimes do my shopping elsewhere." At that, she spun around to show off her light turquoise blue dress with the tulip hem.

"If I may ask, where did you get it?"

"Pittsfield, of course. Sorry to say Miss Smith the store owner likes plain clothes in basic colors. Although I do go in and buy things from time to time just to ease the tension."

I admired Nina's bright clothing choices and was happy to know I didn't have to go back home or New York City to give my wardrobe a freshening up.

"Can you come in for tea?" she asked, opening the gate.

I agreed and admired the lush lawn and the border of daisies perfect for cutting with a stand of irises behind and a clump of white hollyhocks. We entered the unlocked front door, Nina put her hat on a table under a mirror just inside and led me to the study to let her husband know she had returned.

"Hello, darling. Aggie is here with me." She kissed his forehead. "And Mrs. Sturdevant and baby are in good spirits today."

The reverend stood to shake my hand. "Ah, good news."

"Her mother was there and by the skeptical looks she gave me, I have no doubt she thought I was the least qualified to visit a new mother. She took in my figure from head to toe!"

The reverend laughed and turned a bit red in the face.

"I suppose we'll have to do something about that before the entire town has a new topic to gossip about." She stepped forward to squeeze his arm playfully.

Chapter 23

Miss Manley had a church meeting that evening, so she left the house right after we ate dinner. I went to Glenda's house, knocked on the back door—a habit from home—and waited for her to appear.

"Come in," she said, perplexed I didn't just waltz in without announcing myself.

"Have some coffee?"

It looked as if her dinner was over and while the coffee perked, she went into the dining room to retrieve the rest of the dishes.

"Is Sandra here?" I asked softly.

"Yes," Glenda responded, putting the tray down and donning an apron to begin the cleanup.

"Did she say how long she was going to stay?" I asked over the clatter of the dishes. I got up and closed the door of the kitchen to the dining room.

"Until the end of the summer for certain, she said. Landon Whittaker only paid for two weeks of her stay so far and I am pondering how to best approach him for the remainder."

"How about directly: just ask him."

"I meant to tell you Stuart had such a good idea. He said he would mention the availability of a room to his friends who might want to come up in the fall for a week or weekend of fall colors. It is spectacular at that time. And he does know a lot of people."

I didn't comment on this but added, "He's coming up tomorrow for the weekend."

"Yes, I know," she answered, not turning around. It should have given me a clue.

I got up and took a tea towel from the rack and began to dry the dishes as they got rinsed.

"We could go out to Lake Hoosac and have a picnic on Saturday," she suggested.

"It's a lovely idea. Why don't I get the food together since Annie can help me and you can bring the blankets or umbrella if we need one."

Glenda laughed. "It's not like a beach. There are trees almost down to the water line in most places although there are good picnicking spots. We can rent a canoe or a rowboat, too. You do swim, don't you?"

"Of course."

"Don't worry, it's shallow. The river was dammed a long time ago, power for the mills or something. So, it's a reservoir, not a lake as such." She took another towel from the rack, dried her hands and then the last cup.

"This is going to sound funny to you, but ever since I took in a boarder, I noticed I am tiptoeing around, closing doors more softly, not playing the radio loudly, keeping the house extra tidy."

"That last bit has to be a terrific trial for you," I commented.

"Too funny." She turned her attention back to the percolator on the stove, watching the small glass dome to make sure the coffee was strong, as she liked to drink it black while I had to temper mine with milk and sugar. She reached for a plate of cookies on the sideboard and put them on the table.

We sipped our coffee. "I feel bad about my previous judgment of Christine Nash," Glenda said. "I thought she was a spoiled rich girl who wasted her time lolling about or playing tennis or driving to see her friends in Pittsfield. Which she did, of course. But Nina overheard a conversation she had with the reverend, and I'm sure she shouldn't have repeated it to me, but she did. According to Christine, her father and stepmother did not want her to go off to college and limited her allowance to the point that she couldn't do much. She was stuck at Highfields with an overbearing father and a stepmother she hated. According to Nina."

"Wait, if Christine was angry with her stepmother, why would she kill her father? Her stepmother would inherit it all, and she would be worse off than before."

"I didn't say she killed her father! We don't know who did. But it wouldn't prevent Christine from trying to throw suspicion on Mrs. Nash. Poor kid." She took another cookie.

We didn't dare take the line of thinking further, instead we sat silently, suspicions and consequences racing through our heads. The doorbell rang and Glenda practically jumped out of her chair and then laughed at her reaction as she went to answer it. I could hear a man's voice and then footsteps in the hall and up the stairs. Glenda came back in a few minutes.

"It's Doctor Taylor making a house call to Sandra."

We looked at each other wide-eyed with curiosity and trepidation wondering what her health issue was because I certainly did not know. In a surprisingly short time, we could hear his footsteps coming down the stairs and Glenda hastened to intercept him, inviting him to the kitchen for a cup of coffee.

"Hello, Aggie," he said and I responded, avoiding having to call him John in front of Glenda, which would start a raft of questions later.

"I hope you don't mind the informality," she said, indicating the kitchen location.

"Of course not." He seemed relaxed but tired as he rubbed the back of his neck. "It seems like a long week already and it's not Friday yet."

It only made us more curious about the nature of the house call, but we didn't dare ask.

Chapter 24

Friday morning passed in a frenzy of activity, Annie still grumbling about Stuart's returning after she had already washed the sheets and towels from his previous visit. She was loud enough to have her disgruntlement noted but soft enough we could not understand what it was she was saying. I kept out of the way writing letters to my family and postcards to some of the girls from nurses' training while Annie banged the furniture around in the room next door. Miss Manley had the good sense to escape by going out to get food for the evening, taking her time doing so and bringing back a box of Maid of Honor tarts from the bakery. I was sure Annie could have made these just as well as it was her favorite baked sweet, but it relieved her from doing so with the extra work of another person arriving.

Friday afternoons seemed to bring in all those who had put off their medical complaints for the week but now feared symptoms would worsen over the weekend. Of course, Doctor Taylor was available day or night, weekends and holidays, but many of his patients chose not to abuse that except in extreme circumstances. While I had hoped for a busier work environment on some days, this one fit the bill with phone calls, appointments, and walk-ins.

I got to experience what I later learned were the usual farm accidents where the worker either waited until near the close of office hours or until the injury got bad enough to seek medical attention. The doctor spent almost an hour working on a young man who had gotten a dirty cut from some kind of machinery with soil, grease, and chaff in the open wound. I knew it had to have been painful to receive and worse to treat and the young man bore the poking, prodding, and extraction of dirt and pebbles well, but almost fainted when it was over. Once stabilized, the doctor offered to drive him back while I cleaned up the mess in the exam room before going home myself.

Stuart had arrived earlier, ebullient about some professional connection he had made that he was sure would make all the difference in his career. He produced a bottle of gin from his golf bag with a flourish to the headshaking of his aunt and the scandalized face of Annie, a churchgoing, law-abiding person. He telephoned Glenda to come over for an early cocktail and then join us for dinner at the Red Lion in Stockbridge. Miss Manley protested she had already bought a leg of lamb, new potatoes and asparagus for dinner, but Stuart waved it away as Saturday's dinner; it was going to be his treat tonight. She talked him out of the trip to Stockbridge, which would take about an hour, and he agreed to a restaurant this side of Pittsfield that was not as historic or well-known but a shorter drive and less expensive.

Glenda came into the sitting room, inquisitive about the early summons, and was relieved to find nothing amiss but rather a party in the making. I wondered if Miss Manley would imbibe and found she didn't want to squelch the happy mood by refusing and became relaxed and verbose after her first sips.

"Tell us what has happened, Stuart," she asked.

"All in good time, all in good time."

I excused myself to change out of my uniform and into the newly refurbished dress that had just come back from the dressmaker's. I took my time freshening up, combing my hair back into a fake jeweled clip and adding a touch of rouge and lipstick. When Glenda saw me, she realized she had better change into something fancier as well. Miss Manley wore her usual mid-calf length flowered dress, although I was sure she would put on a hat and gloves to complete the outfit. We were just starting in on the second round of drinks when Glenda came back, looking chic with her short blonde hair tousled and an expensive-looking black silk dress. I raised my eyebrows as if to ask where she had got it and she whispered, "My mother's."

Then Miss Manley had to toddle off to finish getting ready, and I certainly hoped Stuart did not have to change his clothes, or we would knock off the entire bottle of gin without any food before the night was over. But she was quick and in our collective jolly mood got into Stuart's Packard, Miss Manley in the front and Glenda and I in the back getting our hair tossed about by the air from the partly open windows. It was still light but cooling off with delightful smells of pine needles from the warm day scenting the air. The ride to the restaurant seemed long although Stuart drove much too fast on the winding roads, so we three women were hanging onto the door handles for balance at each turn. Conversation was impossible with the noise of the wind and it was just as well he wasn't distracted from sharp turns along the unlit roadways of the countryside.

I could tell Stuart was disappointed he didn't get to show me the Red Lion and almost turned his nose up at the Mountain Aire Hotel, a much less famous place, although it suited me just fine. It was a bustling resort hotel with a swimming pool, tennis courts, and brochures about cultural activities in the area and sightseeing. As Stuart glanced around the dining room, it occurred to me it wasn't the reputation of the place, the décor, or probably even the menu at issue—he was expecting to be among a more notable clientele than well-to-do people on holiday from surrounding states. Stockbridge had the allure of hobnobbing with the second or third generation of the robber barons who had built their cottages in the Berkshires although Prohibition had driven parties with alcohol mostly back into private homes. Stuart helped us into our seats and looked around again to see if there was someone of note he had missed in his first perusal. Alas, no, but he put on a pleasant smile, determined to make the best of it.

"What is your news, or do we have to wait for dessert to hear about it?" Glenda inquired.

He was dying to tell us and got right to it. "A publisher was at a party I attended this past week and as we chatted, he became interested in my book series. It seems it is exactly what his publishing house is looking for and suggested they could be modified for a younger audience."

"That sounds interesting," Miss Manley said.

"We met the next day and talked about the idea more and there are so many choices to be made. He could re-publish my books under his imprint and market them to young male readers through advertising in magazines such as *Boys' Life*. Or I could rewrite the existing plots and perhaps insert a new character, a boy hero who helps out."

"It sounds like fun. Perhaps younger readers will identify with the stories more," I said.

"I would make them a lot more fast-paced and interesting than the Hardy Boys books, for example," he said.

We looked blankly at him.

"They are extremely popular, just been out a few years, brothers who solve mysteries. I don't suppose any of you would have seen them," he added.

"My brother is off to college soon, so I think he would have been too old to read them."

We veered onto the topic of colleges, of which Stuart knew quite a lot, having attended boarding school and having definite opinions on the status of various colleges and universities, being a

Yale man. There were a surprising number of colleges in Massachusetts, as well, and he rattled off names and alumni with remarkable recall. Stuart was so talkative that his monologue, interrupted by questions from time to time, took us all the way to dessert before getting back to the topic of publishing.

"Charlie Hudson is the man I was speaking to last week. A few years older than I, also a Yalie, he suggested the imprint for this adventure series be done under the name 'Hudson-Manley.' What do you think, Auntie?"

"I think your father would have been proud, Stuart."

He thought so, too, and launched into the types of bindings, endpapers, typefaces, and dust covers that should accompany each of his books.

"Which is your favorite book?" he asked me.

Luckily, I had just put a spoonful of sherbet into my mouth and held up my hand indicating my mouth was full, so he turned to Glenda.

"I love all of them," she said.

It pleased him and surprised me since I don't think I had ever seen her reading anything other than our textbooks when we were in training and even those did not get much attention. His eyes swiveled back to me.

"To be honest, I've only just begun **The Peril of Dunbar**. Between adjusting to this new place and work, I haven't had much time." I saw rather than his face falling in disappointment, he was more surprised than anything, as if shocked I had not devoured each volume already.

The drive back wasn't as fast because now the road was pitch dark, with the only light coming from the headlights on Stuart's car. He was navigating more carefully now that the effects of the gin had worn off as well as the anticipation of the announcement of his exciting news. What was the publishing industry like? I had no idea, but it seemed New York City was the place to be, which was certainly in his favor, and his penchant for socializing would probably be an asset, as well. Now all he needed was a beautiful young woman on his arm to attract attention and he might do quite well for himself.

When we got back, I offered to make coffee for us all and went to the kitchen while the other three went to the sitting room. On one trip in to bring in cups, saucers, milk, and sugar, I saw Stuart and Glenda had both resumed drinking the gin, this time without ice or water. She raised her glass to me as if to question if I wanted one, but I shook my head and went back to the kitchen. By the time I returned with the pot of coffee, the conversation had become lively.

"Well, the most exciting part of 'Hudson-Manley' is I will be a partner with Charlie."

"Have you been asked to invest in this new venture?" Miss Manley asked calmly.

"It's not a new venture, as I explained. It is an offshoot of an existing business, a roaringly successful one, into a new area of publishing. Charlie has some incredible ideas about how to sell the books."

"In a bookstore, I should think," Miss Manley teased.

Stuart was not amused. "Of course, but there are so many other ways to do it. Advertising is the key—advertising on products young men buy or use."

"Like chewing gum or candy?" Glenda offered. I didn't know if she was being serious.

"It's a possibility. They used to have photos of baseball players inserted into packs of cigarettes to make people want to buy more to collect particular cards. But we could advertise in magazines or even on the radio."

"Gosh, isn't it expensive?" Glenda asked.

Stuart let out a frustrated breath. "I am talking about the future of writing and publishing and you all seem to want to shoot down my ideas and my ambition." His face was getting red.

I was becoming uncomfortable and stood to say, "Thank you, Stuart, for a lovely dinner and evening." I shook his hand and he seemed to calm down.

By the time I had finished in the bathroom upstairs, I could hear the conversation had escalated again. I stopped near the head of the stairs to hear Stuart berating his aunt for not realizing the great prospects ahead of him if she could only loan him the money. Ah, so that was it: Hudson-Manley would need Manley money and Stuart didn't have enough but good old Auntie did. From the softer tones of her replies, although I couldn't hear the actual words, it seemed she was calmly letting him know it was not a possibility at this time. He raised his voice again, and not wanting to hear any more, I tiptoed to my room and closed the door.

***

Whatever the tone of the exchange of the night before, Miss Manley had dismissed it by breakfast and was her usual calm, pleasant self in the absence of Stuart, who had slept late. Miss Manley picked up her marketing basket, maybe to avoid further confrontation, or perhaps I was reading too much into what I had heard last night, and she simply was doing the marketing on a Saturday morning when many people came into town on the same errand.

I packed a few apples and sandwiches and a thermos of lemonade and grabbed the broad-brimmed straw hat I had presciently brought from home, went next door to get Glenda, and Stuart got the car ready to set off for the reservoir. It was not far from the road we had usually taken to Pittsfield, but instead of proceeding due south, we took the left fork in the road and followed the eastern shoreline of a long body of water visible through the trees.

"We'll rent a rowboat and go out to one of the little islands," Stuart suggested.

"We can pretend we're Peter Pan and the Lost Boys—maybe there will be pirates, Indians, mermaids, and fairies," Glenda said.

"It sounds like you want to build a fort," I teased her.

"We used to do that when we were children: forage for branches and try to build a house or teepee. They were pretty flimsy structures, but it was so much fun."

"There is a spit of land, a peninsula at the northern end with some houses on it but the other islands are empty, or were, the last time I was out there. It's where we'll go because the water is a decent depth; the middle and southern basins are so shallow we'd be scraping bottom most of the time," Stuart said.

"Maybe I shouldn't have brought so much for lunch," I suggested facetiously.

"Well, if we become grounded on a sandbar, we can just pitch the food overboard to lighten the load," Glenda suggested.

"Or you," I said.

Now we were giggling while Stuart was trying to remain serious.

"The north basin is deep enough, don't worry. And the water is usually crystal clear."

We pulled into a gravel parking lot next to a man sitting outside a small building smoking a pipe. As we approached, he lifted his head in greeting and got up. He had a distinctive Yankee accent I couldn't begin to duplicate, but that, the corn cob pipe, and plaid shirt added to the quaint atmosphere. He and Stuart went inside to discuss terms of the rental while Glenda and I walked toward a short pier where several rowboats were tied up.

"Oh, dear, I hope he doesn't think we're going to supply the muscle in this excursion," Glenda said.

"It was his idea to take this cruise so to my mind he's the galley slave for the day. Anyway, look how close those islands are," I said, shading my eyes to see better despite the broad brim of my straw hat. It was a perfect day to be out on the water, not too hot with a light breeze. And the reservoir was narrow enough, even if a sudden squall should come up, we could make it back to shore quickly. I had to chastise myself for even thinking about storms and sea calamities, but I blamed it on reading a few more pages of ***The Peril of Dunbar*** where a nautical disaster in the Atlantic has something to do with the hero's later plight.

Stuart emerged from the building and suggested we leave anything we didn't need in the car, which would be locked and under the watchful eye of the building owner; I took off my watch and put it in my purse in the back seat, not wanting to risk getting it wet, and Stuart took off his jacket and rolled up his sleeves, ready to supply the oar power.

"You can swim, can't you?" he asked me.

I answered, "Of course," and then wondered why we hadn't thought of bringing bathing suits except perhaps for modesty's sake. We walked down the wobbly pier and he pointed to a sturdylooking wooden rowboat, its oars laying in the hull. He crouched down, gingerly put one foot then the other, onto the rear seat and, holding both gunwales, stood up while the boat bobbed up and down.

Glenda had her hand to her mouth while watching him make his way to the middle seat, then sit down and take up the oars to put in the oarlocks.

"Well, come on," he said, as the boat continued to shift from side to side in the water.

"You first," Glenda said to me, clearly unnerved by the motion.

"You must have been in a rowboat before," I said.

"Not for a long time," she answered.

I repeated Stuart's cautious approach into the boat, holding on to the gunwales but seating myself in the rear seat more gingerly than was necessary to reassure Glenda everything was safe and steady.

"Come on, you've done this before," Stuart called out to her, still nervously standing on the pier.

"I have, but I was just a child and I think the boat was bigger."

"It was. You were smaller," I suggested. I turned around and held out my hand to her which she took and, making a little yelping noise, bent down and practically crawled onto the boat. By this time, we were all laughing at the ridiculous situation of being in shallow water, our boat bumping into the others on each side as we rocked back and forth.

"I think the pointy end is the front," Glenda said, I hoped in an attempt to be silly.

"Thank you, captain," Stuart said and used one of the oars to push us away from the pier and into the open water. I looked back at the boatyard owner, shaking his head at our ineptitude but knowing under the circumstances we could do little damage to his property.

Stuart was surprisingly strong and with a few strokes had us moving at a steady pace. I noticed his biceps were large and my former impression of him toiling on a typewriter in a dark apartment was dispelled and now I envisioned him as a member of an athletic club in New York making social connections on the tennis courts or in the locker room.

"What fun this is!" Glenda said, although she held onto the rear seat with both hands. I looked down into the clear, shallow water, seeing gravel at the bottom and fish moving past.

"We should have brought fishing poles to bring your aunt something for dinner."

"Good thought, alas, too late," he said.

"Does your hero ever get to use his rowing skills?" I asked.

"He was on the crew team at Princeton, of course, but I think I revealed it in a previous book. Haven't you got to the part where he commandeers a fisherman's boat to cross the loch in a pelting rainstorm?"

"I haven't," I could honestly state.

"Ripping action, if I do say so myself. Had a lot of fun imagining and writing it."

He was starting to get a bit winded, so I left off the questions and enjoyed the breeze accelerated by our propulsion in the water. I wondered if Stuart had rowed crew in prep school or college or if his literary hero got to do all the things he had not accomplished in real life. The lake bottom was darker and deeper as we went on and then a short ten minutes later it became lighter in appearance as we approached the island.

"Treasure Island!" Glenda announced.

"If you remember, the actual name was Skeleton Island," Stuart said, maneuvering the prow onto the gravel. "I'd suggest you take off your shoes."

He took off his socks and shoes, rolled up his pants, clambered to the bow, got out, and pulled the boat more fully onto the shore. We took off our socks and shoes and followed his lead, splashing into the warm inch-deep water and squealing at the sharp gravel under our bare feet. You couldn't call the ten-foot-square patch of small stones a beach, but we sat on it anyway and looked back onto the shore we had left so recently.

"I wonder who owns this island? And if you could build a house on it?" Glenda asked. Restless as usual, she turned her head around to survey what was behind us. "I wonder if that tree house we made has survived?" She got up and walked carefully on the stony ground.

"I imagine some other wild children have been here in recent years to either occupy it or knock it down," Stuart said.

I had the sudden realization Stuart and Glenda had known each other a long time. Of course, she grew up in West Adams and he had mentioned visiting his aunt; they must have been friends from childhood although he was a bit older.

"Do you remember where it was?" she asked, moving further into the shrubbery. I had another realization: we had just rowed across some purposefully flooded valley and the island upon which we sat was once a hill or small mountain, as were the other islands existing above water in this reservoir.

Stuart got up and followed her into the greenery.

"It's not like there are acres to explore or discover, you know," he reminded her. "And I haven't got on my shoes."

"Tenderfeet, both of you," I called out as they disappeared. All I could hear was the rustling of leaves and laughing behind me and I left them to it. After a few minutes, they came back out, Glenda holding a long switch in her hand.

"It's gone," she said. "No replacement structure, either."

"Did you bring lumber out here to build it or just use what was available?" I asked.

"There was a short tree with perfectly climbable branches, and we pulled others up there to create a comfy place to sit and look out over the water. Right, mate?" she said, poking the stick at Stuart like a sword.

"Take that, Long John," he answered, looking around desperately for a weapon and instead falling backward onto the gravel with a thump.

We shouldn't have laughed, but he was usually so stuffy, this seemed funny and he joined in.

"Let's have some of the lunch I brought," I suggested, getting the packet from the boat while Glenda plopped down on the sand next to him.

"No checked picnic tablecloth, we'll rough it." I handed them each a cheese sandwich wrapped in waxed paper and poured out lemonade, which made Stuart wince, not because it was sour but because he was expecting a Tom Collins or something similar.

"Well, very healthy," he commented.

"Let's see if we can go over to the other island," Glenda said.

"Easy for you to say as I am the one doing the rowing."

We finished eating and she and I climbed back into the boat, took our position in the rear seat while Stuart grabbed the gunwales and pushed off from the shore.

"I think I used to call it Enchanted Island to myself,' Glenda said. "I had all kinds of daydreams about setting up a little camp and having my boat to get there." She turned her head and said, "Let's go over to that one." It was as far as we had come already from the shore and as long as Stuart didn't complain, I was game. I trailed my hand in the water and we progressed farther south. Glenda put her face up to the sun, leaned back and trailed her hand in the water as well. Suddenly she yelped, pulled her hand out quickly and stood up.

"What? Sit down!" I said.

"Something nibbled at my hand," she said and in trying to sit down, stumbled into me pitching me into the water.

It was warm with no shock of cold, but the act of having been propelled into it was startling, nonetheless. I took in a mouthful of it before surfacing and reached out to the side of the boat but in falling over, my belt had caught on the oarlock and I couldn't seem to right myself. I could hear Glenda screaming and yelling at Stuart to do something, which consisted of him holding out an oar for me to grasp. Unfortunately, his action drove my belt more tightly into the oarlock and I couldn't seem to get my head above water for more than a few seconds before being sucked under again. I gulped another mouthful of the swampy-tasting lake and flailed my arms. This couldn't be happening to me, I thought, I know how to swim, I took a lifesaving class at summer camp one summer, I can't be drowning. The oar came out at me again and the commotion on the boat made it collide soundly with my head. Now I was stunned and went under, and then finally had the presence of mind to try to undo the belt at my waist. It had been tied with a double knot and I could not see clearly in the now turbulent water where the knot was. I fumbled and tore at the fabric which was now thoroughly saturated and stretchy and was able to partly free myself and bob my head out of the water.

I was gasping for air and grabbed at the oar, looking up into Stuart's horrified face. It was at this point he realized my belt was the object that had kept me from the surface, and he untangled it from the oarlock, then pulled me toward the side of the boat and put his hand over mine.

"Glenda, sit down," he commanded. "We don't need you to go over, too."

She sat and moved to the far side of the boat.

"I'm going to pull her aboard, so the boat will rock a bit. Just stay steady."

I didn't know my clothes could weigh so much and I felt weak with fear of my near-drowning but experienced a jolt of energy that allowed me to hoist my torso out of the water and, putting one leg over the side, pull myself fully into the boat where I tumbled inelegantly into the hull and curled on my side to catch my breath. They both reached out to me asking repeatedly if I was all right and apologizing for the event. I finally slowed my breathing and managed to pull myself onto the rear seat.

"Can we go now?" I asked.

Stuart pulled mightily on the oars and had us moving swiftly through the water.

"Aggie, I'm so sorry," Glenda said, putting her arm around me. "Something was trying to eat my hand."

"Don't," was all I could muster before coughing then vomiting over the side of the boat. I had swallowed so much lake water and didn't want to think about what manner of microscopic life had been in it.

The warm day now seemed chilly to me in my clinging wet clothes made worse by the wind that had picked up. Oh, please, I thought, let's not have a storm on top of all this, but though the wind continued, and the sky clouded over, there was no squall to impede our quick return to shore. We had barely reached the pier when I turned and crawled out onto the wooden structure before standing up. The boatman came toward us, sensing something amiss, and just stared at me.

"Went for a swim," I said.

He had no change in expression. "I hope the boat's all right."

I walked shakily toward the car in my bare feet, holding socks and shoes in one hand while Glenda and Stuart gathered up their footwear and the picnic things and hurried behind me to the car. He unlocked it and took a blanket from the trunk and said he would just settle up with the boatman, which only took a few minutes. Glenda was busy fussing over me, tucking the scratchy woolen blanket in around me and apologizing profusely before getting into the back seat by herself.

"We'll be back soon," Stuart said, turning on the engine.

I began to shiver, not from the cold, wet clothing but shock, I believe. Before putting the car in gear, he reached over to the glove compartment and extracted a hip flask. The ever-present gin, I thought to myself, a lifesaver at that moment.

I don't remember the drive back to Miss Manley's, but it wasn't long, and the shivering had abated as I slugged down the alcohol and fumed at the idiocy of Glenda's impulsive action, Stuart's inept rescue attempt, and more humiliatingly, despite my knowledge and ability to swim, the realization that I had come close to drowning. In a calm, relatively shallow lake, a reservoir, no less.

No sooner had we pulled into the driveway than I pushed the blanket off and walked into the kitchen, startling Miss Manley who, with one long look, took in my dripping clothes, bare feet, and hair plastered on my face. She took my arm.

"I'll get a hot bath started," she said, and we diverged at the top of the stairs, me to peel off my clothes smelling of lake weeds or algae, a slightly fishy odor I couldn't wait to get rid of. I heard the tap water gushing and putting on a robe was thrilled to find the deep clawfoot tub halfway full. She patted my arm and left me, closing the door behind her. I locked it by habit but also did not want to see or talk to anyone just then. The clear, slightly blue tub water looked so innocuous, but I knew people sometimes drowned in their baths, too. How I could not imagine. But I also could never have imagined I, a healthy, hardy young woman who could swim and save others' lives, almost died in water that day.

Chapter 25

The soak was long and luxurious, and I washed my hair twice to eliminate the lake smell before realizing the bathwater was getting cold and my fingers wrinkly. I heard doors opening and closing downstairs, Stuart bumbling around in his room down the hall as I dried myself and got into the bathrobe. Someone had discreetly removed my soggy clothes from the floor of my room and wiped up the mess; I certainly hadn't intended for Annie or Miss Manley to do so, but was thankful, nonetheless. I sat on the bed wondering if I should get into pajamas and under the covers or get dressed and join her downstairs but couldn't make up my foggy mind just then. A knock on the door and Miss Manley put her head around and asked how I was doing. I managed to mumble I was all right, and she asked if I would entertain a visitor. I hoped it was not Glenda again with her effusive apologies or Stuart trying to make amends for hitting me on the head with the oar. But it was neither; it was Doctor Taylor. I gasped at the surprise.

He smiled his wonderful smile, approached, and put his hand on my shoulder.

"I heard you had an accident."

I was embarrassed to note my eyes were filling with tears, so I turned my head away, cleared my throat, and gave a little laugh.

"Yes." I managed to look up into his concerned brown eyes. "It was terrible. It happened so quickly, and my belt was caught on the oarlock so I couldn't get my head above water." Now the tears were falling, and I was mortified to be crying in front of him, but also relieved. He squeezed my shoulder, and I was almost about to blubber into his chest but realized Miss Manley stood there.

"I'll be downstairs," she said, leaving softly.

"Shall we do a quick check?" he asked. "Did you inhale any of the water?"

"No, I don't think so, but I swallowed a lot." I looked up.

"It must have been nasty."

"Tasted like my grandmother's turtle soup."

That got a laugh from him.

"I vomited both up."

He shook his head. "No need to be brave and funny with me. But it was a good joke. Now turn a bit and let me look at your throat." He did eyes, ears, pulse, the usual and suggested I might want to gargle with some strong mouthwash or brandy if Miss Manley had any.

"Thank you for coming over, Doctor Taylor," I said.

He put his head to one side, with the expression my landlady made when considering a curious question.

"John," I corrected myself.

"Much better. Tomorrow is Sunday, so take it easy. I have a feeling you'll be well enough on Monday to start on our usual workweek." He leaned over to say more quietly, "And maybe you want to steer clear of that lunatic nephew of hers." I

managed a wry smile. "Good idea."

***

Miss Manley brought up a tray with tea and cookies later, which made me feel like a proper invalid but also well cared for, reminding me when I was sick with the usual childhood illnesses— chickenpox, measles, and mumps—and was confined to my bedroom for what seemed like weeks and my mother bringing up a tray of food. If I were at home now, she would have done the same but thinking of my family, here was another incident I decided not to share as my mother worried enough as it was. With a bit of a laugh, I wondered what I could write home about that wouldn't startle them: the reverend's sermon or tea with the women of West Adams?

By dinner time I felt silly lying about in my bathrobe and got up, dressed in something casual, and brought the tray back to the kitchen. I found Miss Manley in the sitting room and asked her where everybody was, meaning Stuart, of course. I imagined Glenda wouldn't show her face for another day at least. She always was a bit of a coward.

"Let's see. Stuart has gone to Stockbridge for dinner with Glenda," she said looking at me from above the reading glasses she had on to do her knitting. Reacting to my surprise she added, "I believe he was rattled by your experience."

I finished the sentence for her, "So he had to celebrate with dinner?" Then I thought perhaps he had persuaded his aunt to lend him money and it was cause for celebration.

She put the garment down in her lap. "No, I don't think he is celebrating. He was genuinely upset, and I think he is grappling with not only how to apologize to you but why he didn't have more presence of mind to comprehend what went wrong and complete a timely rescue. After writing all those books," she gestured to the shelf full of them, "full of derring-do and lightning decisions on the part of his hero, it was a shock to find himself in a dangerous situation and not meet the standards he had set for his fictional counterpart."

So like Stuart for this event to be all about him, I thought. "You know he practically knocked me out with an oar."

"He didn't quite describe it that way."

I sat next to her on the sofa. "I don't mean to sound peevish, but I was hanging by my belt, almost upside down in the water and it seemed all they did was yell pointless instructions at each other and worsen my situation."

She patted my hand. "It must have been frightening for you. And I am sorry they were not up to the challenge to help you in time. But it's all right now, isn't it?"

I didn't want to seem as if I were going to hold a grudge against her nephew—although at the moment I did—but I knew I shouldn't drag her into this incident, as she hadn't been responsible or even present, just a down-to-earth woman who was saddled with a rather dramatic relative. Her reaction to my distress just then was: it was over, and let's move on again, a perfectly sensible form of action. She gave me a smile that seemed to encompass her acknowledgment of my feelings while not backing down from her inclinations.

"Let's get a bite to eat, shall we?" she asked, getting up.

The evening went by slowly and I found myself exhausted by eight o'clock and so returned to my room to prepare myself for the week ahead with lights out by nine. Stuart came noisily home sometime thereafter and, listening to him bumping around in his room, I decided to put an end to part of my annoyance with him.

"Can't you be quieter?" I asked loud enough to be heard through the wall. He did not answer but stopped moving for a bit, long enough to allow me to drift off to sleep.

The next day I wasn't surprised to learn Stuart had risen early and left without eating breakfast or saying goodbye to his aunt. He did leave a small note by her place setting in the dining room and one by mine. Mine said, 'Aggie, please forgive me for whatever part I played in the frightening events yesterday. Stuart.'

Frightening events? Is that how he put it? I was beyond trying to understand him or care and dove into my bowl of oatmeal enthusiastically. I noticed Miss Manley read her note, folded it up, and put it back next to her plate without expression or comment.

Glenda tiptoed into the dining room from the kitchen with a bouquet from her garden that she handed me as a peace offering, a sheepish look on her face. How could I remain angry with her?

"Thank you," I said as graciously as I could manage.

She gave me a hug and one for Miss Manley, too, who looked quite surprised at the sudden affection and Glenda sat at the empty place setting.

"Would you like something to eat?" Miss Manley offered.

"No thanks, I ate already. I thought I would join you for church this morning," she said to Miss Manley's astonished face. "That would be nice. We'll go in about half an hour." "I'll just pop back home and get a hat and gloves," she said.

Miss Manley and I looked at one another and shrugged.

Church with Reverend Lewis presiding was entirely uneventful, in a good way. You have to admire Episcopalians for conducting an uplifting, smooth religious experience—no guilt, no fire and brimstone—just the messages you want to hear and in the reverend's case, a little bit of scholarly information. It seemed he liked to read about archaeology and the excavations in the Holy Land so Sunday he inserted a tidbit about what people ate into his description of the miracle of the loaves and fishes, describing what sort of bread they made and what species of fish was available. It may have seemed odd to some people, but I rather enjoyed allowing myself to envision the daily lives of people of biblical times and I thought it brought them closer to us in that way. His soothing voice and topic relaxed me, and I looked around at the other parishioners, Mrs. Nash a few pews ahead, her attention riveted upon his every word. If Christine were here, she wasn't sitting next to her stepmother nor was Richard Fairley. I assumed recent events kept him at a distance from Elizabeth Nash, and they had the good sense or taste not to be a couple just yet, at least not publicly.

Chapter 26

Annie had brought the **Berkshire Eagle** and laid it on the dining table, impossible to ignore and I soon saw why. There was a photo of Mrs. Nash and an accompanying article describing her in sympathetic tones. She was the former Mrs. Tuttle and I wondered if she had been widowed before or divorced, and the author speculated on whether she would return to Boston or stay in 'our beautiful mountains.' Something about the treacly tone of the writer annoyed me, his supposition she was the grieving widow pining away in her 'hilltop home with breathtaking local vistas.' Then I thought back to the inquest and Christine's comment about the criminal gang in Boston and wondered if Mrs. Nash had any connection to them. Suppose *she* was one of the gang's family members? She had no resemblance whatsoever to my idea of a gun moll, or whatever you called a gangster's girlfriend—as if I knew what one looked like—but I had been to enough movies to have formed an opinion. I had to laugh at myself then to think I would base any evaluation on an actress's portrayal of a type of woman who, of course, had peroxide blonde hair, cheap-looking clothes, and an accent to match.

Hardly Elizabeth Nash.

I handed the newspaper to Miss Manley, who shook her head either at the excessive prose of the author or at the notion of Mrs. Nash, I couldn't tell. The remainder of my morning consisted of ironing my recently laundered uniforms—something I felt was not one of Annie's duties—and applying white polish to my shoes. A letter and a postcard from one of our classmates at nursing school compelled me to reply in kind as well as dash off a note to my parents.

Oddly enough, who should come into the doctor's office that afternoon but Mrs. Nash. I greeted her as Doctor Taylor came out to bring her into the exam room, and I made my way back to his office to put the medical journals on his desk. Now, I know people who overhear conversations always claim they were not eavesdropping, not intentionally trying to listen but in this case, it was true. His office and the exam room were separated by a fairly thin wall so I could hear what was being said. Should I have stepped quickly and quietly away?

Yes, but did I?

No.

Mrs. Nash sounded agitated and while Doctor Taylor reassured her it was a normal reaction to her recent ordeal, she countered she routinely woke about three o'clock each morning and had a hard time going back to sleep. While her mind was running over all the arrangements she still needed to make, she heard noises in the house like doors opening and closing and stealthy footsteps. Though frightened, she nonetheless went to investigate the night before, going quietly along the second floor and then down to the first, thinking perhaps the cook or a maid might be about. Although she searched high and low, she could find no trace of anybody around and went back to bed but not to sleep.

I thought in an older house such as Highfields there were bound to be creaks and other noises happening naturally from the expansion and contraction of the wood, but that was my logical brain at work. So many people lived at the house that she could have overheard any number of them either being similarly sleepless or using the bathroom. Then I wondered if she thought she heard the ghost of Judge Nash moving about, a sign of a guilty conscience, no doubt.

The doctor said nothing for a few moments, and I was scared he would come out of the exam room and see me in his office, but I calmed down as he continued talking.

"What would like me to do?" he asked.

"I would like to have some sleeping tablets," she said. "I can't go on settling things up with such a lack of sleep."

I tiptoed back to the reception area and sat to continue opening the rest of the mail, heard the exam room door open, and they both came out toward the front door.

"Thank you so much," she said, and as he closed the door behind her, I noticed she did look haggard from lack of sleep.

Doctor Taylor raised his eyebrows and sighed. "Poor woman."

The rest of the day was uneventful, a quiet dinner, early to bed with one of Stuart's books I had taken from Miss Manley's bookshelf that did not pique my interest no matter how I tried.

I shut it with a sigh, put on a robe, and took it back down to the darkened sitting room, convinced even another year here couldn't persuade me to pick it up again to read, although to relieve my conscience, I thought I might get a signed copy of one of Stuart's books for my brother for Christmas. The house was quiet with Miss Manley asleep upstairs and I perused the titles of travel recollections deciding that I probably wouldn't be visiting the Levant anytime soon.

Conscience was much on my mind as I entered the sitting room and looked around wondering what Stuart had been doing down here last week, opening and shutting drawers while his aunt slept upstairs. Her desk had this afternoon's mail sorted, some of it opened. I replaced Stuart's book on the shelf and turned to look through the afternoon mail to see if there was anything new for me: just a postcard from Tillie who was on vacation in Vermont. Only inches away was the top drawer of the desk and feeling intensely curious and ashamed at the same time, I pulled it open to examine the contents. Some writing paper, envelopes, fountain pen, and stamps were in the shallow drawer; the ink was likely in one of the deeper side drawers. What made me continue to peer into every drawer of the desk? This wasn't like me at all, but Stuart's rustling had awakened my curiosity.

There was a stout pot of glue next to a stack of photos, waiting to be affixed in an album later. The bottom drawer was the one that always got stuck, Miss Manley had said, but I gave it a yank and gasped when it opened so easily. My eyes widened as I saw the words: Margaret Manley, Last Will and Testament.

I had gone this far.

I couldn't stop now, so looking behind me, which was ridiculous since only Miss Manley was in the house and asleep upstairs, I took the handwritten document and began to read.
Surprisingly, it was dated only two days ago, and it indicated 'AGNES BURNSIDE, for her assistance and care of my health and wellbeing' was bequeathed the entirety of her estate.

I dropped the paper and exhaled loudly.

What in the world?

I picked it back up again. At the bottom of the page were Miss Manley's signature and the names and signatures of two witnesses: Stuart Manley and Glenda Butler.

Was this what Glenda had tried to tell me about Miss Manley feeling I was a kindred spirit? How was this possible? I had known her for such a short time! More importantly, what did it mean? I reread the brief document and thought I heard footsteps upstairs. I quickly replaced the will in the bottom drawer, closed it and raced over to the sofa to turn the pages of a magazine on the end table, my heart beating loudly enough to be heard. But all was silent, the noises I had heard likely the settling of the old house. Someday to be my old house, if I had read the will correctly.

I have no idea what I read or rather looked at in the magazine since I was so preoccupied with what I had previously seen. My eyes scanned the pages and my hand turned them by rote. The will had been written two days ago when she wasn't feeling well—had she been insistent with Glenda and her nephew that she wanted to make a change? Why in the world would they acquiesce to such an outrageous change from what her former stated intentions were? Was it her signature? Was she assuming I would be her caretaker in exchange for the house and, if so, when was she going to talk to me about it? A strange idea came to me: did Stuart and Glenda maneuver Miss Manley into changing the bequest to the church and assumed after her passing they could talk me into sharing my inheritance with them?

None of it made sense.

Then I had a more troubling thought. Two days ago. The day I nearly drowned. Had it been accidental when Glenda stood up in the boat, reached out to me, and toppled me into the water? She was my best friend—it was an accident, wasn't it? Was Stuart trying to help save me or was he trying to push my head further under the water with the oar? My God, had they tried to kill me? I stared at the French windows across the room, stood hastily and locked them. Annie had keys to the house, so I had no compunction in locking the front and rear doors as well, my hands shaking all the while.

I breathed deeply to calm my nerves and walked slowly back to the sitting room, then paced as I continued to think. Logically, I knew—or was told—there had been a will where Stuart got something and the church the bulk of Miss Manley's estate. Who had told me? It must have been Glenda as Stuart wouldn't have shared such a thing with me. Knowing his extravagant tastes and aspirational lifestyle, what she had intended to leave to him would probably not be enough, and he wished to have the entirety. How was giving it to me going to solve a problem for him? Was he planning on proposing to me? Ugh, what a thought. But none of it made sense since Miss Manley was much alive. Unless he thought her 'episodes' were an indication of a disability that was bound to get worse. Was he so unscrupulous as to consider hastening her demise in some way? But if she died anytime soon, I would still inherit everything, unless he challenged the will, in which case the former will would prevail where he would get something, but still less than he wanted. Oh, my head was beginning to hurt badly from trying to puzzle this out, the late hour, and the events of the day. I went to the kitchen and warmed up a glass of milk with the desperate hope it would make me sleepy. At least it calmed me down and by the time I put my head on the pillow, I consciously thought about Atlantic City and the waves of water coming into the shore and back out again, soothingly, repeatedly, until I fell asleep.

Chapter 27

Miss Manley was in the sitting room, sifting through the morning mail. She greeted me and handed me Tillie's postcard from yesterday and a new letter today from my parents.

"I haven't told them about the judge's death," I confessed before opening it. "I didn't want them worrying or suggesting I return home immediately."

"They are not the only ones who might be worried, I think," she said with a smile. "I noticed all the doors were locked this morning when I got up."

"I don't know why I was jittery and couldn't sleep. Then I heard noises and felt a good deal better locking up the house. I hope you don't mind."

"Not at all. Too many disconcerting things have been going on lately."

"Good morning," Glenda said, entering the room. "I came to ask you, Miss Manley, about what I should do. I've had my first unpleasant experience as a landlady."

"Did Sandra skip out on you?" I asked, rather liking the slang I had heard somewhere.

"No, she is upset. Mr. Whittaker is paying the rent for her and he gave me a check but the bank in Adams said there were insufficient funds. I know I have to tell him, but do you suppose Mrs. Nash hasn't been paying him?"

"Perhaps the judge's financial affairs haven't been settled enough. Or perhaps under the circumstances, she didn't think to pay him," Miss Manley said.

"Sometimes it takes a few days for a deposit to clear, too," I added.

"I hope that's it." Still, she fidgeted a bit as she walked around the room, touching the drapes, picking up a china ornament from the table and ending up at the bookcase. "I see you finished **The Peril of Dunbar**."

"Yes, thrilling," I lied.

She turned to Miss Manley. "I think I'll go up to Highfields and see if he is there. Aggie, come with me. It might look more natural if we both pop in and then I can have a private word with him."

I agreed, thinking I could somehow tease out the meaning of Miss Manley's will during our walk, but I couldn't reveal I had seen it, or she would know I had snooped. And I wasn't quite sure what it meant if I was the only beneficiary. Why wasn't Glenda angry about being left out of getting something? Was Stuart angry about being cut out entirely? I decided to say nothing just then until I could work it out better.

We set off onto the back path and I wondered if Glenda was so concerned about the rent money—and she had told us that he had paid some in advance—that perhaps her financial situation was tighter than I imagined.

"Isn't summer wonderful here?" she asked as we walked in the shadowy woods. "I am afraid winter is horrible, however. Overcast, snowy, icy, cold, and stuck in the house all day unless you have to go out and shovel more snow."

"I'd have thought you were used to it growing up here."

"Back when we had money, we would take the train down to Florida for two weeks and soak up the sun. I always came back with a fantastic suntan, the envy of everyone at school. The last two Christmases were the first time I had to spend the entire holiday here and it was incredibly boring and cold."

That was the big difference between us. She had always had the money for a private school, midwinter holidays, ski trips, even a transatlantic trip with her mother over the summer one year, she had told me. It was all gone, her parents, the money, the fun times. And now she had to run down a man for a bad check.

We stopped at the edge of the lawn and took in the view of the house.

"I'll never get tired of looking at this place," she said. "Maybe someday I'll have enough money to buy it." Luckily, she laughed at her foolishness.

We rang the bell and the maid, Alice, answered, surprised to see the two of us and more surprised to find we were seeking Mr. Whittaker, not Mrs. Nash or Christine.

"He's not here," she said. "He left for New York Sunday to purchase fabrics or something. Would you like to talk to Mrs. Nash?"

We looked at one another and decided not to pursue the issue further at this time, thanked her, and walked to the turnaround portion of the driveway where the view of Mount Greylock was best, and you could see the valley beyond. Glenda put her head on my shoulder.

"I bet it's spectacular with fall colors," I said.

"Yes, fall is great, so is spring, but there's the long, dark winter to get through in between." She looked up at me. "Don't worry, I'll figure something out."

***

I was just about to open the door to the doctor's office when John flung it open.

"The most extraordinary thing has happened," he said. Do you remember Mrs. Nash came to see me yesterday? I'm not breeching confidence here in telling you she requested sleeping tablets and said she had imagined hearing noises in the night."

"Really?" I said, with a suitable degree of surprise.

"Naturally, I thought it was her frame of mind. Mourning and the terrible way in which her husband died. It turns out she

202

probably was not imagining things; the judge's collection of ivory chessmen has been stolen as well as other items of value. And Mr. Whittaker has flown the coop!"

I gasped. "There's more," I added. "He wrote Glenda a check for Sandra's rent and when she went to cash it, the bank said insufficient funds. I'll bet he got paid by Mrs. Nash and went off with that, too."

I sat at the reception desk. "Poor Sandra. Stranded."

"Changing the topic for a moment, would you like to see our first chickenpox patient for the summer?"

"Here or house call?"

"First, have you had the chickenpox yet?"

"Yes, long ago. And all the other childhood diseases."

"That's good. It is a house call. We can't have the child giving it to the entire town. Although some mothers think it's the best way to get over and done with it."

It's what my mother believed, too, and the reason I had my bout at age eight. I agreed to go with him although why he thought he needed my assistance, I'm not sure. As it turned out, he did not; he just wanted company on the journey.

By ill luck, the boy was Bobby, who had broken his arm, and his mother was distraught because the cast was still on and he was in misery with itchy spots underneath. From my experience, he certainly looked like he had the disease in the early stages of rash formation.

"You're having one heck of a summer," John said to him.

Bobby was trying to look brave, but his eyes welled up with tears, which he swept away with his hand.

"It itches something awful. Can't I put a stick down there to scratch?" he asked indicating the arm with the cast.

"No! You could scrape the skin and get an infection under there and we do not want that."

His mother's eyes were wide with concern. "That would be horrible. Isn't there something you can give him?"

I hadn't noticed when they first came into the office that Bobby was the hyperactive type although the tree climbing accident ought to have been a clue. He was restless in bed, scratching where he could at the incipient spots and wriggling under the covers.

"I have a good way to stop the itching," John said. "Instead of scratching, take your index finger and tap the spot ten times. Not hard, just tap, and it will help a lot." He turned to Mrs. Connelly and suggested she have him drink milk with a little bit of coffee in it several times a day, and when the scabs formed to pat calamine lotion on with a cotton pad.

"The worst is almost over," he said. A younger boy peeked around the corner as we left the bedroom and all I could think was he would be the next one in bed, itching, squirming, and miserable. So, the worst was not almost over for Mrs. Connelly or her children. How well I remember lying in a darkened room, bored, feeling too weak to take an interest in anything, and certain everyone else was out playing and having fun, although in my case it was during the school year and I was missing my schoolwork, too.

We drove back to town and encountered another crisis, this time the reverend who was in a state and wanted to tell someone about his ill fortune, and since his wife was in Pittsfield for the day, he decided the person to share it with was the doctor. He practically burst through the door of the reception room after we had gotten in.

"Gone. Gone. My entire arrowhead collection."

I knew exactly what he was talking about and immediately thought of how Landon Whittaker had admired his collection of artifacts. While not wanting to incriminate the innocent, I mentioned he had suddenly left town.

"What a fool I've been!" He smacked his forehead dramatically and John suggested he call the police about the theft immediately. He hurried out, slamming the door behind him.

"Mrs. Nash must have some contact information for Whittaker," I suggested.

"If what he supplied was truthful. I wonder if he even is an interior decorator," he said.

"*Designer*, if you please. He certainly talked a convincing line. I wonder if Landon Whittaker is even his real name?"

"Too much going on in this town at the moment," John said, retreating to his office to read a journal that had come in the mail.

One more worried mother called about the rash her daughter was displaying and this time John went out on the house call by himself while I stayed back to answer the phone and open the rest of the mail. The envelopes containing payment were usually hand addressed and lumpy but there was a thin one in the pile stuck to another one, and out of curiosity I opened it first. It was what they call a poison pen letter, written in crude capital letters as if to disguise someone's handwriting.

WHAT DOES YOUR WIFE DO IN PITTSFIELD EVERY WEEK?
FROM A CONCERNED NEIGHBOR

I looked at the front of the envelope and saw it was addressed to Reverend Lewis. The postman must have made a mistake and put it in with the doctor's mail. What to do now? Try to reseal it with glue and slip it into the reverend's mailbox? Suppose someone saw me? They would assume I was the one who wrote it. The reverend was having a bad week and I did not want to be part of it. I decided to put it back in the envelope and let John deal with it, coward that I was.

I tried to concentrate on the tasks of logging the payments in the accounts book, putting receipts in the patients' files, and filling out the deposit slip for our trip into Adams tomorrow, but I kept thinking about the letter. What was wrong with people? Was it just this particular town or did gossip run rampant in all small towns?

Perhaps I had led a sheltered life up until now and here I thought I was so sophisticated having lived in New York City for two years. What I had seen and heard there was nothing to several weeks in this bucolic place.

Chapter 28

West Adams was abuzz in the afternoon after news of the two thefts came to light, and by the time I got back to Miss Manley's the phone was ringing incessantly with updates and inquiries about the 'gang' that had burgled two of the town's most well-known people. Naturally, people also linked the concept of a gang with the death of the judge and nasty people from Boston roaming the streets with evil intent. Officer Reed was on the case at once, and because Mrs. Nash was the victim and her husband's chessmen were the more valuable items stolen, Inspector Gladstone was called in for guidance. I saw Glenda out in her garden, not working in it, mind you, but sitting in a chair and I sat to fill her in on the news.

"That's ghastly!" she whispered.

"Why are you whispering?" I asked.

"Sandra is in the house and I don't want her to hear any more of this awful business. Not only was my rent check no good, but her paycheck also could not be honored at the bank."

We shook our heads at the perfidy of Landon Whittaker and the gullibility of young women. The front doorbell rang, clearly audible at the back of the house and Glenda jumped up to answer it. A few moments later she returned with the police at her back, the two men looking serious, the inspector with an added layer of annoyance on his face. I stood up and meant to excuse myself, but they insisted I stay.

"Miss Burnside, do you know this Landon Whittaker?" the inspector asked.

"Yes, but not well." I was puzzled by his question.

"Were you at Reverend Lewis's home when his collection of, whatever it was you would call it, was shown to Mr. Whittaker."

"Yes."

"Who else was there?"

"Mrs. Lewis and Sandra Logan."

"Did you notice him taking anything from the reverend's collection? Palming anything at the time?"

"Of course not! There were so many of us there. And if I had, I would have said something." What an idiotic line of thinking.

He scribbled in his notebook.

"Is Miss Logan at home?" he asked Glenda.

She nodded and went to bring her downstairs.

Sandra seemed put out, not only owing her landlady the rent, but having been cheated out of her pay, and out of a job on top of it. She held her head high, nonetheless, and submitted to the inspector's questions, which were much the same as the ones he asked me before he delved deeper into how she came to be in West Adams.

"How long have you known Mr. Whittaker?"

"Only since May, when I answered an advertisement for an assistant."

"How did you get the job with Mr. Whittaker?"

"I was at school, and he came to campus and we had an interview. He gave me his card and told me about his New York City design business, and he had a wealthy client who wanted as little disruption on her day-to-day life, so speed was of the essence. He said he would find me a place to stay and pay for it and also give me a salary, but it was the experience I was looking forward to."

"Did you suspect anything amiss?"

"No. I didn't know quite what to expect in the process. He had met with Mrs. Nash at least once and having seen the house had an idea of what could be done. He was exuberant in his descriptions of redesigning much of the first floor and had made preliminary sketches and everything."

"What was the nature of your work for him?"

"I took measurements of the rooms, an inventory of the furnishings and artwork since they would be put in storage during the construction phase, and I recopied the designs in ink for a more formal presentation he was making to Mrs. Nash." She was twisting her fingers and I didn't blame her. It was not pleasant being grilled by the inspector. But what did he imagine—somehow she was in cahoots with Whittaker? It hardly seemed likely as she was a college student.

"When was the last time you saw him?"

"Friday, at the end of the workday. He gave me my paycheck, but I couldn't cash it until yesterday because the bank in Adams had closed for the day. I had no idea the check was not good. I fully expected to see him yesterday, but he wasn't at Highfields. They said he had gone to New York to price fabric or something. I thought maybe he had forgotten to put money into his account before he left, and I was a little upset, but then Glenda let me know today the rent check was also not honored by the bank."

The inspector shook his head. "What do you intend to do now?"

"Since I haven't any money, I'll go home for the remainder of the summer. But I'll be sure to have my parents send you the money for the rent," she added to Glenda.

"Thank you."

We assumed the questioning was over and Sandra had stopped twisting her fingers. I noticed she had a gold pinky ring on her left hand, the exact ring I had seen on Christine's finger last week. While the inspector continued to write with Officer Reed looking over his shoulder, I gave Glenda a look which meant, 'follow my glance,' as I deliberately looked down on Sandra's hand. She did and gave me a questioning look in return, not understanding.

The policemen got up and thanked us and Glenda walked them through the house to the front door and then hurried back to where I was in the garden and sat.

"That wasn't so bad now, was it?" I asked Sandra.

"This has been a bad week so far," she said.

"I noticed you have a lovely ring," I said.

"Thank you." She held her fingers out to admire it.

"I saw the same ring on Christine Nash's little finger recently. Were you in league with Landon Whittaker and took her ring as well? What else did you take from Highfields?"

She sputtered. "What are you talking about? This is my school ring."

"Oh?" I said, homing in on the discomfort she displayed, which surely meant she was lying.

"Yes, and Christine has one, too, because we went to school together." She stood up, her jaw tight and her eyes narrowed at me.

"Oops," I said sheepishly. "I didn't know. I'm sorry."

She turned on her heel and walked swiftly back into the house.

Glenda held in her giggles until the back door slammed and I gave her a withering look, making her laugh more.

"After my performance, I think I will go home," I said, thoroughly embarrassed by my assumptions of Sandra as a thief.

I found Miss Manley in the sitting room seated on the sofa working on the tiny sweater she had been knitting. She smiled as I entered, and I sat next to her to confess my erroneous comment to Sandra. Rather than condemning me, commiserating with me, or laughing at me, she said the most curious thing. "That is an interesting piece of information." "Whatever do you mean?" I asked.

"Nothing." She held up the sweater. "Almost done. And it is time for lunch." She got up to assist Annie in the kitchen and I followed her.

"I heard you had a nice compliment today," she said as she reached for the dishes.

"I'm afraid I can't reveal my source, but Inspector Gladstone confirmed the handwriting in the note found under the judge was not his. Just as you had suggested. It took a while to find a graphologist, I think they are called, to analyze the handwriting."

"How interesting," I said, swiping a stick of celery from the condiment dish before bringing it out to the dining room table.

"This is what I think," she said, sitting erectly in her chair. "I think more than one person was involved in judge Nash's death." She demurely cut up a slice of pork chop, put it into her mouth, and had what can only be described as a smug smile on her face.

"First, why do you think that? And second, who do you think those persons might be?"

I was amazed she had been pondering this for some time.

"I think things were carefully planned out—this was not a spur-of-the-moment murder. There are so many details that are confusing, contradictory, or just wrong. For example, the note you noticed seemed to have more than one handwriting on it. You were right but additionally, neither of them was the judge's. Why?"

"To confuse people?"

"I would say yes. Eat your chop, dear, it is delicious."

I did as commanded and she was correct, especially when taken on the fork with the baked beans Annie had made.

"Then the broken wristwatch showing a time that was not the time the judge died according to the doctor's estimate. Please don't take offense at my next observation, but logically, either somebody tampered with the watch or Doctor Taylor was incorrect as to the time of death." She let the comment sit there for a moment. "I think somebody altered the time on the watch before smashing it, making it seem as if the weight of Judge Nash's head had crushed it." She stopped for a moment. "I'm sorry, am I making you lose your appetite?"

"No, not at all," I said truthfully.

"The reverend was alone with the judge's body for a short while so he could have damaged the watch."

"But why? Because the judge was going to challenge him about a few dollars missing from the collection?" I asked. "That seems far-fetched."

"Exactly! The crux is 'who benefits' and the likelihood the reverend would shoot the judge over a few dollars is ludicrous. So, back we go to who benefits?"

She was thoroughly enjoying teasing out the bits of information and making sense of it. I certainly hoped her 'episodes' were a thing of the past because she had a fine, logical mind.

"I'll bet Landon Whittaker was eyeing the judge's possessions since he had Sandra do an inventory before the renovation he envisioned," I said.

"Interesting," Miss Manley said, her head cocked to one side in thought.

"Perhaps the judge suspected he was up to something and was killed before he acted on his mistrust," I suggested, then hastily changed my mind. "No, the timing of the theft was considerably after the murder. I don't think he is a likely suspect. For the murder, at least."

"Sam Campbell was suggested early on due to an onerous sentence that the judge imposed on him," Miss Manley reminded me.

"If you think more than one person was involved, then Elsie would be his accomplice. Elsie could have easily taken the gun from Richard Fairley's studio and given it to Sam. He would have had to somehow sneak into Highfields, not a likely scenario considering he was persona non grata already. I don't think someone in his position would have risked it just for revenge."

"Revenge can be a powerful motive," Miss Manley stated.

I agreed with her, but somehow, in this case, it fell flat. We continued eating.

"What if somebody brought the gun into the house and left it for someone else to use?" she asked.

"Who are we talking about?"

"What if Richard Fairley brought his gun into the house and left it for Mrs. Nash to use? Perhaps he gained access to the house and left it in the study somewhere."

"And he was nowhere near the house at the time of death. Hmm, how clever," I said.

"From what I've heard, there were a lot of people in the house at the time, scattered among many floors and rooms, moving from one place to the other performing their normal activities at the time of the murder. The only events people seemed to remark on, as I noticed in at the inquest, was the time they first were made aware of the death of Judge Nash, which was a full thirty minutes after it occurred."

"Good point," I said. After thinking a bit, I concluded, "Then it could have been anyone. The cook or one of the maids."

"If they had a motive to do so."

I used my fork for emphasis. "What about the judge's history in Boston and the possibility of a former felon or disgruntled gang member? A relative of the cook, for example?"

"Oh, no. I know her family. They are local people. Very upright."

"Alice and the chauffeur are locals, too, aren't they?" I asked.

"Yes. It leaves one maid and the housekeeper. I wonder if Officer Reed or Inspector Gladstone has looked into their backgrounds?"

"If they haven't, perhaps you might suggest it to them."

She gave me a strange look. "I don't know how much credence they would give to my musings as they haven't so far.
But in the interests of justice, it is worth a try."

***

My mind was whirling with possibilities about the events at Highfields and although the theory of vengeful gang members or parolees was a good one, it didn't seem to hold much water. The judge would have recognized them unless it was an accomplice taking the vendetta. Now there was a plot Stuart Manley should pursue! He could call it ***Blood Feud in the Berkshires***.

Thomas Kirby came into the doctor's office in the afternoon with color in his face and a broad smile to match. He was either getting better or was in a state of remission from the dreadful cycle of fevers and debilitation. He greeted me pleasantly and I could tell from John's expression he detected a definite improvement in his patient's condition; it was always a wonderful thing to see and experience. Their consultation was brief, from which I assumed he was just in for a checkup and when he came out he told us he was going to be resuming his duties at the church that afternoon for a service being held.

When I got back home the house was empty with a note on the kitchen table saying Miss Manley had gone to an evening church service with Glenda—a bit of a shock—and they would be back for the dinner Annie had prepared before she left for the day. I changed leisurely and took a book, not one of Stuart's, out to the garden, sat and began to read. I wasn't there long before I saw Mrs. Nash leave the studio next door and, pretending not to see me, walk along the path toward town. To be fair, I was sitting quite still, and she may not have known I was there, but my thoughts returned to the supposition Miss Manley had of who would benefit from the judge's death. Why, Mrs. Nash, of course. She may have had problems sleeping, but she didn't appear to be the mourning widow to me, especially with a handsome, young boyfriend to visit.

Not too much later Glenda and Miss Manley returned through the front garden and came out back to where I sat, each removing her hat as she did. They had startled expressions on their faces, and I could not imagine what it was they had seen or heard. Coming closer they sat and spoke in lowered voices because they didn't want anyone in the reverend's house to overhear them.

"The reverend just gave the most blistering sermon I have ever heard from him," Miss Manley said.

"Reverend Lewis?" I asked, thinking perhaps it was Thomas Kirby who had preached.

Glenda nodded and I could not imagine him doing so, but Miss Manley elaborated.

"His topic was mendacity and gossip ruining the fabric of a community, a suitable enough sermon, but rather than the measured, academic tone he usually uses, this was a brief homily and forcefully spoken. He even suggested gossip was a thief who stole the soul of the town."

"I wonder what prompted that?" Glenda asked.

I think I knew that he had finally read the poison pen letter inadvertently delivered to Doctor Taylor, but I said nothing.

"He was so angry," Glenda added. "And those who were at the service were either puzzled or looking guilty."

"He's not wrong about the gossip part and I hereby confess to being a party to it," I said holding my hands up in surrender.

"What? Do you mean our speculations on who killed the judge? That's not gossip, it is an exercise in deductive reasoning," Glenda said.

"Well, the sermon was an extremely unsettling experience. Highly out of character," Miss Manley concluded, getting up to go into the house.

Alone with Glenda, my mind went back to the issue of the will I had found in Miss Manley's desk and I thought the moment would be a good one to ask what she knew of my landlady's financial situation. But then I stopped myself. I still hadn't figured out why there was a new will and why I was designated the sole recipient. If I started asking questions Glenda might wonder if I had seen it. Or was it her intention?

"Whatever is the matter?" she asked me. "Your forehead looks like thunderclouds are gathering inside your brain. You'll get wrinkles," she said, getting up. "Dinner time for Sandra and me."

Pushing aside my ruminations I asked her when Sandra was leaving.

She shrugged. "I hope by the end of the week. She did say her parents would send me money for the rent so I can't just make her leave before then."

I closed the book and began to think about Sandra, who knew Christine before she came to West Adams. Was it a coincidence? And had they had a cheerful recognition of the serendipitous event, had they been quiet about it for some reason, or had it been planned?

Who gains, Miss Manley had posed to me. Surely Christine got out from under the thumb of her overbearing father once he was dead. And what if she could cleverly direct the attention to her stepmother and Richard Fairley as the possible culprits? Someone had effectively put the police off the scent through the timing of the murder and the known whereabouts of everyone, but where were Christine and Sandra except also at Highfields? Christine had just returned from the Lewises' house and Sandra was somewhere upstairs busy with the designer's instructions. The two young women could have orchestrated something where the gun was stolen from Richard, hidden in the room, and either Christine or Sandra slipped in—probably Sandra— because we knew Christine was at the parsonage for at least some period of time but returned to Highfields before her father's body was discovered. Sandra could have fired the shot, set up the bogus letter, adjusted the watch, smashed it and stolen back out again in a matter of minutes. Something nagged at me about the entire thing that remained unsolved but might continue to be an unsolved mystery forever.

Chapter 29

As I was getting ready for bed, I began to mull over the notion of more than one person's being involved in killing the judge. What irked me was the police seemed to have given up on finding out who had committed the crime whereas I, who had no vested interest except incessant curiosity and the abhorrence of things left unfinished, couldn't seem to let go of it.

The next morning Miss Manley had two pieces of news. Thomas Kirby had confessed to Reverend Lewis that he had indeed taken the money from the collection plate, had offered to resign, and had had his resignation rejected. The other item was that she saw Sandra Logan walk toward the center of town, suitcase in hand, presumably to get the morning bus to Pittsfield. Now that I had appointed myself one of the neighborhood busybodies, I dashed over to Glenda's to make sure she was aware of this. She was sitting at the kitchen table, drinking coffee, when I knocked on the back door and then came in.

"Well?" I asked.

Glenda looked puzzled, looked over my shoulder and quickly got up to shut the cabinet door where she had stashed the brandy. I hoped she was not drinking this early in the morning.

"I assume you know Sandra has left."

"Oh, yes. And good riddance. All she did was mope around for the last few days. At least I'll get the rent money. Sit down and have some coffee."

"No thanks on the coffee." I sat and leaned forward in my chair. "Did anyone ever think to check Sandra's suitcase for the stolen chessmen and other items?" I asked.

Glenda's mouth popped open. "Do you think?"

"Why not? We don't know Landon Whittaker took those things. She saw the reverend's collection and knew about the ivory chess sets at Highfields. The valuables were gone and so was he—

216

but coincidence? I think I'm going to share my suspicions with the police," I said.

"Do you think you should?" Glenda asked, her forehead wrinkled.

"I'll just call Officer Reed and suggest I have some thoughts to share with him early this evening." I left Glenda goggle-eyed, but I was determined to at least share my concerns with Miss Manley.

"Would you mind if I asked Officer Reed over for a chat after work today?" I asked her, catching her at her knitting in the sitting room.

"Certainly not! I have been thinking of the judge's murder and I believe I have solved it." I

was speechless.

"It took a great deal of planning, lightning speed, and coldhearted determination, but I believe I know who the two people were who committed the crime."

"Should we ask for Inspector Gladstone, as well?"

"It's a good idea, my dear." She smiled smugly and resumed knitting.

I had a hard time concentrating on my duties that afternoon, with several booked appointments and several drop-ins. Chickenpox had mercifully not overwhelmed the town yet, but there were the usual aches and complaints, some shared with me at the reception desk that might have been better told in confidence to the doctor. John kept giving me strange looks and I finally asked him why.

"Is something troubling you?" he asked.

This took me by surprise because in my experience with men they were not too perceptive of moods and didn't bother to ask if something was the matter, even when there was ample reason to do so. But those were all young men and too absorbed in themselves and how they appeared to others to be concerned with observing the moods of female companions. John was in his mid-thirties and either his chronological age, life experience, or maturity made for a pleasant contrast to my experiences.

"This is going to sound a bit crazy," I said. "But there is something about Sandra Logan that I can't put my finger on, and her leaving today further raised my suspicions."

"What do you mean?"

"It is more than a feeling, so I've asked Officer Reed to come by after work to talk to me. Was it overstepping, do you think?" I asked, suddenly embarrassed by my assertive attitude about a topic in which I should have had little or no interest.

"Maybe. Maybe not." It was all he had to say about it, and we did not discuss it further. It doesn't mean I didn't continue to ruminate about my suspicions the entire afternoon while keeping one part of my brain actively on my work and performing my duties as usual.

At five o'clock I was anxious to get back home and change out of my uniform to face Officer Reed with what I hoped were not idle suspicions. When I got there, Miss Manley was in the sitting room, lying down, in the throes of one of her episodes though this one was not so severe. Annie and Glenda were in attendance and I called John to ask if he could come over. Now there were five of us in the room when the doorbell rang, and Annie escorted Officer Reed and Inspector Gladstone in and tried to find them places to sit. They were surprised to see Miss Manley stretched out on the sofa, so she made an effort to sit up despite all our imploring her to be still. Despite a degree of disorientation, she was oddly agitated and after instructing Annie to bring in refreshments, took a handkerchief from her pocket and held it tightly in her hands.

"Gentlemen, I believe I know what happened at Highfields on the day the judge was murdered." Naturally, their eyebrows shot up and they leaned forward to hear what she had to say.

"The observation was made earlier that probably more than one person was involved in the murder. What makes this case particularly difficult is there were so many people in the house at the time, some of them with a strong motive. And there were others with compelling animosity who were not at the house—as far as we know. I assume you have eliminated Sam Campbell from your list of suspects?" she asked.

They nodded reluctantly as he would have made an appropriate culprit.

"There is no way he could have sneaked into the house unnoticed, I should think, although he also had an alibi. Both the reverend and Thomas Kirby had the motive of keeping the judge quiet about the missing collection funds, but I hardly think it was enough reason to kill him. Besides, Mr. Kirby was much too unwell at the time to have done anything about it. And the reverend was out and about in the countryside due to a bogus telephone call, so we can count him out, as well. Christine certainly had a motive of resentment toward her father but there was no one to help her. I don't think Landon Whittaker had a reason to kill the judge; after all, the Nash family was the goose that laid a golden egg for him, according to his vast plans for spending their money on a redesign. Three of the staff—the cook, Alice, and the chauffeur—are local people and they didn't have any reason to dislike the judge. The other maid and the housekeeper, although previously not known to us, were found to have solid references and were not related to anyone the judge committed to prison, isn't that so, Inspector?"

He nodded his head but wondered how she knew it, as did we all.

"It leaves Mrs. Nash and Richard Fairley."

"What!" Officer Reed and the Inspector Gladstone fairly shouted at the same time.

"I thought they were exonerated because of the time of death and Mrs. Nash's flimsy and false confession," John said.

"Yes, how clever on their part to throw suspicion on themselves so they could be eliminated as suspects early on. This is what I think happened. Richard Fairly had been up to Highfields the day before to seek payment for at least one of the two portraits he had completed. While he was there, he hid his gun somewhere in the study and likely had an unpleasant conversation with the judge. The next day, while everyone in the house was busy, Mrs. Nash stepped away from whatever she was doing on the second floor, went down to the study where her husband was waiting for the reverend, took the gun from its hiding place, and shot the judge. She then raced back upstairs, and her absence was hardly noticed by the maid with whom she was working on counting linens."

"But no one heard a shot," John said.

"Doctor, of course you were right about the time of death. I suspect a silencer was used on the gun, as you observed, Inspector. Now the interesting part is Richard Fairley waited a suitable amount of time so he would not be implicated in the deed, came into the study, changed the hands on the watch, smashed it and put it under the judge's head just before the reverend got there." Glenda gave a little gasp at the image.

"And then substituted whatever the judge was writing with that nonsensical and phony note, just to confuse everyone. Then he picked up the gun, wiped Mrs. Nash's fingerprints off and stashed the silencer in his pocket to be disposed of later."

Here Glenda and I looked at each other remembering our walk in the woods and seeing Richard Fairley seemingly searching for something in the underbrush.

"I think I know what happened to the silencer," I said.

"Richard ran out the door, running into the reverend in the driveway." She had a small smile on her face. "He acted distressed, hysterical, and went quickly away, leaving the reverend to discover the body."

We were quiet for a few moments and then there was a torrent of questions. Miss Manley held up her hand for silence as she intended to continue.

"And cleverly, when the reverend and the maid put up the alarm, everyone came running from their places in the house, with Mrs. Nash acting the shocked wife. As far as anyone knew, she had been upstairs the entire time with a maid, going from the linen closet to one room or another. Richard Fairley was in the clear because he was observed in town somewhere at the time of the murder. His confession was seen as a noble act of sacrifice, although later disproved by the doctor's evidence. Mrs. Nash's confession was also contrived to seem as if she were protecting her lover although all the details were purposefully wrong."

Inspector Gladstone whistled in appreciation. "How can we possibly prove this?"

"I have an idea of how we can set a trap for them."

I cleared my throat at this point. "I hate to interrupt, but I have an alternative theory."

Heads swung in my direction and I confess I was taken aback by my bold assertion.

"Miss Manley, you have rightly asked who gains, and there are more people who gain than Mrs. Nash and Richard Fairley. Probably the person who gains the most is Christine Nash."

Glenda gasped again. She always was an enthusiastic audience for me.

"We know Roger concocted the phony telephone call to get the reverend out of the house that afternoon, so he and Christine could keep an amorous appointment." I don't know why I dressed up the obvious with such colorful language. "Mrs. Lewis was in Pittsfield; however, she returned earlier than everyone expected to look in on Thomas Kirby, about whom she was concerned. A poison pen writer in town had suggested she was up to something else in Pittsfield, which I think was just malicious gossip, but someone saw her going up to Mr. Kirby's apartment and thought the worst. But it's irrelevant. The point is Christine was at the parsonage with Roger when her father was shot." I waited for the puzzled faces to turn their gaze to me.

"Shot by Sandra Logan."

Another storm of questions and protests. Now it was my turn to have a small smile.

"Sandra Logan and Christine went to boarding school together. They wear the same school ring. While Sandra was able to pursue a college education at Wellesley, Judge Nash forbade Christine from going, whether because he was against higher education for his daughter or he suspected she had an improper relationship with one of her fellow female students."

"Wait, you just said she was with Roger when her father was shot," Officer Reed said. "He was her beard."

Uncomprehending looks all around except for John, who tilted his head as if to wonder where I picked up such terminology.

"He was her cover story. In any event, the judge thought he could control her by keeping her at home, which only made matters worse between them since she did not get along with Mrs. Nash. It was probably Christine who suggested Landon Whittaker for the job of the Highfields redesign and who directed him to Wellesley to seek an assistant for the summer. And guess who applied for the job? Christine's friend and former classmate, Sandra. Christine stole the gun from Richard's studio, unlocked like everyone's house around here, and she stashed it somewhere in the study as you said, Miss Manley. Somehow either she or Sandra managed to purchase a silencer. And it was Sandra who stepped away from her work with Mr. Whittaker for a few minutes to race down the back stairs, shoot the judge, tamper with the watch, and plant the bogus letter on the desk. Nobody would suspect the interior designer's assistant had anything to do with it, and Christine had an alibi for the time of the murder and was at home later to join everyone in the aftermath of the discovery. When Richard Fairley stopped by to talk to the Judge, he found him dead with his gun on the carpet. He also saw the silencer attached and took both away, thinking Mrs. Nash had used it and wanting to protect her. He hid the silencer somewhere along the path in the woods and intended to hide the gun as well, but thought better of it and turned himself in. When everyone discovered the timing was wrong—that he couldn't possibly have done it, nor could Mrs. Nash, he wanted to retrieve the silencer, fearing fingerprints might still be on it. Glenda and I saw him mucking about in the leaves on one of the forest paths. That should give you some solid evidence."

Now everyone was quiet.

"Interesting," Inspector Gladstone said. "Again, how do we prove this?"

"I will bet you Sandra did not go back home this morning and she is probably at Highfields even as we speak. She took a suitcase with her to town this morning and there is a good chance the ivory chessmen and other valuables are in her suitcase. She has returned them to who she thinks is the rightful owner, her lover, Christine. It can probably finance Christine's college education if her father somehow left her too little in the will. The beauty of their scheme is Mrs. Nash and Richard would be the likely suspects except they did a ridiculous double confession that exonerated them."

"How can we prove this?"

"Go to Highfields, see if Sandra is there, and see what is in her possession," I said more confidently than I felt.

There was a tremendous commotion as a result of my comments, and Miss Manley nodded her head. "It could have happened either way, I suppose," she said.

I admitted it was possible, but I had one other card up my sleeve. "Glenda, have you cleaned out Sandra's room yet?" Knowing, of course, she wouldn't get to it for days.

"Why, no."

"I bet we may find some of the reverend's collection somewhere in her room," I said.

Glenda's eyes were large again. "If it's true, she might have stolen something from me, too."

"I don't think she was interested in his collection, per se, she just wanted to throw suspicion on Mr. Whittaker."

Officer Reed and the inspector shook their heads at the two theories offered as to why and how Judge Nash was killed and quickly proceeded to their car and up to Highfields to see who was

223

in residence, leaving John and Miss Manley behind. Glenda and I went back to her house and ransacked the guest room. Granted there were not many places to hide things, but Sandra was not an original thief, for she had put the reverend's arrowheads in the most obvious place possible: between the box spring and the mattress. Luckily, none of the more fragile specimens had been damaged because Sandra probably got into bed carefully each night after she had taken them.

Glenda plopped down in the armchair in the room and put her head in her hands. "I hope you are wrong, Aggie. I don't want to think I was harboring a murderer all this time." She stood up and sat quickly. "I don't feel so well. The excitement, I suppose."

"You know the drill," I said, "head between your knees and deep breaths. I'll get some water."

I went to the kitchen and was about to get a glass of water and then remembered the brandy she had hidden up in the high cabinet. I could just about see it but in reaching for it, pushed it farther back. I pulled one of the kitchen chairs over to use as a makeshift stepladder and climbed up. Yes, there was the brandy. But there was another bottle there, as well, unlabeled and stoppered with a cork that looked like Miss Manley's tonic. I sniffed. It smelled familiar and I sniffed again. What was it doing here?

"What are you doing?" Glenda said from the doorway, her face still pale from her previous near-fainting spell.

"What is this?" I said holding up the bottle.

She may have been weakened, but she was angry, and she rushed at me, toppling me off the chair, where I landed on the counter, but I managed to hold onto the bottle.

"Why are you such an infernal busybody?" she said, making a grab for it.

"Did you switch out Miss Manley's medicine?"

"No, it's an extra prescription."

"Why?" I held it away from her and took the cork out carefully to sniff the contents again. It smelled strong and alcoholic— that was as specific a determination as I could make.

"I guess that stint working in the pharmacy last year *was* helpful, Glenda, wasn't it? Is that where you learned about soporifics? Or poison? Here, you drink some," I said, holding it out toward her.

She slapped it out of my hand, and it fell to the floor and shattered.

"Oops," she said.

"I don't understand. Were you trying to kill Miss Manley *and* me?"

"What?" she protested.

I looked into her eyes, those pretty blue eyes people always commented on and I searched for a glimpse of remorse.

"Killing her slowly with an extra dose at teatime every now and then. And trying to kill me by pushing me into the lake?"

"I did not push you. It was an accident. I would never do such a thing."

"You mean you could never do the deed yourself. Instead, you concocted a new will for Miss Manley, with me as the only beneficiary. You knew I would be suspected of having orchestrated her overdose because if she were no longer living I would inherit everything. Then, when they looked at the will, they would see her signature was forged as were yours and Stuart's. Everything would point to me—I live in the same house and have access to everything including her medicine. The will. Perfect. You didn't want to get your hands dirty; however, it was all right to set all these events in motion and let a jury decide my fate."

"Well, yes," she said with a simpering smile as if it made it all right. "It was Stuart's idea, anyway," she added.

"You didn't have to go along, you know."

"But I did. You see, we've been married for some time."

I collapsed into the chair and stared at her. Who was this woman whom I had called my best friend? About whom I knew so little.

"And the secret New York boyfriend?"

She nodded. "Stuart."

She had played her part well, pretending indifference, no latenight rendezvous in West Adams—or had there been? Solicitous of Miss Manley while she had full access to her house and personal papers. Fooling me all along.

"But I don't understand something. The previous will left him so little."

"Where did you get such an idea? The previous will gives everything to him," she said.

"Where did I get that idea? From you, of course." Then I had to laugh at my naivete at believing everything she had told me. "You two have been clever. But if Stuart was going to inherit everything anyway, why create this elaborate ruse of the phony will and dosing Miss Manley's tonic?"

Glenda sighed with exasperation. "Stuart needed the money for the publishing enterprise now and his aunt wouldn't even lend it to him."

"Wait. Were you going to poison her?"

"Not exactly. But if anything happened to her...." "Stuart's brilliant plotting," I said.

"Of course. You know I don't have a head for puzzles."

I stared at her. She seemed to be entirely without guilt or remorse.

"How could you?" I asked.

"Don't be silly, Aggie. They don't execute women anymore. Do they? You'd just spend a little time in prison and then you'd be free. If you have any money troubles, we could always help you."

This was a surreal conversation. "I would lose my nursing license for certain. I would have a criminal record. I would be unemployable. It would ruin my life and my family's name."

"Hmm. I hadn't thought of that. But I'm sure you could work somewhere."

Her glib responses were quintessential Glenda, but under these circumstances with lives on the line, mine and Miss Manley's, they were utterly heartless.

"Well, what now?" she asked me defiantly.

"We go tell Miss Manley what you've done."

"Absolutely not! And she'd never believe you, anyway."

As she turned away, I grabbed her arm and dragged her through the kitchen toward the back door, not an easy feat since she braced her feet and clung onto every object in the way, whether chair or door handle, finally sitting down on the floor thinking I would give up. I was taller and stronger and released her hand, grabbed her by the feet and towed her across her back garden while she screamed I was trying to kill her. If it weren't so serious, it would have been a funny sight, me walking backward, pulling her by her legs, she partly sitting up to pull her skirt down until I tripped on something and fell. I was hoisted up almost immediately by John, who demanded to know what was going on.

"Go ahead, tell him."

Miss Manley had joined the three of us by that time and had her head cocked to the side.

"We found the reverend's collection," Glenda said, getting herself upright.

"No, not that part!" I scolded.

Glenda burst into tears, which lured Miss Manley to her side for sympathy.

"Fess up," I said, hands on my hips.

Glenda was doing a masterful job at blubbering her apologies, blaming Stuart for any evil intent, then dismissing his efforts as inconsequential, ending up running out of excuses.

"What she is trying to say is she and Stuart manufactured a will—"

"Oh, that," Miss Manley said.

Her casual admission took us by surprise, most of all John who didn't have a clue what we were talking about.

"I finally got the darn drawer open and found the absurd piece of paper. I can't imagine what Stuart made you do to create an absurd forgery that would never hold up in probate, but it has already met its fate in the fireplace." She took Glenda by the arm and led her back to the sitting room and positioned her on the sofa next to herself.

"It was naughty of you," Miss Manley chided. Glenda had the decency to look sorry, at least. John kept looking back and forth trying to make sense of the scene.

"I fully intend to lend him the money for his publishing venture, absurd as it is, because all I own is going to be his anyway at some point in the future, so why wait?"

The sun broke through the clouds on Glenda's face and she gave her benevolent neighbor a heartfelt hug. Well, at least they were both happy with the outcome, and I wasn't going to spoil their happiness with the mention of a separate bottle of tonic laced with whatever that lay broken on Glenda Butler's kitchen floor.

The phone rang and a few moments later the astonished Annie came in to report the inspector had been on the phone and Sandra Logan was indeed at Highfields. As were the judge's chess pieces and confessions were in progress.

"What is going on?" John asked.

"Why don't we go to your place, and I'll tell you all about it?" I said, taking his hand. It was probably about time I became more familiar with the inside of his house.

Read more of Aggie Burnside when she encounters
The Girl on the Doorstep
Coming soon
www.Andreas-books.com

Printed in Great Britain
by Amazon